Property of Lisa Mett

D0385351

THE PRODIGAL HUSBAND

THE PRODIGAL HUSBAND

Jacquelin Thomas

BET Publications, LLC

NEW SPIRIT BOOKS are published by

BET Publications, LLC
c/o BET BOOKS
One BET Plaza
1900 W Place NE
Washington, DC 20018-1211

Copyright © 2002 by Jacquelin Thomas

All rights reserved. No part of this book may be reproduced, stored in a retrieval system, or transmitted in any form or by any means without the prior written consent of the Publisher.

BET Books is a trademark of Black Entertainment Television, Inc. NEW SPIRIT and the NEW SPIRIT logo are trademarks of BET Books and the BET BOOKS logo is a registered trademark.

ISBN: 0-7394-2515-3

Printed in the United States of America

To Brenda (BJ) Woodbury

*You believed in this story from the moment I shared it with you.
Thank you for your loyal support and for all of your fabulous reviews
of my books. I truly appreciate your support and your friendship as well.*

ACKNOWLEDGMENTS

Bernard—I have to say thanks yet again for all of your love and support. I wouldn't be the woman I am had it not been for you. You are my best friend and my most cherished treasure.

My children—The three of you are my best work ever. We have had our ups and downs, but I want you all to know how proud I am of each of you, and I wouldn't give up a minute of being your mother.

Vanessa Woodward and Tina McCray (JE Publicists)—You two are the best publicists a girl could have. Thank you! Thank you! Because of you both, it's been a busy year for me, but I'm not complaining. It's all been well worth the effort. I am grateful for all the time and energy you've put into promoting me and my books.

The Childcare Division of Wake County Human Services—I am forever grateful for the patience and understanding shown to me when I'm on deadline and/or traveling for book-related events. I am overwhelmed by your unwavering support.

My readers—Please know that I love you and am blessed by each of you on a daily basis. Your support and earnest letters are forever etched in my heart.

Prologue

Charleston, South Carolina

Jake would remember this night for the rest of his life. Tonight his desire to control had cost him his daughter's life and the love of his wife.

Lying in the cold hospital room, Jake could still hear his wife's grief-stricken cry reverberating in his head. Although he hadn't been told yet, he knew Tiffany was dead. Putting a trembling hand to his bandaged forehead, Jake began to sob. His little girl was gone, and it was his fault.

Guilt surged out of every pore on his body. None of this was supposed to happen. Jake still couldn't believe that he'd allowed himself to get so drunk that he would end up in bed with Sheila. Hell, she was his business partner. Thoughts of that fiasco three days ago resurfaced. He could still see the look of devastation on Tori's face when she'd walked in on them in bed.

Although Jake had tried to keep her from leaving, his wife would hear none of it. When he'd come home, he'd found Tori and Tiffany gone. She hadn't even bothered to leave a note, but he'd had an idea where to find her. Jake had driven to Charleston, South Carolina, where Tori was staying with her Aunt Kate, and tried to convince her to give him another chance.

All he'd wanted was for Tori to return home with him. When she'd refused earlier tonight, Jake had impulsively grabbed Tiffany, taking her with him. He'd known that if he and Tiffany were back on Edisto Island, Tori would follow. *His master plan.* Terrible regrets assailed Jake, and a knifelike pain squeezed his heart as he thought of his fifteen-month-old daughter.

Tori had not come to see him yet, and Jake understood why. It was because she blamed him for the death of their only child. Jake sat up gingerly in the bed. He had escaped the car accident with nothing more than a few deep cuts and bruises. *It should have been him. He should have been the one to die.* Then the realization hit him. He was doomed to live a lifetime of guilt. One where forgiveness would never come.

There was a light rap on the hospital door and a woman stuck her head inside.

"I-I came as soon as I heard," she stammered.

Concern was etched all over Sheila's face. Tears bordered the eyes of his partner. Sheila Moore was a tigress when it came to business, but seeing her like this . . . Jake had never seen her look so distraught. She had loved Tiffany as if she were her own daughter.

She walked briskly into the room, saying, "I'm so sorry, Jake. I'm so sorry." Huge tears slipped from her eyes and slid down dark chocolate-hued cheeks.

"I killed her," he croaked. "I killed Tiffany."

She sat on the edge of the bed, embracing him. "No . . ." Sheila whispered. "Jake, this isn't your fault. The other driver ran a red light. He was drunk. You would never hurt Tiffany. Tori knows that."

In a desperate gesture, Jake gripped her by the arms and said, "Sheila, I need your help."

"What is it?"

"I need to get out of here. Now."

She looked surprised by his request. "What about Tori?"

Jake shook his head sadly. "She blames me for Tiffany's death, I know it. Tori hates me."

"No, she doesn't," Sheila denied. "She's just upset right now."

He wasn't convinced. "I don't blame her, because I hate myself."

"Are you sure about this, Jake?"

He nodded, ignoring the ache throbbing in his head. Easing his feet out of bed, Jake stood up. Pain shot downward, and the bandage covering the gash on his thigh became tinged with his blood. His badly stained pants had been ripped by the paramedics at the scene. Jake imagined he must look a sight, but at the moment, he didn't care. All he could think about right now was escaping. He couldn't stay in the hospital a minute longer.

Although Jake kept telling himself that he wanted to spare his wife the torment of his presence, deep within, the real reason behind his leaving was that he couldn't face Tori.

He groaned in agony.

"How's your leg?" Sheila asked. "You look like you're in a lot of pain."

"I'll be fine," he managed to get out. His leg was killing him, but Jake had to get out of the hospital. He wanted to escape all that had taken place this evening.

Jake moved as fast as his injuries would allow. Every now and then he would groan in pain, but with Sheila's assistance, he made his way out of the hospital and into her car.

As Sheila drove away from the hospital into the endless night, only once did Jake glance backward. "Tori, honey, I'm so sorry. I just wanted you and Tiffany to come home," he whispered. Those words weighed upon him, choking him.

"You should go check on your husband," Linda Samuels-Dawson advised her daughter. "We've been here for hours, and I'm sure he's wondering where you are."

"Mama, how can I face Jake right now?" Tori asked in a low, tormented voice. "I have to t-tell him that Tiffany's g-gone. H-how can I do that?" Grief and despair tore at her heart.

Patting Tori's hand, Linda suggested, "I could tell him for you, sugar."

Tori shook her head woefully. "No, I have to do it. Mama, he's going to blame himself. I know Jake." A blade of guilt lay buried in her breast, and she broke into fresh sobs. "He came to Aunt Kate's house demanding that I come home. I refused." Tori paused slightly before continuing. "I don't know why I just didn't agree to go back home with him. Maybe . . . maybe none of this would have happened."

"You and Jake shouldn't blame yourselves for what happened. It was an unfortunate accident."

"Mama, I walked out on my marriage. I did, and it was wrong. I shouldn't have left just like that. If I'd stayed home . . ." Tori gestured toward a room at the far end of the corridor. "Now I've got to go in there, and tell the man I love more than anything that our daughter is dead. How are we going to get through this? Mama, I have to be honest. I'm not sure we can. Our marriage hasn't been on solid ground for the past year or so. I don't know if I can survive losing Jake, too." She closed her eyes, feeling utterly miserable.

"Honey, you don't have to worry about that. You and Jake love each other. You need him right now and he needs you, too. Put this situation in the Lord's hands, sugar." Linda embraced her daughter. "Right now, we're all grieving for our precious little girl, but Tiffany's gone home. She's in heaven." Wiping away a tear, she tried to smile. "In time, everything will get easier. It doesn't seem like it right now, but it will."

Tori glanced down at the stuffed teddy bear she was holding. "This is . . . w-was Tiffany's favorite toy." She gulped hard, hot tears slipping down her cheeks. "Oh, Lord, my baby. I'll never get to hold my little girl again. Sh-she won't ever see her second birthday or . . ." She yielded to the compulsive sobs that shook her.

Tori was vaguely aware of the presence of her cousin and aunt. When she was all cried out, Tori went to the bathroom to wash her face. When she came out, she found her mother talking to her Aunt Kate and her cousin, Charlene. Wiping her nose with a damp tissue, Tori announced, "I need to go see Jake."

"Do you want me to go with you?"

Tori shook her head. "Thanks, Mama, but no. This is something I have to do on my own." She placed a trembling hand on her face. "Do I look okay?"

Charlene nodded. "You look fine, honey."

"Remember, now, I'll be right out here if you need me." Linda hugged her daughter once again before saying, "You go on down there to your husband. At a time like this, you two shouldn't be apart."

Tori nodded. "You're right, Mama." She strolled down the long, narrow corridor to the room where her husband lay. How was she going to get through this? She needed to be strong, she silently reasoned. Jake would need her. Just as she neared his door, Tori prayed for the right words to come.

She was totally unprepared for what she found. The bed was empty. Where was her husband? Tori searched every inch of the room. Frantic, she rushed out of the room, almost colliding into a nurse pushing a cart laden with sterile medical supplies. She tore past the woman and ran to the nurses' station, asking, "Where is my husband? His name is Jake Madison. Did someone move him? Did they take him to X ray or something?"

The nurse standing there looked as bewildered as she did. Her eyes seemed to soften as she took in Tori's overwrought expression. In a calming voice, she replied, "Mrs. Madison, I'm sure he probably left the room for a minute. He shouldn't be out of bed, but . . ."

"No, he's not here," Tori insisted. "I know it. I've looked everywhere for him. Jake is not here."

Tori walked up and down the corridor, peeking in rooms. Flustered and frightened, she turned and went in the other direction. Charlene spotted her and told the others. They rushed toward her.

Her mother reached her first. "Tori, what's wrong, honey?"

Tears streaming down her face, Tori answered, "He's gone, Mama. Jake's disappeared." Tiffany was gone and now her husband had walked out of her life. The truth sank through her, twisting and hurting. The shock of everything that had happened was unlike anything she'd ever experienced. It spread through her, wave after wave until there was nothing left except the raw sores of an aching heart.

Chapter One

One year later

"Where would you like to go, sir?"

Jake gave the airline representative a blank stare. He wanted to go home to Charleston, where the streets were narrow, some paved with cobblestones, and traditions were set in stone. Jake even missed the one-way traffic that could be frustrating during rush hour.

It was the month of March. By now, the wind was warm and the trees fully clothed and fertile with new life stirring at the tips of aging limbs. It was also time for the annual charity ball hosted by his mother. Jake had not talked to her or his younger brother, Shepard, since the night he left the hospital. He'd been too ashamed to face them. Sheila was the only person with whom he'd kept in contact. At the moment, Jake was debating whether or not to call her now and inform her of his intentions. He finally decided to surprise all of them.

"Sir?" the representative prompted.

"Savannah. I'm going to Savannah, Georgia." Before he went home to South Carolina, he wanted to see Tori. Sheila had told him that Tori had returned to Brunswick, Georgia, right after the accident with her mother. She'd even buried Tiffany there. From

7

Savannah, Jake would rent a car and make the hour-long drive to Brunswick. He didn't want to go another day without seeing Tori's face. He missed her bright smile and her big beautiful brown eyes.

For months now, Jake had awaited this moment with an eagerness of a young man on his first date. He knew he wouldn't get close enough to touch her ever again, so Jake resolved to be content with stolen glimpses of Tori. He needed to see for himself how she'd fared over the past year. Did she hate him still? How could she not? he reasoned.

Jake allowed himself to briefly imagine what it would actually feel like to be in the same room with her once again. In his fantasies, they were still a family. Even Tiffany was alive.

Jake shuddered as he took his airplane ticket and boarding pass. No, he would never see Tiffany again, and Tori would no longer be a part of his life.

He was tired. Jake was tired of running, and tired of living out of a suitcase. He'd spent the last year traveling all over Europe and the Caribbean. But not even his love for exotic travel could help Jake achieve the sense of peace that he desperately sought.

He took a seat and waited for boarding to begin. Jake opened the magazine he'd brought with him to read but couldn't concentrate. He finally gave up trying altogether. Over and over in his mind, Jake asked himself, *Am I really ready to go back home?* The truth of the matter was that he wasn't sure, but it was time he did.

When the boarding began, Jake rose to his feet. Moving slowly, he got in line.

Fifteen minutes later, Jake was in his seat and they were preparing to take off. He closed his eyes, hoping sleep would come quickly. Flying always made him uncomfortable.

As the plane made its ascent toward the heavens, Jake experienced a small measure of panic. He wished desperately that Tori were sitting beside him. She'd always been able to distract him during their airline travel. Never in his life had he felt more alone.

Jake reached down to rub his thigh. The wound he'd received in

8

the car accident bothered him still and had left him with a permanent limp.

The airplane hit an air pocket and Jake swallowed his anxiety. He would be elated when this plane ride was over. Shifting uneasily in his seat, Jake drummed his fingernails on the armrest and glanced across the aisle to the woman sitting there. She looked completely relaxed.

Jake felt silly for being afraid of flying, but it did nothing to ease the fear. This particular weakness was a souvenir of his youth, a remnant of the tragedy that tainted his childhood and had stolen his father from him.

On a business trip, Jake's father died in a plane crash. Jake's fear of flying started from that moment on. He had never been one to be controlled, so he'd set out to conquer that fear. But it seemed no matter how many planes he'd taken, the fear remained. It was only after he was miles into his flight that Jake would begin to relax.

Hours later, Jake rejoiced when the plane landed in Savannah. After making the necessary arrangements for a rental car, he decided to stay in town for the night and drive to Brunswick in the morning.

Jake checked into the Gastonian, a hotel in the historic district on Gaston Street. After a quick shower, he was finally able to relax. He hadn't eaten anything on the plane, so Jake was hungry.

What was the name of the restaurant Tori loved here in Savannah? The question hammered at him. He remembered that it was somewhere near Trustees Garden. "The Pirates' House," Jake murmured to himself. "That's it."

Picking up the phone book, he quickly located the number and called to make reservations for dinner. It no longer felt odd making reservations for one since Jake had been alone for most of the past year. He'd even celebrated his thirty-eighth birthday by himself. Sheila had offered to join him, but Jake had refused.

Every other month, Sheila would fly to wherever he was staying at the moment. Jake was grateful for her friendship. Although she'd hinted that there could be more between them, he never pursued it any further outside of satisfying moments of lust. The only woman on his mind was Tori.

He'd tried to forget about her, but found he couldn't. When Sheila told him that Tori had decided to move back to Brunswick, Jake pretty much figured that his marriage was over.

It had taken time, but he'd finally come to accept that fact. But that acceptance did not void the love he felt for Tori. His feelings were akin to an addiction, fueled by his need for her. Jake knew he was taking a risk by seeing her again, because he knew once he had a glimpse of her, walking away would not be easy.

Chapter Two

Charleston, South Carolina

Tori stared up at the burgundy- and gold-colored letters gracing the tall glass structure of modern architecture housing her husband's company. The Web design and marketing firm of Madison Moore Creative Visual Solutions, Inc., had been a dream of Jake's since his college days. She refused to believe that he would just walk away from all of his hard work. He had been obsessed with making Madison Moore a success. There had been times in the past when Tori had strongly suspected the company meant more to Jake than his own marriage.

While making the drive over, she'd felt she was doing the right thing by coming to Sheila's office, but now that she'd arrived, all she felt was a sense of dread. Tori glanced down at the clothes she'd chosen with care this morning. The khaki skirt that nearly reached her ankles and the crisp, white linen shirt looked fine, but the clean white Keds and the white cotton socks suddenly felt wrong.

She turned to leave but changed her mind. Tori told herself what she was wearing did not define who she was as a woman.

Tori strode into the four-story building with purpose. The receptionist in the lobby area greeted her with a smile.

"Mrs. Madison, how are you?"

Tori returned the woman's smile with one of her own. "I'm fine, Selma. How about you?"

"I'm okay." Selma paused for a minute before saying, "We all miss Mr. Madison so much around here."

Tori felt ice spreading through her stomach. She had no idea what the employees had been told, and scrambled for an appropriate response.

Selma's next comment spared her. "We all hope he'll be ready to return back to work real soon."

Nodding in agreement, Tori said, "Me, too."

They talked for a few minutes before Tori took the elevator to the fourth floor. She was there to see someone in particular.

As she stood in the doorway of Sheila Moore's office, Tori swallowed the bitterness that threatened to spill forth. Sheila's designer clothes and meticulously applied makeup made her look like a high-powered corporate executive. Unconsciously, Tori placed a hand on her own face, which was completely devoid of makeup—the way Jake liked it. Fighting the swell of anger and the strong smell of betrayal, she took a deep calming breath before saying, "Hello, Sheila."

Looking up from her seventeen-inch flat-screen monitor, Sheila appeared a little unsure at first, but immediately relaxed. An easy smile formed on her lips as she slid gracefully from behind her desk. "Tori, what a surprise. How are you?" she inquired pleasantly.

Tori took a step backward as Sheila neared. She would never trust this woman again. "Have you heard from Jake?" she asked, getting straight to the point of her visit.

Drawing a blank expression, Sheila answered, "No, I haven't. Tori, you didn't have to come all the way here to ask me that. When we last spoke on the phone, I gave you my word that I would call you if I heard anything."

"Obviously, I don't believe you," Tori stated coldly.

One of the employees passing by glanced at them.

Sheila hastily closed the door to her office. "I never meant to hurt you. Jake and I were entertaining potential clients and we drank too much—"

Tori cut her off by saying, "I didn't come here to talk about that, Sheila."

"I just want you to know it never meant anything."

Changing the subject, Tori inquired, "How is it that you're Jake's partner—his right hand—and you have no idea where he is?" Tori ran her fingers along the edge of Sheila's desk before picking up a crystal picture frame, containing a photo of Jake and Sheila. They were huddled close together and laughing during one of the many company functions they often attended, leaving Tori at home alone with Tiffany. One could easily assume they were a couple.

Swallowing her despair, Tori put the picture back on the desk, all the while conscious of Sheila's gaze. If she was waiting for Tori to react, then it would be a long wait. She wasn't going to give Sheila the satisfaction of seeing her fall apart.

The chill between them seemed to grow.

"Jake signed over his interests in the company to me. It was all arranged by his lawyer."

Tori still didn't believe her and told her so. "I can easily make a call to our attorney and find out if you're telling the truth. I can't imagine Jake just signing over his interests to you. He loves Madison Moore too much. Nor do I believe for one minute our lawyer would do something like this without informing me."

"If I hear from Jake, I'll call you. I promise," Sheila said smoothly, with no expression on her face.

Tori didn't bat an eye when she responded, "Your promises mean nothing to me, Sheila."

A muscle quivered at Sheila's jaw. "We were friends. I really miss you."

"You were never *my* friend, Sheila. If you were, you wouldn't have slept with my husband."

"You're wrong. I was . . . I am your friend," Sheila managed through stiff lips.

Folding her arms across her chest, Tori stated, "If that's true, then prove it. Tell me where I can find my husband."

"I'm sorry . . ." Sheila began.

Tori's throat ached with defeat. "Jake's always said you were extremely loyal." Turning, she strolled toward the door without a backward glance.

Inside, she was steaming. Sheila was lying, and Tori knew it. Jake wasn't using any of the credit cards they shared. He hadn't touched any of their joint accounts either, so he had to be using an account of which she had no knowledge. Jake had several business and personal accounts. Tori was sure she didn't know about all of them.

Not knowing where her husband was ripped Tori's patience. She couldn't go on much longer. She needed to find Jake, even if it meant the end of her marriage. The message he was sending by his absence seemed pretty clear to Tori. He obviously didn't want to be with her.

It took a minute to realize that Tori had been so consumed with her thoughts, she hadn't pressed the button to summon the elevator. She pressed it now.

The elevator arrived a few minutes later. Tori stepped inside, grateful that it was empty. When she reached the lobby, Tori waved at Selma. She wanted desperately to reach the comfort of her car before she humiliated herself by bursting into tears.

Inside her black Ford Explorer, Tori allowed her tears to fall. Calling to mind the photograph sitting on Sheila's desk, she cried harder. When would this nightmare ever end?

Tori pulled a tissue out of her purse and wiped her face. She planned to visit her mother-in-law next, and she didn't want Gwendolyn Madison to know she'd been crying. Tori didn't want to upset Jake's mother.

She pulled down her mirror and stared into it. The woman who stared back looked older than her twenty-eight years. Her copper complexion was an unnatural pale color, her face was puffy, and the dark circles beneath her eyes didn't enhance her appearance at all.

Tori brushed her hair back away from her face and pulled it into a ponytail, but it didn't help. She still looked tired and unhappy. She dug into her purse for her sunglasses and a metal clip for her unruly dark hair.

She composed herself and started the car. Tori glanced back at Madison Moore before pulling out of the parking lot. "How could you treat me like this, Jake?" she whispered.

Chapter Three

Tori greeted her mother-in-law warmly with a kiss on the cheek. "Della let me in downstairs."

"Oh, my goodness, it's good to see you, dear. I was so glad to get your call earlier. I'm happy you decided to move back into your house."

Smiling, Tori said, "It's good to see you, too. There was no way I'd leave Charleston without seeing you." She was surprised to see how frail her mother-in-law had become in the last couple of months. Gwendolyn Madison used to be a tall, full-figured woman, but now she looked much too thin. The king-size bed almost seemed to swallow her. Concerned, Tori inquired, "How are you feeling?"

"I have good days and bad." Gwendolyn tried to smile, but her eyes were bleak. "The cancer has spread to my brain. Doctors have given me six months." Shrugging, she said quietly, "I just take it one day at a time. Me and the good Lord above."

Easing down onto the bed beside her mother-in-law, Tori announced, "I went by Madison Moore earlier to see Sheila. She's still claiming that she hasn't heard from Jake."

"She's his partner, so how can she not know?" Gwendolyn sighed heavily. "I don't understand my son. I used to try and warn him about Sheila. That woman never had his best interests at heart. She's not his friend."

"Jake is naive where Sheila is concerned." Tori shook her head regretfully. "I thought he would eventually contact you and Shepard though." She resisted the urge to wrap herself in a cocoon of anguish.

Gwendolyn leaned back against a fluffy stack of pillows, eyeing Tori. "Tell me, dear. Do you still love my son?"

"Mother Madison, he's my husband and he was Tiffany's father. I will always love Jake, but I'm really not the one you should be asking that question."

"I know my Jake. He's going to come home, dear." Gwendolyn reached over and gently touched Tori's face. "Stop your tears. Jake's coming home."

"But will he come home to me or Sheila?"

Gwendolyn's almond-shaped eyes widened with astonishment. "I know things look bad, but one thing I know for sure. Tori, he doesn't love Sheila Moore. *Jake loves you.*"

Tori's eyes became tear-bright and her mind was languid, without hope. "But Sheila's got her hooks in him. She's probably the only one who's spoken to Jake in this last year." She paused a moment before continuing. "Who knows how close they've become?"

"I don't believe it. *Jake and Sheila?*" Gwendolyn shook her head. "No. He wouldn't."

"Jake and I were having lots of problems before Tiffany died," Tori admitted. "He wasn't happy and neither was I. After I found out he slept with Sheila—I just couldn't stay in the same house with him. I took Tiffany and moved out." Her voice was filled with tears and her eyes darkened with pain. "Maybe Jake blames me for her death. Maybe he hates me."

A soft gasp escaped Gwendolyn. "You can't really believe that. Surely, you know Jake much better than that."

Tori's back ached between her shoulder blades, so she shifted her position. Her shoulders were tense, as if she was bracing herself against the impact of what she was about to say. "He wouldn't have left me if he'd really loved me, Mother Madison." Her voice sounded weak, not her voice at all.

"Well, well, well," a deep voice boomed behind them. Tori knew without turning around that it was her brother-in-law, Shepard.

She glanced over her shoulder, gazing at him in despair. "Shepard, I didn't know you were home." Tears stung Tori's eyes, turning everything into a blur. Just looking at her brother-in-law brought a stab of pain to her heart. He looked so much like Jake. Over six feet tall, his handsome features were chiseled in a sun-tinted golden brown. Shepard and Jake both had sparkling, soft brown eyes and full lips like their mother.

Strolling into the room, he stated, "I left the office to check on Mother." Leaning down, Shepard planted a kiss on Gwendolyn's cheek. "How are you doing?" he asked.

"I'm feeling fine, son," she replied with a smile.

Tori asked, "Have you been able to find out anything about Jake?"

Shepard looked from one woman to the other, then shook his head. "No. Sheila's sticking to her story."

Gwendolyn wore a look of disgust. "I really don't understand that woman."

"I don't, either," Shepard agreed. "I told her about Mother's cancer spreading and she still wouldn't tell me anything. Sheila's loyal to Jake, if nothing el—" He caught sight of the pain in Tori's face. "I'm sorry."

"It's true, Shepard. No matter how much it hurts. I have to accept the truth." She was facing a lightless future, and her sense of loss had begun to weigh her down.

Taking Tori's hand in her own, Gwendolyn said, "Don't say that, dear. You can't give up hope."

"I just wish I knew if he were safe. It doesn't matter whether or not he comes home to me—I just want to know that he's well."

"Come closer, Shepard," Gwendolyn requested. "Why don't we come together right now as a family and pray for Jake's safe return home?"

Tori stood up and moved to stand near the head of the bed. Shepard strode over to the other side. Holding hands, the three bowed their heads.

Gwendolyn started to pray. "Most gracious Father, we come before You to ask Your forgiveness of our sins. We come before You to say thank You for blessing us every day, but especially today. Today is the only day that counts because it may be our last. Lord, we pray for the safe return of my son, Jake. Comfort him and give him strength to make the journey home. Thank You, Lord. I ask this in Jesus' name. . . ."

"Amen," they chorused.

Tori gloried briefly in the shared moment. Glancing over at the clock on the bedside table, she spent a few more minutes talking before she finally said, "I've kept you up long enough, Mother Madison, so get some rest. I know you want to be ready for the charity ball. I can't believe you are throwing a big party like this."

"I'm not dead yet, dear. This year Shepard chaired the committee and handled most of the arrangements for me. I didn't have to do anything. You know how much it means to me to raise funds for the terminally ill children and the Make A Dream Come True Foundation. God willing, I'm going to be there. When I'm gone, I hope Shepard will continue to hold the ball each year. It's a big fund-raiser."

"Della's fixing dinner right now," Shepard announced. "Why don't you stay and eat with us?"

"Thanks, but I'm going to have to take a rain check. Aunt Kate and Charlene are at my house waiting on me." Tori embraced her mother-in-law. "I'll give you a call tomorrow. You take it easy now."

Meeting Shepard's eyes, she asked, "Walk me out?"

He nodded. "Sure."

When they left the bedroom and were out of Gwendolyn's earshot, he asked, "Are you writing my brother off, Tori?"

She stiffened under his glance. "No. I'm just trying to face reality and move on with my life. If Jake wanted me, he would come home," she snapped out of frustration.

Immediately feeling guilty over her outburst, Tori said, "I'm so sorry. I shouldn't be taking my frustration out on you."

He embraced her. "It's okay, sis. I understand. I miss him, too. Mother sent invitations to everybody, including all of Jake's friends. Someone out there is bound to know how to contact him."

"You think he'll come home? Just like that?"

"I hope so," Shepard confessed. "Jake loves you, Tori, and I'm counting on that love to bring him home." He gave her another hug. "Tell Charlene I'll give her a call later this evening."

"I will."

As Tori headed to the door, she kissed Shepard on the cheek. "I'll see you later." She made her way to her car and climbed in. She drove away without looking back. If Shepard was right and Jake did indeed come home, what would happen then?

More important, what would she do?

Chapter Four

Tori was a lover of African-American history, and the Low-country region of South Carolina was rich with it. Even the building at 91 Broad Street, which she'd just driven by, figured prominently in history.

In 1886, it housed the first black law firm in America. It was the law firm of William Whipper, Macon Allen, and Robert Brown Elliot. Elliot was also the editor of the oldest black newpaper in America, the *Missionary Recorder*.

She followed Route 17 out of Charleston, driving along the narrow strip of land along the coast. She stuck a disc into the CD player and relaxed for the forty-five-minute drive to Edisto Island. It wasn't until Tori reached Highway 174 that she slowed her speed.

On her left as she entered Edisto Island was the Zion Baptist church, built in 1810 by Hepzibah Jenkins for the plantation slaves. She continued her drive, passing both elegant plantation homes and smaller, modular houses nestled on generous squares of grass.

While she drove, Tori played around with the idea of forming an African-American heritage trail along coastal Carolina. The more she thought about it, the more she grew excited over the idea of exploring what her ancestors never imagined would become history. She could start the tour in Charleston and follow the trail back to Edisto Island.

At last, she came to the two-story Colonial-style house that Jake had conceived, designed, and built for her. It looked exactly as it had when she'd left a little over a year ago. Moss furred the trees guarding the sparkling pond behind the house, and the grass was so green and healthy, Tori knew that if she took off her shoes and walked through it, the lawn would feel like she was walking on a cloud.

She parked her car in the driveway and got out, slowly appraising her surroundings. Edisto Island was still one of the real jewels of the South Carolina coastline. During her stay in Georgia, Tori had missed the picturesque area that consisted of moss-covered oak archways and the antebellum plantation estates that successfully managed to retain the atmosphere of the old South.

Strolling toward the house, Tori heard a car passing by with a loud muffler. It brought to mind the old cars that sat rusting in a few of the front yards along Highway 174, wrapped in honeysuckle and wisteria vines. A smile formed on her lips. It felt good to be home.

Charlene met her on the front porch. "Well, how did it go? Did you find out anything from that witch?"

Tori didn't miss the bridled anger in Charlene's voice. She shook her head. "No. Sheila's still not telling me a thing. I stopped by to visit Mother Madison, and she hasn't heard from Jake, either."

"What about Shepard? He told me he was going to talk to Sheila, too."

"No, nothing." Tori followed her cousin into the house. In the entry hall, an English chaise and American sofa, covered in a neo-classical damask, sat on opposite walls facing each other, with a mahogany sofa table holding an elaborate floral arrangement.

She fingered one of the roses, which had been cut from her own garden in the back of the house. Jake had had a colorful arrangement of rosebushes planted there right before they were married. It was one of his wedding gifts to her.

"Why on earth did you and Jake buy such a big house?" Charlene asked. "Mama and I are plum wore out trying to get this place cleaned."

"Humph. I wonder that myself," Kate muttered as she joined them in the living room. "Tori, I didn't know you were back. How did your little visit go?"

Laying her keys and her purse on the sofa table, she replied, "I just got back. Mother Madison looks so fragile, but she's got such a strong spirit, I can't imagine her letting the cancer get the best of her. I saw Shepard, too. He thinks that Jake may come home in time for the charity ball."

"If Jake wanted to come home, he would. Wouldna been gone all this time, either."

Her aunt's comment sent a stab of pain through her, although Tori had expressed the same sentiment earlier. It seemed to hurt more when someone else said it.

"Mama made dinner," Charlene announced abruptly. "Hope you're hungry."

"I'm starved," Tori confessed as she followed her cousin to the kitchen. After washing her hands in the sink, she picked up an empty plate. Her aunt had prepared collard greens, cornbread, and catfish. There was also a pitcher of fresh lemonade on the marble countertop.

Seated around the oak dining-room table, Tori bowed her head and prayed over their dinner. When she was done, they attacked their food with relish.

"There's a nice young man at church who has had his eye on Charlene for a while now. She don't pay him any mind, though," Kate announced.

Without lifting her eyes from her plate, Charlene stated firmly, "I'm not interested in Sammy Banks."

Tori took a sip of the cool, refreshing lemonade before saying,

"She's in love with my brother-in-law. Besides, they're engaged, so why in the world would she be interested in another man?"

"You didn't tell her?" Kate demanded.

"Tell me what?"

"Shepard called off the wedding. Those Madison men don't do anything but break a woman's heart."

"Mama, that's not true! Shepard and I decided to postpone the wedding, that's all."

Tori was surprised. This was the first she'd heard of this. "I didn't know about your postponing the wedding. I was under the impression you hadn't even set a wedding date."

"We hadn't," Charlene confessed. "We're just taking some time to think about some things."

"My child's in denial," Kate announced. "She refuses to believe that Shepard dumped her."

Charlene's eyes flashed in anger. "No, he didn't."

Kate's face went grim and she started to mutter under her breath.

"What was that, Aunt Kate?" Tori questioned, a smile trailing her lips. Her aunt had always been opinionated, but when it came to the Madisons, it seemed she could never say anything nice about any of the Madison men. What was up with that? she wondered.

"I said that you both should have your fill of Madison men. They bring a girl nothing but heartache."

"Mama . . ." Charlene's expression grew hard and resentful. "Why do you always have to—"

"Aunt Kate," Tori asserted quickly, hoping to deflect the argument that was sure to come. "Jake and I both are to blame for what went wrong in our marriage. He and Shepard are two very different men. You shouldn't lump them into one pile like that."

Kate cut her eyes at her niece. "I don't care what you say, young lady. I've known the Madison family from way back. Long before Simon married Gwendolyn. Heck, I've known Jake and his brother since they was knee-high to ducks. They both want things their way or no way."

"Mama, nobody wants to hear about that stuff," Charlene complained.

Kate ignored her daughter. "When I worked as a housekeeper in the Madison household, Jake and Shepard were pure terrors. There were many times I wanted to take those boys out to the woods back behind that big fancy house and whup 'em good."

Memories of Jake as a little boy skipped through Tori's mind. She recalled how she used to follow him around, hoping he would notice her. He never did.

After her mother married Leroy Dawson, they'd moved to Brunswick. Tori had had to settle for spending summer vacations on the island with Aunt Kate and Charlene. Despite visiting every summer, she hadn't seen Jake again until her sixteenth birthday. Although Tori had sensed that he was attracted to her, Jake hadn't vocalized his feelings until the following summer.

Caught up in memories of a much happier time, Tori finished her dinner. Jake was the only man she'd ever loved and she would never love another.

Sheila slammed down the telephone in frustration. She'd called every number she had for Jake, but was unsuccessful in locating him. Shepard's news regarding their mother's health motivated her into making this call. However, she had no intention of telling Jake about Tori's visit. She made it a point to avoid even mentioning her name to him. It was in her best interest that Jake continue to believe Tori wanted nothing to do with him.

Sheila and Jake had attended college together, both studying engineering. Back then, she had done everything she could to get close to Jake, but he'd paid her no mind. During those days, no one had paid her much attention. Her hair was short and nappy, her eyeglasses thick; she was reed-thin and her clothes unfashionable.

It wasn't until a few months after Jake married Tori that Sheila had run into him again. By then, she'd had a complete makeover.

Hair, cosmetic surgery, and a wardrobe of expensive clothes. She'd manipulated a meeting with him through a mutual friend and presented him with the proposal to start Madison Moore, knowing all along that Jake had always envisioned such a company. Sheila had also known that something so simple as using a combination of their last names was also part of the appeal for him. It gave Jake a sense of control.

Until he'd run into Sheila, he had been unsuccessful in his business ventures. Part of it was due to incompatible partners, and the other was his lack of motivation when it came to seeing a project through. The son of the founder of Charleston's only black-owned bank, Jake had the money and the vision, but Sheila had the ability to see it through. She had a way of making him feel just as excited about a project as she was. Sheila's enthusiasm about a project always spurred him into action. Those were the qualities that made them a great team.

After Tori gave birth to Tiffany, she'd suffered a severe case of postpartum depression. As she and Jake had drifted further apart, he and Sheila had begun to get close. She'd quickly become his confidant.

When Tori didn't lose all of the weight she'd gained with Tiffany, her insecurities had mounted and she'd begun accusing Jake of cheating on her. Sheila had been thrilled when he'd begun to vent all of his frustrations to her. It had enabled her to use all he'd told her against Tori. Sheila had been able to provide Jake with the attention he'd lacked from his wife.

Sheila smiled at the memory of the first night of passion she'd shared with Jake. They had thrown a party in the penthouse of the Hotel Augustus after landing a huge account. After the guests left, Jake and Sheila had decided to stay a little longer to drink more champagne.

He and Tori had had a big argument right before the party, which was why Tori hadn't come with him. When Sheila had kissed him, Jake had offered no resistance. Things had grown more passionate between them, and soon they'd found themselves in the bedroom.

After making love, Sheila had ordered more champagne for them. Everything had been perfect until Tori had shown up at the door instead of room service. Caught with his pants down, Jake had been filled with remorse and kept his distance for the next couple of days. She'd felt all hope was lost until the night Tiffany died. In his moment of grief, he'd sought her out. Not his wife.

Over the past year, Sheila had been the only one who knew of his whereabouts. She had even managed to spend a few stolen moments with Jake every now and then. But he'd always become consumed with guilt afterward. Once his marriage was finally over, all that would change, however.

She stared over at the phone. "Jake, where are you?" Sheila asked. In her mind, she replayed their last conversation. He'd been thinking about coming home. . . .

Sheila jumped to her feet and grabbed her purse off the sofa table. "That's it. Jake's on his way home. No, he could already be there." She ran out of her luxury town house and climbed into her silver Mercedes-Benz.

Jake had given her a set of keys to his house on Edisto Island. Sheila decided to drive out there and wait for him. Excitement flowed through her as she considered the idea that he might already be home. If things went according to plan, Sheila would be moving in permanently.

It had taken some doing, but she believed she'd been successful in getting Jake to realize how much he needed her. Sheila was his friend, his confidant, but that wasn't enough for her. She wanted more. Much more.

She sang to herself as she drove along Highway 174 to Edisto Island. Sheila hoped desperately that she would find Jake safe at home. The last time they'd talked had left her with an uneasy feeling because it was clear that he was struggling with his desire to come home.

In her panic, Sheila had suggested they move the company to London or France. Jake was totally against the idea and had voiced it. She couldn't understand why he was being so adamant.

Although Jake had cried that he hated being so far away from his mother and brother, Sheila didn't believe that was the only reason. Tori was very much a part of the equation.

She was genuinely saddened over Tiffany's death, but on the other hand, Sheila was relieved the bond between Jake and Tori existed no longer.

Chapter Five

Tori walked through her house, trying to figure out how she'd embarked along the wrong path. "What could I have done differently?" she whispered to the silent living room. "How did my marriage end up like this?"

Without an answer, she made her way up the curving staircase to the second floor. Charlene had made sure the windows and doors were all locked before she'd gone to her own room. Tori glanced at the keypad on the wall in the master bedroom, but decided against setting the alarm. Part of the reason was that she hoped Jake would suddenly show up.

She showered and changed into her nightgown.

Arms folded across her chest, Tori stared over at the bed she once shared with Jake. "Lord, what was I thinking by coming back here? This house is filled with so many memories. . . ." Her thoughts died when she heard footsteps in the hallway.

Strolling toward the door, Tori wondered what Charlene was still doing up. It was well after midnight. Her aunt had retired to her room hours ago. When the knob turned and the door opened, Tori's mouth dropped open as she stared at her visitor in shock.

Sheila appeared just as astonished.

"What are you doing here?" they asked in unison.

"*This is my home*," Tori sputtered with indignation. "Wh-what are you doing here?" she asked a second time. She couldn't believe the nerve of this woman. Sheila was acting as if this were her house.

"I . . . I come by every now and then to check on things."

Tori grabbed her robe from the foot of the bed and slipped it over the thin nightgown she wore. "For Jake?" she questioned.

Sheila gave a loud sigh. "Tori—"

"Give it up, Sheila!" she snapped. Giving her a hostile glare, Tori became breathless with rage. "I know that you're in contact with Jake. Now, where is my husband?"

"If he wanted you to know, don't you think he would've told you?" Sheila's curt tone lashed at her.

Tori stiffened. Sheila's barb hurt.

"I'm sorry. I shouldn't have said that."

Although she hated to beg, Tori couldn't help herself. She desperately wanted to find her husband. "Where is he, Sheila? Please, I need to talk to Jake."

"I don't know where he is." Sighing in resignation, Sheila continued, "I tried to reach him earlier, but he'd checked out of the hotel. I have no idea where he went."

Comprehension dawned, leading Tori to ask, "That's why you came here, isn't it? You were hoping to find Jake here. I'm right, aren't I?"

Sheila didn't respond.

"Now, why would you think that Jake's come home?"

"As I told you earlier, I come out here often to check on the house."

"You're lying, Sheila." Tori's voice was quiet, yet held an undertone of cold contempt.

With a look of defiance, Sheila met Tori's gaze. "How long will you be staying here?"

"This is my home, Sheila. I intend to *live* in it."

Surprise registered in Sheila's eyes for a brief second before it quickly disappeared. "Of course." Backing to the door, she said, "I should be going."

"Good night, Sheila."

Charlene appeared in the doorway, blocking Sheila's exit. "What's *she* doing here?"

"*She* was just leaving," Sheila sniped. Walking briskly, she brushed past Charlene, her expensive Adrienne Vittadini suit contrasting with the wrinkled oversize burnt-orange-colored T-shirt Charlene was wearing.

Tori called out to her. "Sheila, wait one second."

"What is it?"

She walked over to Sheila and held out her hand. "I need the keys to the house. You won't be needing them anymore."

Sheila dropped them into Tori's hand, her mouth twisted into a frown.

Charlene escorted Sheila to the front door while Tori stood watching from the top of the stairs.

Before she left, Sheila glanced up at her and gave a small smile. Tori kept her expression blank.

After Sheila drove off, her cousin met her back inside her bedroom. "I can't believe that woman," Charlene commented. "She never gives up, does she?"

Tori shook her head. "That's one of the qualities Jake admires most in Sheila." She climbed into the bed, saying, "Charlene, I thought you'd already gone to sleep. I didn't know you were still up."

"I was drifting off until I heard voices." She sat down on the edge of the king-size bed. "Why was she here?"

"Sheila thought Jake might have come back."

Inclining her head, Charlene asked, "Why would she think that?"

"She's been in touch with him all this time."

"I knew she'd been lying to you." Anger flashed in Charlene's eyes. "That conniving little witch."

Tori bit back a smile.

"So, where is Jake?"

Tori repeated what Sheila had told her.

"And you believe her?"

"I do. *This time.*" Tori leaned back against a stack of pillows piled against the headboard. "There was something in her face. She looked worried."

"Maybe he's finally coming home."

"If only that were true," Tori murmured softly. "Then at least I would know where I stand with him."

"You know, no one would blame you if you filed for a legal separation or even a divorce. Jake walked out on you. It's abandonment."

Tori nodded. She'd thought about it several times over the past three months, but she could never summon the courage to go through with it. "I've thought about it, Charlene, but it's something I have to really pray on."

"Well, I'm gonna go to bed," Charlene announced. "It's late and I'm worn out."

"I'll see you in the morning. Oh, do me a favor. Remind me to call and change the alarm code tomorrow—Jake gave Sheila keys, so he may have given her the code as well." When her cousin left, Tori burrowed under the covers and lay staring up at the ceiling, blinking back hot tears. When she realized that she was sleeping on *his* side of the bed, Tori quickly scooted to the other side. She turned on her side and closed her eyes, but not because she was sleepy—she was crying.

Chapter Six

"You two look like you could use a tall glass of iced tea. Hard day?" Kate stepped aside to let Tori and Charlene enter the house. "Y'all must have worked hard today setting up that bookstore. You both look worn out."

Tori embraced her aunt. "It's been an exhausting day, but at least we got most of the books unpacked. It's such a good feeling having something that belongs to you. I guess I can understand some of what Jake was feeling when it came to Madison Moore. This bookstore belongs to me and Charlene. It's ours. We work for ourselves, and I love it."

Charlene agreed. "I don't think I've ever worked so hard for anything like I do for this store. I can hardly wait for the doors to open."

"I almost forgot," Kate announced. "Your mother called to see how you're doing. She told me that she really wasn't sure about your coming back, Tori. Linda thought being back in this house might bring back too many memories. She's real worried about you."

"There are a lot of good memories here, Aunt Kate. I just wish

things were different, you know? With Tiffany gone . . . and Jake."
She gave a sad smile. "The one good thing that's come out of all
this is that my relationship with God is a much closer one. I couldn't
have made it without Him."

Charlene nodded in agreement. "Isn't it wonderful? He's always
there for us, no matter what. And no matter where we are in our
lives."

"Bringing Jake home has been my prayer for the past year."

"What would you do?" Charlene questioned. "After all that's
happened, could you just take him back just like that?"

"My heart would tell me to throw my arms around him, but my
head would caution me to wait, and let Jake make the first move."
Tori looked over at her cousin. "My biggest fear is that Jake doesn't
love me anymore."

"What would you do then?"

Shrugging, Tori replied, "Then I guess I move on with my life,
but as painful as that would be, at least I'd know for sure. The way
things are now, there's no closure for me. I'm ready to move forward and start living again, but then I think about Jake and I can't."

"You still love him?" Kate asked.

"Aunt Kate, I'll never stop loving him. Jake is my husband. He's
the man I vowed to love forever."

"Why don't we change the subject?" Charlene suggested.
"Mama, don't worry about making dinner, because I'm taking Tori
out. Do you want to go with us?"

Kate replied, "No, hon. Y'all go out and have a good time.
Mingle with the young folks."

In truth, Tori would have preferred to turn in early with a good
book, but she didn't want to disappoint her cousin. "So, where are
we going?"

"I thought we'd go to Willow's. I remember how much you used
to like to eat there."

Uneasiness gripped her stomach, and Tori carefully phrased her words. "Sounds good. I can't wait." Willow's was her and Jake's favorite restaurant. He'd proposed to her there. . . . A lot of wonderful memories had taken place in that restaurant.

She'd known all along that returning to this house would bring to the front all that was reminiscent of her life with Jake. God had been her source of strength for all of her life, so she was counting on him to get her through this. It was time she prepared to make new memories. Ones that didn't include Jake.

After her shower, Tori strolled into the large walk-in closet in search of something to wear. Arms folded across her chest, she stood inside, eyeing her clothes.

Tori pulled out a forest green-and-navy multicolored dress with an ivory lace collar that tied in the back. Frowning, she put it back. Next, Tori pulled out a black pantsuit. "Too conservative," she murmured.

Everything in her closet was black, brown, navy, or ivory. She made a mental note to add some colors to her wardrobe. Something bright.

She finally settled on a simple black sheath in a matte jersey fabric. Tori selected a silver necklace and matching bangle. She chose a pair of silver hoop earrings for her ears. Continuing her silver theme, Tori stuck her feet into a pair of silver strappy sandals.

After pulling her hair into a ponytail secured by a silver-and-black barrette, Tori was ready to go. Charlene was waiting for her downstairs, so she grabbed her purse and left the bedroom, but not before taking another long look in the mirror. She didn't even own a tube of lipstick. Tori considered asking Charlene for some, but changed her mind.

Willow's was still as crowded as Tori remembered. She and Charlene didn't have to wait long to be seated, however. Mrs. Willow was there, and she seated them personally.

Charlene grinned as she picked up her menu. "It's good having friends in high places, isn't it?"

Tori nodded woodenly. She didn't need to look at the menu, because it was ingrained in her memory, so her eyes bounced around the room. Every now and then she glimpsed a familiar face and waved.

"You okay?"

Her cousin's question drew her back. She raised her eyes to meet Charlene's concerned gaze. "I'm fine. Why do you ask?"

Putting down her menu, Charlene responded, "You looked kinda sad for a minute there."

Tori gave a slight shrug. "I'm okay. I was just remembering the last time I was here with Jake. We came over to talk about where we went wrong in our marriage."

Charlene was apologetic. "I didn't know. We can leave and go somewhere else," she suggested.

"It's okay," Tori reassured her. "Edisto Island is filled with so many memories that Jake and I made. There's no escaping that."

A waitress arrived to take their food orders.

A tall muscular man made his way over to where they were sitting. Tori glanced up, drawn by the man's gray eyes and bright smile. Surprise gradually gave way to excitement. "Nicholas Washington? Oh, my goodness, it really is you."

He nodded and smiled. "I haven't seen you in a long time, Tori. How have you been?"

"Fine." She introduced her cousin to Nicholas. "He and I attended Glynn Academy together. Now he's a famous author."

He laughed. "I don't know anything about being famous." Nicholas shook Charlene's hand.

"It's nice to meet you," Charlene stated. "I read *Deadly Secrets*. It was a great book. I could hardly put it down."

"Thank you. I'm glad you enjoyed it."

"So, Nicholas, how are you? When did you get here?"

"I'm fine, Tori. I've actually been on the island for a couple of weeks now."

"What brought you here?" She paused. "I hope I'm not being too nosy."

He gave an easy laugh. "I came down here to do a little research for a book I'm working on."

Tori stared into his incredible eyes. He had always been handsome. If her heart hadn't belonged to Jake, maybe things would have turned out differently. "The last time I saw you, it was at one of your book signings."

Nicholas nodded. "My first book had just come out."

She suddenly looked sheepish. "I have a confession to make. I haven't read it yet. I feel bad about it."

"Don't. I heard about you losing your daughter right after that. It's been a hard year for you, I'm sure. I appreciate your support though."

"You will always have that."

Nicholas gave her a brilliant smile. "Well, I just wanted to say hello to you. I hope to see you again soon."

She returned his smile and said, "Take care of yourself."

"He's cute," Charlene commented when Nicholas was out of hearing range.

"Yes, he is handsome," Tori agreed. She stole a peek in Nicholas's direction. He was seated alone at a table a few feet away from where they were sitting. "Why don't you go over and talk to him?"

"Because I think he's more interested in you."

Tori gasped in astonishment. "Charlene, I'm a married woman."

"With a husband who's been missing in action for a while."

"I don't intend to break my vows, Charlene." But even as she said the words, Tori couldn't resist another peek at Nicholas. When she turned back around, she found Charlene watching her, an amused expression on her face.

The waitress arrived with their dinner.

"I could strangle Jake for all he's put you through."

"Jake's in pain also," Tori reminded her as she buttered a soft roll. "I'm sure this has been just as hard on him."

Charlene poured vinegar over her collard greens. "I think you're giving Jake too much credit."

"Now you're sounding like Aunt Kate." Tori picked up her glass of iced tea and took a sip. "Why don't we change the subject? We came here to have a good time."

Charlene agreed.

The evening ended on a pleasant note, as Tori and her cousin ran into a couple of their friends. After dinner, they all decided to drive over to a local jazz club. Tori enjoyed herself immensely. It had been ages since she'd allowed herself to have a good time. She threw her head back and laughed at the story Charlene was sharing with them about the good ol' days.

It wasn't until well after midnight that Tori and her cousin finally made it home. She was so tired, it didn't take long for her to fall asleep.

The next morning, Tori woke up early. She had breakfast ready by the time Charlene and her mother came downstairs.

"It sure smells good in here," Aunt Kate said. "Do I smell your famous chocolate chip muffins?"

"You sure do. I had a craving for chocolate, so I thought I'd whip up a batch."

"And you made ham and cheese omelettes, too," Charlene observed. "I'm gonna have to take you out more often."

Tori laughed. "Do me a favor and pour the orange juice for me."

After breakfast, she convinced Charlene to go with her to morning Bible study at her church. Tori hadn't been to Greenwood Baptist Church since moving to Brunswick. This would be her first time back, and she had to admit that she was looking forward to going. She needed to focus more on God and less on her absent husband.

Chapter Seven

Jake stood before the tiny grave, his eyes filling with tears. "I'm sorry, baby. I n-never meant for . . ." He couldn't finish the sentence. Nothing would ever bring his little girl back.

Since his arrival in Brunswick a week ago, Jake had made daily visits to Tiffany's grave site. Although he felt as if he didn't have the right to be there, he knew he couldn't leave without visiting. So far, Jake had driven past his mother-in-law's house almost daily, hoping to catch a glimpse of his wife. He'd seen Linda a couple of times, but no Tori. His heart hungered for just the sight of her. Jake missed her deeply. At least he could come here and visit with Tiffany.

Sinking down to his knees, Jake sobbed loudly. He didn't care what anyone passing by might think—he'd lost his only child, and he would never stop grieving for her.

"Tiffany, I miss you, honey. There has not been a day that's gone by that I haven't thought of you. You wouldn't be here if I hadn't acted so stupid that night. Can you ever forgive me, darling?"

Jake wiped his tears. His sorrow was a huge, painful knot inside his chest. The pain was so excruciating, he felt as if he couldn't breathe. He was experiencing another attack. Trying to brace himself, Jake again fought the panic. Since Tiffany's death, he'd been plagued with panic disorder.

He wondered what Tori would do if she were in his shoes. How did she survive the pain of Tiffany's death? It came to him in one word. *Prayer.*

Looking upward, Jake felt defiant. "Why would you want to hear anything I have to say?" he questioned. "It's not like I've ever been a praying man." In his mind, he wondered, though, if maybe praying would help him find the peace he sought. "Look, I'm not good at this. In fact, I don't even remember the Lord's prayer. It's been such a long time. . . ." His voice drifted, and Jake felt uncomfortable. He sat quiet for a moment, as if listening for a response.

Clearing his throat, he tried again. "I'm sorry. I don't really know what I'm doing, so here goes. Dear Lord, I . . . I'm in a lot of pain. I wish it had been me that died. Not Tiffany. Since that night, I haven't felt whole. Like a chunk of me is missing. I miss my wife. I need her." Jake's eyes welled up with tears. "I don't know if I'm doing this right. I'm just asking You to help me. This probably doesn't make sense to You. I'm not sure I even understand. All I know is that I can't keep living like this. I need help, Lord. I want to feel whole again." Not able to think of anything else to say, Jake ended with, "Amen."

He glanced around expectantly. He felt the same as before. Nothing had changed; all Jake felt was disappointment, then anger. He'd poured his heart out, yet he felt the same emptiness. He believed that God had abandoned him. That feeling of abandonment hurt him so much that he didn't think he could ever come back to the grave site again. Tiffany's death was his fault, and God wanted nothing to do with him. He'd abandoned Jake when his father had died, and now he was doing it again. Jake had to wonder if this was the same loving God that his mother worshiped.

Rising to his feet, Jake turned around to find his mother-in-law standing a few feet away. He wondered if she'd witnessed his pitiful attempt at praying.

Linda quickly closed the distance between them. "Jake, I thought it was you. How are you doing?" she asked.

He scanned her face for some hint of disappointment. Jake didn't find any, to his amazement. Shrugging, he responded, "As well as can be expected, I guess." Jake glanced over his shoulder at the grave. "It's hard to believe that it's been a year."

She nodded. "We've all been very worried about you, Jake." Then she questioned, "How could you just run off like that? Not a word to your wife—not even your dear mama."

Her rebuke was mild, but it didn't matter. Jake couldn't utter a word, his shame choking him into silence.

"Why did you come back here?"

"I . . ." Jake paused for a second before continuing. "I don't know, Mom. I feel it was the right thing to do. Time to face the music, I guess."

Linda eyed him for a moment. "Did you come to Brunswick to get your wife? Or did you just come to visit Tiffany's grave?"

Jake didn't dare hope there was a chance to reconcile with Tori. Too much had happened. "I want to see her. Tori and I have a lot to discuss."

Folding her arms across her chest, Linda stated, "I won't let you hurt her, Jake. Not anymore."

"Despite of the way it looks, I never wanted to hurt Tori."

Linda studied him for a moment. Finally she responded, "She's not in Brunswick."

He was surprised. "Where is she?"

Linda looked as if she were silently debating whether or not to tell Jake anything.

"Please . . . I need to see her, Mom."

"Tori went home."

"*Home?*" Shock coursed through him. "She's on Edisto Island?"

"Yes. She went home, although I think she's making a big mistake."

Without asking Linda, Jake knew the reason why. He had walked out on his wife when she'd needed him the most. Now she was back in the house they'd once shared—the very house where Tiffany had been conceived.

"I don't have any right to ask you this, but I'm going to anyway. I need you to do something for me."

"What?"

"I don't want Tori to know that you've seen me. At least not yet. I need some time."

Linda looked skeptical. "I don't know, Jake. I don't keep secrets from my daughter."

"It won't be for long," he said quickly. "I promise. I just need a few days before I see Tori."

A pregnant silence followed.

"I'll give you two weeks, Jake," Linda stated quietly. "You have exactly two weeks, and then I'm going to call Tori. She's worried sick over you."

"Thanks, Mom."

She placed a firm hand on his arm. "Jake, if you are not going to stick around for good, then at least be honest with Tori. My daughter deserves to move on with her life." Giving him a quick hug, Linda started to walk away, then stopped and turned back to face him. "So do you."

The past few days had been filled with all sorts of surprises.

Sheila had not been prepared for Tori's return to Edisto Island. In fact, it bothered her a lot. She couldn't help but wonder if Jake's leaving Aruba and Tori's sudden reappearance in town could be connected.

She wasn't going to let that stop her though. She'd worked too long and too hard just to let Jake go without a fight. Sheila loved him and vowed to make him love her in return.

Tori wasn't woman enough to handle a man like Jake, Sheila mused. She could not delude herself about Jake's love for his wife.

He was head over heels in love with Tori. Sheila decided the best way to keep a wedge between the couple was to play on Tori's insecurities.

It was going to be easy enough since she and Jake had already made love. Tori would never be able to trust him again. Sheila intended to see to that.

Her imagination running wild, Sheila smiled. Maybe she was worrying for nothing. It was possible that Tori wanted a divorce. She had been successful in convincing Jake that his wife wanted nothing to do with him thus far. But Sheila had not been able to push him into filing for a legal separation.

Tori's reappearance worried her, but Jake's disappearance bothered her even more. Sheila didn't like not knowing where he was. She didn't want Jake and Tori running into each other just yet. Their connection was still too strong.

Chapter Eight

Tori was craving garlic shrimp, so she stopped off at a local fish market. She spotted Nicholas inside the corner store, standing with his back to her at the end of the counter. She walked over and tapped him on the shoulder, saying, "I'm beginning to see you everywhere."

"Are you following me?" he teased.

"No," she answered quickly. "I didn't realize you were still on the island."

"I've rented a condo for six months not too far from here. I'm doing research for my book, remember? So you're going to be seeing me around for a while."

Tori nodded with a smile. Aware of his heated stare, she pretended to study the jumbo shrimp displayed on a bed of ice behind the glass counter. Not since Jake had a man shown so much interest in her. She stood, her hands nervously pulling at the navy calf-length linen dress she wore. It hung loosely on her since she'd lost so much weight.

"I don't mean to make you uncomfortable, Tori."

She glanced up at him. "Don't be silly." Tori spied two women standing nearby, watching them.

Nicholas leaned over and whispered, "Think we're going to be the subject of a scandal?"

Tori burst into laughter.

"Those old birds have nothing to gossip about. I know your heart belongs to Jake Madison," Nicholas assured her. "It's always been that way."

He was peering at her intently, his gaze as soft as a caress.

One of the women behind the counter took Tori's order. She didn't realize how grateful Tori was for the interruption. She was by no means blind to his attraction, and she found herself extremely conscious of his virile appeal.

She paid for her purchase while Nicholas ordered a pound of trout.

"I love fish," he said. "I don't eat beef or pork anymore. Just chicken and fish."

Feeling at ease, Tori responded, "I've never cared much for any kind of meat. I like ham, but I love seafood myself."

They launched into a dialogue that lasted for fifteen minutes before Nicholas asked, "Tori, would you like to have dinner sometime? It would just be two former schoolmates getting together for old times' sake." With a laugh he added, "We could have fish."

"Sure, Nicholas. I'd love it." Turning, Tori accidently bumped into a woman standing nearby. "Oh! I'm so sorry—" she began. "Sheila!"

"Hello."

Tori took a deep breath, trying to collect herself. "What are you doing on the island?"

"Relax, Tori. I haven't been to your house. I was visiting a friend and decided to stop here for some fish." Sheila's eyes strayed to Nicholas. Grinning, she asked, "Who's your friend?"

Keeping her temper in check, Tori answered, "This is Nicholas Washington. He's a good friend of mine from Brunswick." She saw no need to elaborate any further.

Sheila's eyebrows rose a fraction. "I see." Shaking Nicholas's hand, she added, "It's so nice to meet you. It really is."

Tori didn't like the way Sheila was acting. "Well, I have to go. Good-bye, Sheila," she said in a clipped, even voice.

"It's always good seeing you," Sheila called out. "And you, too, Nicholas."

Tori walked out of the store with Nicholas by her side. "Is she a friend of yours?" he asked.

"Sheila Moore is my husband's partner," Tori explained.

"Oh, I see. And how is Jake?"

She glanced up at Nicholas. "I have no idea."

He frowned. "Why did you say it like that?"

"You may as well know. I haven't seen my husband in a little over a year."

"I didn't know you two had separated," he murmured. "Hard to believe. You and Jake were the golden couple."

Tori's throat closed up and it became hard to speak. "I thought so, too. I guess we were both wrong, huh?" She kept her tears at bay one trembling breath at a time. "I'm sorry, Nicholas. Jake walked out on me and I guess I haven't gotten over it."

He gave her an understanding smile. "You have reason. The end of a marriage is hard. Especially when the couple was so in love." Nicholas scanned her face. "You sure you feel up to having dinner, Tori?"

She nodded. "Nicholas, you're my friend. Of course we're going to have dinner. It's going to be so good having you in town. I've really missed you."

"I missed you, too." Nicholas pulled out a pen and wrote on the back of his receipt. "Here's my phone number. Call me whenever you need to talk."

Tori wrote down her number on the back of her receipt and gave it to Nicholas. "Here's mine."

* * *

The next morning, Tori told her cousin about her dinner plans.

"I can't believe you're having dinner with Nicholas." Charlene handed a stack of books to Tori. "That's a handsome man, I have to tell you."

Arranging them on a bookshelf, Tori responded, "It's not a date or anything. It's just dinner between two friends, that's all."

Leaning against the bookshelf, Charlene said, "Tori, be honest with me. Aren't you just a little bit attracted to him? Those gray eyes of his would drive a woman crazy."

"I'm human, Charlene. I think Nicholas is drop-dead gorgeous. But the fact remains that I'm not looking to get involved right now—just tired of being alone. I need to start living again. Spending time with a good friend is a good way to start, I guess. If anything more develops later . . . I'll just have to take it one day at a time."

"Sounds like you're giving up on your marriage."

Glancing over her shoulder, Tori asked, "Why would you say that, Charlene?"

"You're certainly singing a different tune."

Tori's voice became hoarse with frustration. "I don't have much choice, Charlene. Jake walked out on me, and only God knows if he's coming back." She pulled a set of books out of a nearby box. "I can't take much more of this." She pressed a hand over her eyes to stop her tears.

Charlene's arms encircled her. "Honey, I'm so sorry."

Wiping her face, Tori shook her head in resignation. "It's okay. I keep trying to be strong, but sometimes it's so tough." She peered over at her cousin. "I'm so tired, Charlene. And I hurt so bad inside. I keep thinking that I shouldn't still love a man who walked out on me. I feel like I should be angry or something. Instead, I've been living with a broken heart and praying for him to come back to me. I'm probably the biggest fool on this island."

"Why don't we take a break? Let's go grab something to eat,"

Charlene suggested. "We've been working in the store since seven this morning nonstop."

"Would you mind just picking something up? I want to stay here and work on the young adult section."

"You're sure?"

Tori nodded. "I'd like to get home a little early tonight. Just get me the same thing I had yesterday?"

"Sure." Charlene crossed the room in quick strides and picked up a set of keys. "I'll be right back."

When she left, Tori locked the door behind her. She went to her office and sat down. At her desk, she began to pray. "Praise God. Thank You, Lord, for all that You have blessed me and my family with. And please forgive us our sins. I know that nothing is owed to me, and that I am the one who owes You. All You ask is that I seek You every day and put my total faith in You. I pray for continued faith and strength in You, Lord. I ask this in Jesus' name. Amen."

No sooner had she spoken the words than Tori began to feel an enormous sense of peace wrapping her in its warmth. Smiling, she murmured, "Thank You, Lord."

She hurried back to the selling area. Their bookstore was due to open in a few days, and Tori wanted to have everything in place.

Fifteen minutes later, Charlene returned with their lunch.

After dining on fish and chips, they returned to the task of unpacking the last box, a shipment of Bible study aids. They finished up around four o'clock.

"Well, TC's Books and Gifts is ready for business," Charlene announced.

Surveying the large storefront area, Tori nodded in agreement. "Pastor Allen will be in on Monday to bless the store." She and Charlene had decided to use just the initials of their first names when naming their bookstore.

"Everything's ready. We just need customers to walk through those doors next week. Lots of them."

"It's going to happen," Tori stated. "Now, let's get out of here." She navigated her way to the office and returned with their purses. After giving the store a final once-over, they set the alarm and left the building.

"I think I'll stop by and visit Mother Madison before I head home. The charity ball's in a few days, and I promised her I'd help her with some last-minute projects. Want to come with me? Shepard might be there."

Charlene shook her head no. "I think I'll head on to the house. Shepard and I aren't on the very best of terms right now."

Leaning against the wall, Tori inquired, "What's going on between the two of you?"

"There are some things we need to settle between us, that's all."

"To the point of calling off your marriage?"

"Yeah. Marriage shouldn't be entered into lightly. Shepard and I haven't exactly called off the engagement permanently. We just have some things to seriously consider."

Tori couldn't imagine what problem her cousin and Shepard were having, but she hoped that they would be able to find an amicable solution. Those two belonged together.

Shepard was already home when she arrived and greeted her at the door. After spending a few minutes with her mother-in-law, Tori was ushered into Shepard's office to finalize the plans for the charity ball.

"Do you still think Jake will come?" Tori asked once they cleared up the details. She tried not to sound too hopeful.

"I haven't heard anything, but I do."

Tori wasn't so sure. Rising to her feet, she said, "If that's everything—I need to get going." She embraced him. "I'll see you all at the ball next Friday." Tori headed to the door with Shepard following.

As soon as Tori stepped outside, the hair on her neck stood up. As casually as she could manage, she carefully surveyed the area.

The air suddenly seemed thick with tension, and it threatened to choke her. She'd never felt this way before. It was almost as if someone was watching her.

Walking quickly, Tori made her way to the car and climbed inside. Driving home, she tried to convince herself that it was simply nerves and anticipation. But deep within, she had a feeling it was something more.

Chapter Nine

Jake had parked his car where it couldn't be seen. On foot, he'd headed through a battalion of trees that led to his boyhood home. He still wasn't ready to make his presence known to his family.

As he stood on the edge of the woods, hidden from view, Jake had clear sight of the house. When a black Ford Explorer came rolling up the circular driveway, curiosity got the better of him, and he stood watching as a lone figure got out.

Jake's mouth dropped open. He couldn't believe it. It was Tori. And she looked great. Slender, with dark brown hair that fell a couple of inches below her shoulders—even from this distance, Jake could tell she hadn't changed a bit. Her smooth copper complexion was void of makeup. He remembered how Tori never liked wearing it.

She disappeared into the house much too soon for Jake. He yearned to see more of her, so he waited. Tori couldn't have been inside more than an hour. When he saw the door open and she came out, he moved closer, being careful to stay out of sight.

Jake stared at her, trying to photograph her with his eyes. He fought his overwhelming need to be close to her. Even though he was standing yards away, he felt a lurch of excitement within. Just this glimpse of Tori brought senses to life that he'd thought were long dead.

When she paused and starting searching the area with her eyes, Jake ducked behind a huge tree, breathing hard. Was it possible she'd sensed him out there? Disappointment washed over him when she rushed to her car and sped away. Tori was gone. Making his way back through the woods, Jake trekked back to his rental car and unlocked the door. Just as he was about to get in, he felt a tightening sensation in his chest. It was suddenly difficult for him to breathe. Leaning back against the car, Jake waited for the anxiety attack to pass.

Although it still surprised Jake that Tori had decided to move back into the house, he was relieved. He'd had the two-story house custom-built for her, and he knew how much she loved it. He loved the house just as much.

Jake's eyes strayed back to the house in which he'd grown up. He was back, but could he ever really go home?

Chapter Ten

Tori put away the book she'd been reading. Restless, she got up off the chair and made her way over to the mirror. Under intense scrutiny, she decided it was time to make some changes. Running her hands through her thick hair, Tori made a decision that the long locks would be the first to go. She'd always wanted to cut her hair, but Jake wouldn't let her before.

Placing her hands on her flat stomach, she smiled in satisfaction. Tori had finally lost all the pounds she'd gained during pregnancy—although none of it was due to dieting. She was now much smaller than she'd been when Jake had married her.

Tori's eyes rose back to her reflection in the mirror. Jake had never liked makeup either, so she never wore any, but that was going to change, too. She wanted to enhance her appearance, not overshadow it.

For the first time since Jake's leaving, Tori realized that throughout her marriage, she'd never had any real sense of who she was or where she truly belonged. If she was destined to start a new life without Jake, then she would do it looking the way she wanted to. The woman who had been only Jake's wife and Tiffany's mother would finally come into her own.

* * *

She woke up early the next morning and drove to the hair salon. When Tori walked inside, she said, "Morning, Denika. I want you to cut all of my hair off."

Dropping the magazine she'd been reading, the woman gasped in shock. "What?"

She laughed. "Well, not all of it, but I want it short. Something cute and funky."

Denika raised her eyebrows in surprise. "I don't believe it. You want to cut all that beautiful hair off."

Tori glanced around the small-town beauty shop housed in a chic corner storefront inside the brand-new strip mall on the island. Denika was another cousin who'd decided to return to the South after spending ten years in New York. Her unique and innovative hairstyles afforded her the reputation of being the most sought-after stylist in all of South Carolina.

Sitting down in one of Denika's chairs, Tori said, "I want a complete makeover."

"Whaat?" she drawled. "I don't believe it. Girl, what's done got into you?"

"I'm making some changes in my life."

Denika placed a black plastic drape around Tori's shoulders. She turned her so that Tori faced the mirror. "Honey, you sure you want all this pretty hair cut off?"

"Cut it," Tori said evenly. "I want it gone." She was trying not to think about what was about to happen.

"What's Aunt Kate doing these days?" Denika asked.

"Still fussing as always. You know how she is."

Laughing, Denika tilted the chair so that she could wash Tori's hair. She worked quickly and steadily.

Two hours later, when Tori opened her eyes to look into the mirror, she found a stranger staring back. Her hair was so short, it lay in natural curls, emphasizing her large eyes and thick eyebrows. . . . Tori glanced over at her cousin. "Can you arch my eyebrows?"

Denika nodded. "Sure can. Gonna hurt a little though."

"I don't care. When you're done, I want you to show me how to put on makeup and still look natural." Tori held up a magazine. "Like this. The model's makeup looks like she's hardly wearing any."

At 6:30 that evening, Tori opened the door to let Nicholas inside the house. They were having dinner at the Taste of New Orleans restaurant in Charleston. After leaving Denika's salon, Tori had made a trip to the department stores and gone on a shopping spree in the cosmetics department. She had also decided to splurge on a fuchsia-colored silk dress that sported spaghetti straps and fell just a few inches above her knees. Tori had never worn a dress this short.

Her eyes clung to Nicholas's, trying to analyze his reaction. For a moment he studied her intently, his gaze roving and lazily appraising her. A smile formed on his face before he spoke. "Wow! Tori, you look stunning."

She placed a hand on her hair. "Thank you. I really needed to hear that." Tori picked up her purse. "We should leave now if we want to make our dinner reservations."

He smiled and offered her his arm.

Placing her hand through his arm, Tori laughed. "You are a true southern gentleman."

Traffic wasn't heavy, making the drive to Charleston a smooth one. Tori and Nicholas talked about their parents, mutual friends, and old times. She was careful to avoid talking about Jake and their marriage.

At the restaurant, Nicholas held out a chair for Tori. When she was seated, he sat down in the chair facing her. "I have to tell you, I really love your haircut."

Grinning, she said, "You're so good for my self-esteem." Tori stared at the menu, trying to decide what to order. The restaurant served generous portions of down-home southern cooking with a New Orleans flavor.

"Have you decided on what you're going to order?" Nicholas inquired.

"No, not quite. Everything sounds so good."

"Have you eaten here before?"

"Only twice. My husband didn't like to eat here." Tori was suddenly quiet.

"Are you having a good time?"

Playing with her water glass, Tori responded, "Yes, I am. I'm having a great time. It's been a long time since we've talked like this."

His hand reached across the table and covered hers. "Much too long."

Tori eased her hand away from his and placed it in her lap. She raised her eyes to meet his gaze. "Nicholas, it's nice being here with you."

"But . . ." he interjected.

She gave a tiny laugh. "I'm nervous. I know we're friends, but I feel like we're on a date."

"I guess you could call it that. I won't lie to you, Tori. I'm very attracted to you. I've always been attracted to you. However, I respect your marriage."

"I've accepted the fact that Jake is gone for good. He's not coming back, Nicholas."

"Do you really believe that?"

"Yes, I do."

"I'm sorry."

Tori gave him a smile tinged with sadness. "Thank you for saying that, Nicholas. It's been so hard trying not to give up hope, but . . ." Her voice died as the waitress arrived to take their order.

When she left with their selections, Nicholas asked Tori, "What are your plans?"

She gave a slight shrug. "I don't know. For the moment, I'm just preparing to move forward." Taking a sip of water, Tori suggested, "Why don't we change the subject?"

"What would you like to talk about?"

"Tell me about this new book you're working on. I've already started the other one and it's great. I'm so sorry I didn't read it earlier."

"It's okay, Tori. I told you, I understand." Nicholas lapsed into a discussion of his latest project, pausing only when the food arrived.

Tori listened attentively. She didn't want to think about Jake. Tonight she refused to allow thoughts of him to darken her mood. She was going to have a good time, even if it killed her.

Jake parked a block away from the restaurant where Tori was having dinner with Nicholas Washington. He'd met the man last year when he and Tori had attended one of his book signings. He knew that Nicholas and Tori had grown up together in Brunswick.

It had been purely by accident that he'd found out they were having dinner together. Jake had been driving by the restaurant and seen Tori getting out of Nicholas's car. He almost didn't recognize her with her new look. He wasn't so sure he liked it.

Jealousy oozed out of every pore. His wife was half dressed and having dinner with another man while he sat in his car spying on them. Jake was angry, although he really had no right to be. In all the time he'd been away, he'd never once considered that Tori would get involved with another man.

Hell! She was still his wife. He and Tori were still legally married. Balling his hands into fists, Jake fought the urge to storm into the restaurant and yank Tori out of there. She sure didn't wait long before moving on with her life, he thought selfishly.

Curiosity was getting the better of him, and Jake wanted to go inside the restaurant, but to do so would be a mistake. Tori still didn't have any idea that he was back in South Carolina.

His cell phone started to ring. Jake knew it was Sheila calling, and decided not to answer it. He didn't feel like talking to her right now. The only thing he wanted was for Tori to leave the restaurant and go home. Without Nicholas Washington.

Jake felt a surge of fury unlike anything he'd felt in his life. He sat very still, his hands still in tight fists. In his mind, he saw Tori—this new Tori—writhing beneath Nicholas's naked body, kissing him and moaning in pleasure. Was she doing this to get back at him? he wondered selfishly.

From the first time he'd met the man, Jake could sense Nicholas had feelings for Tori that ran deeper than the bonds of friendship. Right now, his wife was in a vulnerable state, and Nicholas could take advantage of her.

Jake didn't want that to happen, but maybe it was already too late. He couldn't help but wonder just how involved they were. Out of all this, one thing had been decided. It was time to make his presence known. Jake was going to attend the charity ball.

Chapter Eleven

Nicholas was a sweetheart. Not to mention extremely sexy. Tori was flattered by his interest in her. She found she'd really missed being the center of attention for a man. It had been a long time. But in the condition she was in, such an attraction could prove perilous.

Standing in front of the full-length mirror, Tori ran the fingers of her left hand through her short hair, fluffing up the curls. The movement caused her wedding ring to gleam beneath the bright bedroom lighting. Her feelings of elation deflated and soon turned to shame.

She was still a married woman. This attraction she felt toward Nicholas was wrong. "I can't do this, Lord. I'm lonely and I don't know if I can take much more of this. Please bring Jake home. Please."

Tori changed into a pair of pajamas and climbed into bed, bringing her wedding album with her. Turning the pages slowly, Tori stared down at the pictures, calling to mind all of the happiness she'd felt on the day she married Jake. The photographs were memories of a lifetime at the very moment their life together began.

Tears filled her eyes and ran down her face. Tori closed the photo album when the pain of seeing the pictures became too much to bear.

Gazing up toward the heavens, Tori prayed for the courage to face the future. Her future without Jake Madison. Unconsciously, she played with her wedding ring and leaned back against her pillows. Before she could go on with her future, she needed closure on her past. On Monday, Tori would make a visit to her attorney. She was going to file for a divorce.

She fell asleep with water glistening on her eyelids and the trail of dried teardrops staining her cheeks.

Chapter Twelve

Gwendolyn graced Tori with a peck on the cheek. "You look wonderful, dear. I love your haircut. It's absolutely stunning."

Tori released a slow sigh of relief. She still felt a little self-conscious after cutting all of her hair off, but her mother-in-law's words quickly put her at ease. "Thank you. I'm so glad to see you out of bed, Mother Madison. You look beautiful yourself." She ran a hand down the long silk metallic silver gown she wore. Tori felt the plunging neckline was a little daring, but Charlene had convinced her to buy the dress.

"Thank you, dear. I feel so good right now. I'm just so thankful." Patting Tori's arm, she said, "We'll talk in a little while. Right now, I need to greet more of the guests."

Tori was joined by Charlene over by a long narrow buffet table laden with shrimp, stuffed mushrooms, Swedish meatballs, and an assortment of cheeses. Looking over the food, she acknowledged, "Mrs. Madison looks great, doesn't she?"

Tori nodded. "I think this ball has worked wonders for her." Her eyes met Charlene's. "Where's Aunt Kate?"

Gesturing over to her left, Charlene answered, "She's over there talking with the Willows. They want Mama to make more of her famous pecan pies for the restaurant."

Smiling, Tori stated, "That's right up her alley. Think she'll do it?" She picked up a plate and started to fill it with food.

Charlene nodded. "You know she will."

Tori fingered the deep purple gown her cousin was wearing. "Girl, this dress is beautiful. Where did you find it?"

"I bought it when I was in New York last month. When I saw it in the window of this boutique, I knew I just had to have it." Charlene gave a tiny smile. "You don't think it's too sexy, do you?"

"No, it looks fine. You look beautiful, Charlene," Tori reassured her. "You really do."

Charlene bit into a piece of cheese. "You look great yourself. That haircut suits you to a T." Pulling a tissue out of her purse, she discreetly wiped a smudge of lipstick off Tori's cheek. "Much better."

Tori murmured her thanks.

Gwendolyn came up behind them and greeted Charlene. The two women embraced.

"It's so nice to see you, Charlene. I have to tell you though, I'm a little put out with you," Gwendolyn stated.

Tori and her cousin exchanged puzzled expressions.

"But why, Mrs. Madison?" Charlene asked.

"I thought by now you and Shepard would be good and married. My son needs a wife and children. He needs to settle down before he gets too old."

Tori burst into laughter while Charlene gave a small smile, but there was something in her eyes that Tori couldn't define. She surveyed her cousin's face, but whatever she'd seen a few minutes ago was now gone.

Apparently Gwendolyn hadn't noticed.

"Shepard and I are going through some things right now. On top of that, he's been so distraught over Jake's disappearance and Tiffany's death. We both decided to put our relationship on hold for now." Breaking into a wide grin, Charlene added, "I haven't given up, believe me."

Gwendolyn's smile was bright. "That's so good to hear. Now, I'd like to see you two married before I leave this earth. If the doctors have their way, I'll be gone in a matter of months. But only the Lord knows how long He's given me."

"You three beautiful ladies wouldn't be talking about me, would you?" Shepard asked as he joined them. He greeted each of them with a kiss.

Placing his arm around Charlene, he prompted, "Well?"

Gwendolyn was the first to speak. "It's no secret that I think you and Charlene are made for each other. I simply don't know what's taking so long. She just told me that you two are putting your relationship on hold. Why?"

Shepard gazed pointedly at Charlene. "We have our reasons, don't we?"

She nodded stiffly.

Tori didn't miss the faint show of sadness that swept across her cousin's face. Her eyes met Charlene's. She wanted to question her, but that would have to wait until they were home. What was going on between Charlene and Shepard?

"My goodness, did you two have a fight?" Gwendolyn inquired. "I've never seen two more unhappy people in my life."

"We just had a disagreement, Mother. We'll work it out one way or the other."

Charlene cut her eyes at him.

Gwendolyn was still talking. "There's only one thing that would make this night absolutely perfect. And that's the return of my eldest son."

Tori nodded in agreement. She spied Nicholas as he strolled into the ballroom wearing a black tuxedo with an Afrocentric bow tie and cummerbund. Catching his eye, she waved.

Smiling, Nicholas made his way to her side. She introduced him to her mother-in-law. "Don't you look handsome."

Tori accepted a champagne flute from one of the passing waiters. Nicholas did the same, his eyes never leaving her face.

"Your dress is exquisite." He smiled. "I really like this new you."

"I do, too," Charlene interjected. "I think she looks great."

Nicholas complimented both Gwendolyn and Charlene.

"He's a true southern gentleman," Tori teased.

"Think maybe this southern gentleman can persuade you to have one dance with me?" Nicholas asked with a smile. "It's for charity."

Tori broke into a grin. "Sure, let's have that dance."

She allowed him to lead her to the center of the dance floor. Nicholas gathered her in his arms.

"You look different tonight, Tori," he said. "And happy."

"I don't know if happy is the right word. I feel a sense of peace though. I'm filing for a divorce on Monday. It's time to move on."

"I don't understand Jake. He really doesn't realize how lucky he is."

Tori glanced up at him. "Nicholas, I don't want to talk about Jake. Especially not tonight."

"I understand. My wife left me three years ago, but it's only been in the last year that I was able to get past all my hurt and anger in order to move on with my life."

She looked up at him. "Oh, Nicholas, I had no idea. I'm so sorry. I thought the divorce was something you both wanted."

"No, Diana met another man. They got married eight months ago." He looked down at her. "I want you to know that regardless of what happens between us, I will always be there for you, Tori. I'm only a phone call away."

She smiled her gratitude. "The same goes for me."

His hands slipped up her back, bringing her closer. The mere touch of his hand sent warming shivers through her. Tori reveled in his embrace as they danced.

When the music ended, Nicholas escorted her off the floor and over to where Charlene was standing.

Nicholas eyed them both. "The two of you could pass for sisters. You look a lot alike."

Smiling, Tori replied, "People are always telling us that. We're as close as any two sisters could be though."

Charlene agreed. "Tori's my best friend, too."

Sheila sauntered into the room wearing a bloodred gown with a daring back drape and a split that ran almost to her crotch.

"I can't believe the nerve of that woman," Charlene muttered to Tori. "I bet she paid an arm and a leg for that dress and it's hardly nothing there. Look how sheer it is—you can see right through it." Charlene's mouth dropped open. "She's not wearing anything under it."

She followed her cousin's gaze. Tori wasn't surprised to see Sheila. She'd had a feeling she would be here tonight. She cringed inwardly when her nemesis spotted her and began to walk in her direction.

"Here she comes. . . ." Charlene whispered without moving her lips.

Sheila glared at Charlene before speaking to Tori. "Wow, I can't believe it. You cut all of your hair off. It's cute." Running her hands through her own shoulder-length hair, she added, "I guess it's good Jake's not here. You know how much he loves long hair."

Tori ignored the barb. Smiling, she said, "Your dress is quite interesting."

"Thank you. I was just thinking the same about yours. I didn't realize you'd lost so much weight. You really look great!" Nodding in Nicholas's direction, she said, "There must be a new man in your life."

"*I'm a married woman, Sheila.*"

"I didn't mean . . . it's been a year, and I saw you out there dancing—I thought maybe he was your date." Her tone was not even remotely apologetic.

"Why don't you go mingle?" Charlene suggested. "That is, if you can get that foot out of your mouth."

A loud gasp sounded across the room, preventing further conversation. It was soon followed by a rush of excitement.

"What's going on?" Tori asked. She grabbed Shepard's arm just as he was walking by. "Has something happened?"

"I don't know," Shepard replied. "I was just on my way to find out."

The sea of people began to part and Tori's expression froze. Standing there, amazed and very shaken, her senses whirled, as if she might faint, but she didn't. All Tori finally managed to utter was, "Oh, my goodness. I don't believe it."

Her mother-in-law strolled over to her. "What's all the excitement about, dear?"

"Mother Madison, he's here," Tori exclaimed. "Jake's here."

"*What?*" Gwendolyn Madison swayed, but before she could fall to the floor, she was caught by Shepard. He stood beside Tori, staring wordlessly. Charlene motioned for one of the waiters to bring over a chair for Gwendolyn.

Tori couldn't believe her eyes. Her husband was here. Just when she'd decided to let him go, Jake had come home. She took a quick breath of utter astonishment.

Chapter Thirteen

Jake kept his eyes trained on Tori. People were whispering and staring as he walked through the parting crowd. The only thing that mattered to him was his wife. He wanted to see her reaction—he needed to see the look on her face.

He was too afraid to breathe. Jake didn't have any idea what to expect, but he knew he couldn't delay this any longer. As he neared Tori, he could see the shock on her face. His eyes searched for signs of anger, hurt, or hatred. Instead, she found that she seemed almost relieved to see him.

Jake's courage faltered and he stopped a few yards away from her. His eyes met those of his mother, and he gave her a tentative smile. He raised them once more to Tori's face. She looked so different now. Jake's eyes slid down to the neckline of the gown she wore. He wanted to find a shawl or something to cover up her breasts, which looked as if they were about to pop out of her dress at any moment.

How could one woman change so drastically in a matter of a few days?

* * *

Throwing her hands toward the heavens, Gwendolyn's voice cut through the thick silence in the room. "Thank You, Lord. Oh, thank You so much for bringing Jake back to us. You are a great and merciful father. Thank You so much."

Tori felt Charlene's arms around her, lending her the strength she needed. She remained off to the side as Jake, his mother, and Shepard shared a tearful reunion. Tears of happiness filled her own eyes and she murmured a silent prayer of thanks. A few minutes later, Tori found herself face-to-face with her husband.

She was acutely aware that the room had grown silent and everyone was watching them, but she didn't care. The only thing that mattered was the fact that Jake had returned. Her gaze traveled over his face, searching his eyes. For what, she had no idea.

"Hello, Tori," he said quietly.

"Jake, I've . . ." She paused for a moment. Being this close to him unnerved her. For so long she'd dreamed of being crushed within his embrace. But for now she could only drink in the comfort of his nearness. "I'm so glad to see you."

There was a long, brittle silence. Tori watched the play of emotions across his face, wondering what was going through his mind. Was he as nervous as she? Tori wasn't sure. Jake appeared very calm and cool on the outside.

She continued trying to assess his unreadable features. Was he happy to see her? she wondered this time. Awkwardly, she cleared her throat, then moved restlessly. This was not how she'd envisioned their reunion to be. They were being so distant with each other. The man she'd loved all her life was now nothing more than a stranger to her.

Chapter Fourteen

Sheila made her way over to Jake, not caring that she was intruding on the private moment between him and Tori. That was exactly her intention. Pressing her body brazenly against his, she whispered, "Oh, it's so good to see you. I'm so happy you're home. I—"

Jake immediately stepped out of her grasp. "Hello, Sheila."

Her back deliberately facing Tori, she questioned, "Why didn't you tell me you were coming home?"

Jake's gaze moved past her and met Tori's. "I wanted it to be a surprise."

It was obvious even to Sheila that Jake only had eyes for his wife. A wave of embarrassment washed over her at this public display. He was ogling Tori like a schoolboy experiencing his first crush.

Sheila decided to surrender temporarily with her dignity intact. Steaming, she glanced over her shoulder at Tori. "I'm sure you and your wife have a lot to discuss, so I'll let you get back to your little reunion."

"Thank you," Tori commented drily. "*We* would really appreciate it."

Sheila's mouth turned down. "I'll talk to you later, Jake."

He nodded absently, his eyes never leaving Tori's face. It was revolting watching him drool over his wife like that.

Sucking her teeth, Sheila walked briskly past him. As she strode past Tori's aunt, the woman stopped her by roughly grabbing her arm.

"Jake is Tori's husband. Leave the man alone," she ordered.

Sheila glowered at her while snatching her arm away. She resisted the urge to rub the spot where Kate's nails had dug into her skin. "If he were truly hers, she wouldn't be worried, now would she?" she countered.

Kate permitted herself a withering stare. "You are disgusting!" She was shaking with anger. "Remember God's watching you, girl."

"Get out of my way, old woman," Sheila demanded. "I'm not so desperate for a man that I'd try to break up a marriage. Jake and I are partners, and we are also close friends. *Now, you remember that.*"

Kate rose to her full height. "You'd better consider yourself lucky I don't slap you down right here in this ballroom."

A few of the guests standing nearby overheard them and inched closer.

Sheila glared at Kate. "I'm not afraid of you."

Rancor sharpened Kate's voice. "You don't have to fear me, witch. You'd just better stay away from me and my family."

Sheila broke into a laugh. "Enjoy the party, Miss Kate." She spat out the words contemptuously before stalking off with her head up high. She heard a few snickers coming from the crowd and stiffened.

Her heart was pounding and she shivered a little, even though the night was warm. Jake was home, and she wasn't going to let anyone steal her joy. Sheila just wished she'd been the first to know, instead of finding out along with half of Charleston. And especially Tori.

Jake had practically ignored her, and Sheila was somewhat hurt. She'd been too good of a friend for him to dismiss her as he had. She deserved much better.

THE PRODIGAL HUSBAND

* * *

Jake didn't really know what to say, or how to explain his long absence. He knew Tori expected some type of explanation, but he didn't really have one. Standing in the center of the room with his wife, he searched for the right words.

Tori was watching him. Did those eyes hold wariness or judgment? Did he dare hope that she still cared for him? He grew warm beneath the stares of the growing crowd surrounding them. Jake suddenly wished they were in a less public arena. Maybe this hadn't been such a good idea.

"Well, if it isn't the return of the prodigal husband," Kate uttered snidely. "What you come back for now?" Circling around Jake, she folded ample arms across a full bosom. "You're not gonna hurt my niece no more."

"Aunt Kate, this is between me and Jake. Stay out of it," Tori said firmly.

When she returned her gaze to him, he smiled in appreciation of his defense. She did not return that smile. Instead, she said, "You look well."

"So do you," he responded. He tried without much success to tune out the steady buzz of whispers and murmurings moving around the room. This had been a bad idea, he decided.

Jake resisted the urge to reach out and touch Tori's face. He wanted to relish in the feel of her soft skin. He craved the sensation of her body in his arms. "I decided it was time I came home."

"I agree."

Jake's eyes traveled past his wife. Behind Tori, Nicholas stood there watching them. His eyes returned to Tori's. "I didn't think it would be so awkward."

"I wasn't sure this was ever going to happen."

"You thought that I wasn't coming back?"

"Jake, you seem surprised."

He was. He'd assumed Tori knew him much better than that. It was never his intent to stay away as long as he had. It had just gotten easier as time had drifted by. "I was going to come home, Tori."

"How would I have known that?" she asked in a voice too low for the others to hear. "It's not like you kept in touch—" Tori stopped herself. "I'm not going there. This is not the time or the place for this discussion."

"Looks like I came home just in time," Jake announced. His eyes slid over Nicholas. "I see we have a whole lot to talk about."

Chapter Fifteen

They were standing there making small talk. How could this be? Tori wondered silently. And what had he meant by his last comment? In a low voice, she replied, "Yes, we do. We need to talk, Jake."

"Soon," he whispered back.

"Tonight, you should spend time with your family, though." Tori inclined her head in Gwendolyn's direction. "They're very anxious to spend time with you. How about tomorrow morning? You can come out to the house."

Jake nodded. "That's fine."

Tori shifted uneasily, wondering why he was watching her so intently. "What is it, Jake?"

"You look very different than I remembered."

"I'm a very different person now." Tori turned away, fighting back tears.

"Are you okay?" he asked softly.

Tori nodded. "I'm fine, Jake." Turning to face the crowd for the first time since Jake's arrival, she said, "Everyone, we have another reason to celebrate tonight. The return of my husband, Jake

William Madison." Tori signaled to the musicians to began playing.

Scanning the room, Tori turned around and found Nicholas. He was standing a few yards away and gave her a small smile of support, but in his eyes, she saw something else. Disappointment, maybe.

For the rest of the evening, Tori watched Jake as he circulated throughout the room, nodding and speaking to various guests. Over and over in her mind, she gave thanks for the miracle of seeing him again. Her prayers had been answered. But what did it mean?

Nicholas eventually wandered over to her. Standing with his hands in his pockets, he asked, "What did I tell you?"

Tori gave a tiny laugh. "Okay, so you were right. Jake's home. What happens now?"

"What happens next is up to you and your husband." Inclining his head, he asked, "Happy?"

"Relieved that he's okay." She took a deep breath. "Nicholas—"

He leaned down and whispered, "Everything will be okay, Tori."

"I hope you're right."

Tomorrow morning she and Jake would talk. Tori was afraid to think beyond that fact. She looked up to find Jake coming her way. She excused herself from Nicholas and met him halfway.

"Have you eaten?" she asked.

Jake shook his head. "I'm not hungry." He glanced uncomfortably around the room. "It feels kind of strange being here. I'm not sure I like being the center of attention."

"I know what you mean." Tori's eyes bounced around the room. "Maybe we should give them something to talk about."

"Like what?"

"Would you like to dance?"

"Sure."

Tori allowed Jake to lead her to the dance floor. She enjoyed the feel of his arms around her. It felt almost familiar, but strange, too.

When the music stopped, they walked over to where Gwendolyn was sitting.

"You two looked beautiful out there, dancing like old times. I remember the first time Jake brought you to the ball. Dear, you were so nervous and so terribly shy."

Tori stole a peek at her husband. He was smiling, so she let her guard down and relaxed.

They danced three more times that night. When Jake escorted her off the dance floor the third time, Sheila stood in the aisle, blocking their path. "Are you going to keep Jake all to yourself, Tori?" she inquired. "I promise not to run off with him."

Tori stared at her, too stunned to respond. The woman had absolutely no manners.

"Dance with me, Jake." Without waiting for an answer, Sheila grabbed his hand and led the way back to the dance floor.

Inside, Tori was so mad, she could spit nails, however, she decided to seek out Nicholas instead. "How about another dance?" she asked.

Jake could barely concentrate for watching her and Nicholas. Tori took perverse delight in the jealous look on his face. As soon as the music stopped, he made his way over to her despite Sheila's efforts to steer him in the other direction.

Nicholas immediately excused himself.

"Having fun?" Jake asked tersely.

"Actually, I am. What about you?"

"I'll be glad when this night is over. I'm sick and tired of people staring at me."

Tori embraced him. "You can blame it on your grand entrance tonight."

Jake smiled ruefully. "You're right."

She nudged him in the arm. "Why don't you go over and talk to your mother? She's looking over here."

"You don't mind?"

Tori shook her head. "I'm going to talk to the Willows for a moment."

Around midnight, she decided to call it a night and went in search of Charlene and her mother. She glimpsed Jake back on the dance floor with Sheila. She tried valiantly to ignore the feelings of jealousy raging within her. Finding Charlene, she said, "I'm thinking about leaving. You and your mom ready to go?"

"Mama was complaining about the corns on her feet not too long ago, so I guess we'd better head out. You don't want her kicking off her shoes here."

Tori laughed. "Aunt Kate won't do that."

"Humph! You must not know my mama."

Jake suddenly blocked their exit. "You're not leaving, are you?" he asked.

Tori nodded and said, "I'm tired. It's been an emotional night. You're coming home . . . to the house tomorrow morning, right?"

"I'll be there." Jake took her hand in his. "Come on, I'll walk you to the car."

Tori said her good-byes as she and Jake headed to the door. In tense silence, they made their way to her car. Climbing into the Explorer as gracefully as she could manage in her gown, Tori said, "I want you to know that I'm really glad you're home."

He nodded. "Drive safe. You know how the roads can be."

"She won't be alone. Charlene and I will be with her," Kate announced curtly. "More than a soul can say for you."

Jake smiled ruefully. "How have you been, Aunt Kate?"

"I'm fine. And don't you try sweet-talking me, 'cause it ain't gonna work," she replied sharply. "I—"

"Jake, I'll see you tomorrow," Tori interjected quickly. She didn't want her aunt upsetting him. She was grateful when Charlene climbed up front with her. "What took you so long?" she asked in a low whisper.

"I was talking to Shepard."

Tori glanced over at Jake and waved. She waited until he headed back into the house before driving off.

"Don't you let that man back into your life until you know for sure he's back to stay," Kate cautioned. "I don't trust those Madison men."

Tori stared ahead, not saying anything. She didn't want to ruin this night by fussing with her aunt. The woman always had to have the last word.

Sheila released an audible sigh of relief and smiled to herself in satisfaction. Tori was going home without Jake. She waited until he was coming back inside the house before she abandoned her hiding place.

"I've been looking all over for you," she lied. "I thought maybe you'd gone home with Tori."

"No. She's not ready for that."

Her arms folded across her chest, Sheila inquired, "So that was your intent then?" Inwardly, she held her temper in check.

"I don't know," Jake admitted. "Right now it's too soon to tell."

His response didn't sit right with Sheila. Jake was still too emotionally involved with Tori, she surmised. If she wasn't careful, she could send him running straight into the waiting arms of his wife.

Softly stroking his arm, Sheila assured him, "You're doing the right thing, Jake. You can't just expect to rush back into Tori's arms."

"Do you think she's still angry?" Jake asked. "I couldn't really tell tonight."

"Oh, I'm sure she's still very angry. But you know your wife.

Tori's much too *Christian* to admit it. She'll just pray it away."
Sheila handed Jake a glass of champagne.

He took a huge, gulping swallow of the golden liquid.

"Give it time, Jake. Things will work out for the best. You'll see."

He smiled and finished his champagne. Jake signaled to a passing
waiter for another one. His eyes traveled around the room, searching for Nicholas. He found him on the dance floor with a woman
Jake didn't recognize. He was glad Tori had gone home. At least for
tonight she was safe from the clutches of that man.

Tori was his wife, and she belonged to him.

Chapter Sixteen

"I thought this day would never come. Seeing Jake come through the door like that. Girl, it was kind of eerie." Charlene dropped down on the edge of Tori's bed. "It must have freaked you out a little."

Seated at a Queen Anne–style vanity, Tori combed her fingers through her hair. "Well, I'm glad he's back. At least I know he's alive."

Sitting cross-legged on the bed, Charlene asked, "What are you going to do?"

Tori glanced over her shoulder. "About what?"

"About your marriage. Jake's back now."

Shrugging, she stated, "We're going to talk tomorrow. I don't know what will happen after that."

"What would you like to have happen, Tori?"

Tori turned around in her chair. "To be honest, Charlene, I'm not really sure. Jake's changed. So have I."

"You're certainly not that timid little mouse anymore."

She turned back to face the mirror. "You're right about that."

"I hope it works out the way you want."

"Me, too, Charlene. With God's help, I know our love can be restored. A part of me still wants us to be a family again. When I stood before the church and pledged to love Jake forever, I meant it. I made a vow to him and to the Lord, but it takes two, Charlene. I can't do it alone."

"It's so easy for some people to forgive, but for others..." Charlene's voice drifted. "But for others, it never comes."

Tori gazed at her cousin. "What are you talking about? Does this have something to do with Shepard?"

"I can't talk about it right now." Charlene stood up. "I'm tired, so I think I'll go on to bed. I'll say a prayer for you and Jake."

"Good night." Tori wondered for a second time that evening what was going on between her cousin and Shepard. What on earth could be keeping them apart? It was obvious they both loved each other.

She changed quickly, readying for bed. Her nerves were on edge from the fact that she and Jake would be discussing their future in the morning.

On bended knees, Tori prayed. She prayed for strength to forgive and to be forgiven. She prayed for unity between Jake and her. She prayed for peace and understanding.

When she climbed into bed, she allowed her mind to replay all of the happier times in her life. She didn't want to focus on the sad times, but they were necessary. She needed them to help comprehend what went wrong with her marriage. What had led Jake to cheat on her? Had she pushed him into Sheila's arms?

Tori had been able to avoid those questions in the past, but now that Jake was back, she needed to find the answers.

Upstairs in the bedroom he'd occupied as a child, Jake paced the floor. What on earth was he going to say to Tori? Somehow an apology just wasn't enough, but it was all he had.

He cautioned himself not to get his hopes up. Just because she was willing to talk didn't mean she wanted to stay in the marriage. *What marriage?* There hadn't been a real marriage for quite some time now. And too much had happened.

He wasn't the same man, but he figured Tori couldn't have changed that much on the inside. Still, Jake wasn't sure they could ever find their way back to each other. Their differences would still be there. But no matter what, he would always love her.

Shepard burst into the room. "You really don't want your marriage, do you?" he demanded.

"What are you talking about?"

"How could you disrespect your wife like that? Sheila was all over you."

"She was all over me, not vice versa," Jake responded quietly. "What was I supposed to do? Knock her on the ground?"

"That's a start. Man, I've told you that Sheila's up to no good. I can't believe you're blind to her games."

"I've been gone a year. When I left, you were singing this same old tune. How many times do I have to tell you that I love my wife?"

Shepard strode over to the door. "If you love her, then act like it!" Without another word, he left the room.

A few minutes later, Della knocked on his door before peeking inside. "Mr. Jake, I'm glad you had the good sense to come home. Your mama sure has missed you."

He smiled at the plump housekeeper, who was also his mother's companion. "I missed her, too. And you."

"Do you need anything, Mr. Jake?"

"I'm fine, Della. Have a good night." He lay down across the bed, staring up at the ceiling. He hadn't tried to pray since that day at Tiffany's grave. God hadn't answered him. Maybe it was because he was a stranger to God. Jake decided he wasn't the sort of man the Lord wanted anyway. In this situation, he was alone.

It was strange. Throughout all his life, he'd wanted to control situations. Now that he craved guidance and leadership in his life, none was forthcoming. Tori always used to tell him that God was there for everyone. All a person had to do was ask. Well, he'd asked. Now where was God? Jake couldn't wait on God. His marriage was at stake.

Chapter Seventeen

The next morning, Tori was so nervous she couldn't eat a thing. Charlene finally convinced her to drink something. She poured her a glass of cranberry juice. "Here, drink this. You need something in your stomach. Try to eat a slice of toast, at least."

"I don't have an appetite." Her stomach churned with anxiety and frustration. Tori was afraid that if she ate anything, she would be sick.

Aunt Kate sat down across from Tori. Placing a napkin in her lap, she said, "Charlene and I had a talk this morning. We're going home today. The house is clean and ready. Jake's back—we should go home."

"You don't have to leave. Jake's staying with Mother Madison for now." In a small voice, she added, "I hate being in this big house all alone."

Charlene bit into a slice of bacon. When she finished chewing, she wiped her mouth with her napkin. "For once, I agree with Mama. As long as we're here, it might make things awkward for you and Jake. You don't need us underfoot while you're trying to work things out with your husband."

"We're only a phone call away, sugar."

Clenching her hand until her nails made indentations in her palm, Tori said, "I know, Aunt Kate. I know you're right, but I would still prefer you both stay until Jake and I decide what we're going to do."

Kate's expression eased into a smile. "The sooner we leave, the better it'll be for you."

Tori wasn't so sure about that. Her breath seemed to have solidified in her throat and she couldn't speak.

"It's going to be fine," Charlene assured her. "By tonight you and Jake could be having a second honeymoon."

She shook her head. "No. It's not going to be that easy for me to just let Jake come back here. Aunt Kate said something last night that made a whole lot of sense to me."

"What was that?" Charlene questioned.

"Yeah, what in the world did I say?"

Tori gazed across the table at her aunt. "You said that I shouldn't let Jake move home until I know he means to stay."

"But you *are* going to give him a chance, right?"

"Charlene, we don't know if he even wants a chance." Tori took a sip of her juice. "He may not. I'm not assuming anything where Jake is concerned."

The phone rang around 8:30 the next morning. "Good morning, Jake."

"Hello, Sheila," he mumbled. He glanced over at the bedside clock.

"How did you sleep?"

"Okay." In reality, Jake hadn't slept much at all. He'd spent most of the night trying to figure out what he was going to say to Tori.

"I was thinking about taking you to breakfast. We could go to the Middleton Place Restaurant. It'll be like old times—"

"No," Jake interrupted. "I appreciate the offer, Sheila, but we can't do that. At least not today. I'm driving out to Edisto Island. Tori and I . . . we need to discuss our marriage."

There was a long brittle silence.

"Sheila, you still there?" he asked.

"I didn't realize you'd planned to do it so soon."

"You consider this soon?" he asked. "It's thirteen months past due, Sheila." Jake sat up in bed, trying to get comfortable.

"You know what I mean. Don't you think you should take a moment to really think this out? You could use me to bounce your thoughts off of."

"I don't think that's a good idea, Sheila. Thank you, however."

There was a slight pause. "I was only trying to be a friend." She sounded hurt.

"I realize that." Jake's tone was apologetic. "I'm sorry, Sheila. I'm just a little edgy about meeting with Tori this morning."

"It's okay. I understand. Jake, I hope you aren't getting your hopes up. You and Tori have been apart a long time."

"I know that," he muttered as he climbed out of bed.

"Just be careful, Jake," Sheila warned. "That's all I'm saying. Your wife has changed a lot over the last year. She's not the same woman she was when you left."

"I'm not the same man I used to be, either. Tiffany's death changed both of us." Even as he said the words, Jake doubted Tori could change that much on the inside. She'd changed her outer appearance, but surely she was still his sweet, forgiving Tori.

"Good luck with your talk, Jake."

"Thanks, Sheila. I'm not sure what to expect, but whatever happens happens."

Jake hung up the phone and headed to the shower. He felt cautiously optimistic about the meeting after last night. Tori had appeared very happy to see him, but he'd also seen the way she'd looked at Nicholas Washington.

Chapter Eighteen

Sheila couldn't just sit at home while Jake was with Tori. Fear and anger knotted inside her, gnawing at her confidence.

"Jake, why did you have to come home now?" What would she do if he and Tori reconciled? Panic welled inside her, and Sheila tried to keep her fragile control. She needed to find something to take her mind off Jake, so she decided to visit her mother, whom she hadn't seen in a couple of months.

One hour later, she was dressed and walking out of her condo.

Sheila headed on Route 21 to the tiny village of Frogmore. The inhabitants of the South Carolina coast, including her own family, were part of a distinct group of African-Americans who were able to trace their roots to the villages of the Sierra Leone territory in West Africa.

A half mile from the center of Frogmore was the Penn Center Historic District. This was the first school established in the South to educate the freed slaves, but Sheila had little appreciation for the historic landmark. She hated Frogmore and everything it represented.

Sheila parked her car and got out. She couldn't stand coming out here, but her mother refused to be uprooted from the only place in which she'd ever lived. As she walked up the worn steps to the uneven wooden porch, she could hear her mother's loud laugh and then her words.

" 'E mus'bz . . ."

Her voice lowered until Sheila couldn't make out what she was saying. Suddenly another round of laughter rang out.

Frowning, she took note of the haint blue painted on the rotting wooden doorjambs and window trims. It was supposed to keep the evil spirits away. Sheila knew that her mother still got up before the sun came out to sweep her yard. It kept Doctor Death on the other side of the road.

Distaste colored Sheila's expression. Her descendants—the Gullah people—had made the horrific passage to South Carolina as slaves, but now . . . she shook her head in frustration. It was time to move out of the past.

The land her mother had lived on was once owned by white planters who did not return to reclaim the land after the Civil War. Everything about this place made Sheila sick. It wasn't so much that she hated her lineage—it was the refusal of her people to move forward. She couldn't understand their sense of pride in the past. An ugly past.

Conversation died abruptly when Sheila strolled into the tiny room that served as living room, dining room, and kitchen. Her mother stood near a rusting stove that had seen better days while two of her friends sat at the dining-room table.

"Hey, Ma."

One of the women visiting her mother stared at her multicolored tank top and matching pants by Jean Paul Gaultier, then let her eyes roam on down to her Anne Klein shoes before her bullfrog eyes traveled slowly upward, displeasure forming on her lips. "Da gal 'e don' see nobody else in dis house?"

Sheila held back her retort. "Hello, Miss Minnie. Miss Dorie."

"W'y you don' come'yah ta see your mama? Don' you know'um 'e not feeling too well thees days?"

A soft gasp escaped her. "Ma?"

"I doin' fine. No need for you to worry."

Sheila's concern for her mother overshadowed her feelings of disgust in being in this house, listening to the mixture of Gullah and English. "Are you sure you're okay?"

Her mother flicked an imaginary speck from the dull gray dress she wore. Sheila couldn't understand why her mother refused to wear any of the new clothing hanging in her closet.

Miss Minnie grumbled under her breath in Gullah while Miss Dorie just sat there, rolling her eyes. Sheila ignored them both. She glanced down at the worn couch covered in a horrendous plaid pattern before taking a seat. Her mouth took on an unpleasant twist as she sat down.

"That chair probably cleaner than you," Minnie said snidely.

" 'E my gal, Minnie. Leave her alone."

"Humph! 'E disrespectful." Minnie rose to her feet. "Dorie and I goin' to the fish market. You need anything, Essie?"

Her mother shook her head no.

Sheila put on a fake smile and waved to them as they ambled out of the house. She was glad they had the good sense to leave. Out of the corner of her eye, Sheila spied movement.

A roach! The hair on her skin stood at attention. Sheila gritted her teeth to keep from screaming. She hated the ugly little disease-carrying creatures with a passion. As a child, she used to listen to them moving about beneath the loose wall paneling that one of her mother's former boyfriends had half installed.

Sheila had had the entire house redone on the inside as soon as she'd landed her former job with Pioneer Systems. She also had quarterly exterminations done, but the unsightly little bugs simply wouldn't go away. She made a mental note to call the exterminator as soon as she made it to her office.

"Ma, why won't you let me buy you a real house? I don't under-stand why you want to live in this old musty shack." Sheila glanced all around in disgust. "The clothes I'm wearing cost more than what this whole place is worth."

"I was born in this house, chile. This be the place where I die, too."

"I don't get it, Ma. I hate this house. The way it smells. I hate everything about it."

"You trying to forget where you come from. Chile, you are who you are—you can't be somebody else."

Sheila pulled out a wad of hundred-dollar bills and held them out to her mother.

"I don't want that money!"

"Why do you always act like this, Ma?" Sheila screamed. "I'm not selling drugs or whoring. This is my hard-earned money. All I'm trying to do is help make your life easier. Just look at this place. You got roaches running around here like family."

"This is my home, Sheila." Essie sighed heavily. "Try and make yourself happy, chile. That's what you can do for me. That's all me want. To see my chile happy."

"I am happy, Ma. Why can't you see that? I'm in love with a wonderful man—"

Shaking her head, Essie cut her off. "He's a married man, chile. No good can come from that."

"Jake's not going to be married for long, Ma. You'll see. He's going to leave his wife and marry me."

"He is not in your future, chile. Minnie done tole me so. He is not the one for you."

Sheila shook with anger. "Stop saying that, Ma. Ol' Minnie doesn't know what she's talking about. She needs to mind her own business and leave mine alone. I don't trust that old root woman."

Pointing to the huge black pot on the stove, Essie inquired, "Hungry?"

Sheila shook her head no.

"Chile, you too good to eat my food now?"

Standing up, Sheila said, "I'm not going to do this. I'm not letting you ruin my day by arguing with you. I came all the way out here to drop off this money." She dropped the wad of cash on the pine coffee table and stormed out before her mother could say a word.

Now that her duty as the good daughter was done, Sheila drove as quickly as she could, trying to escape her past.

While she waited for Jake to arrive, Tori changed clothes three times. She wanted to look her best when Jake finally arrived. Standing in her latest choice, a jade-green shirred-waist slip dress, Tori had to wonder if all her efforts would be lost on her estranged husband. Jake wasn't used to seeing her in dresses like this.

She heard the sound of a car pulling up. Tori stole a peek out of the bedroom window. It was Jake.

By the time she quickly assessed herself in the full-length mirror and made her way down the stairs, Jake was knocking on the door. Tori rushed to answer it. She didn't want to risk him changing his mind and leaving.

"Hello, Jake. Come on inside." Tori stepped aside to allow him entrance into the house.

"Good morning."

Jake followed her through the foyer and into the living room. She settled into the love seat while Jake sat down in one of the matching wing chairs. Tori spoke first. "I'm glad you came over. We have a lot to talk about."

He assessed her from top to bottom. "How have you been, Tori?"

"I've had good days and bad, but I managed. By the grace of God I managed." She glanced down at her hands. Jake was staring at her, and it made her nervous.

Leaning forward, he questioned, "What did you do to your hair?"

Tori didn't bat an eye when she replied, "Isn't it obvious? I had it cut."

Jake frowned, disconcerted by Tori's answer. He had never known her to be so flip.

When he had imagined this moment, it was with the old Tori, not this stranger sitting across from him. Taking another look at her hair, Jake decided it wasn't too bad. He still didn't like it though. At least it would grow back.

"Would you like some coffee?" Tori asked.

"No, I'm fine."

Silence fell.

Jake was beginning to wish he'd rehearsed this more, but he hadn't expected Tori to make it so difficult. Sitting up straight, he decided just to go to the heart of the situation. "I made a big mistake."

"Uh-huh."

"Okay, I made several mistakes."

Tori sat there, staring at him, her mouth drawn in a thin line. Her silence made him uncomfortable. "Can you forgive me, Tori?"

"Jake, I hope you realize that this is not one of those moments where you can say you're sorry and it's all over. It's just not going to be that easy."

"Don't throw away all those years we—"

"I didn't *throw* away anything, Jake. I wasn't the one who left."

He nodded. "You really have changed a lot. When I came out here, I thought you would hear me out and then throw yourself in my arms," he confessed.

Tori looked up at him sharply. "I grew up while you were gone, Jake."

Her gaze was uncomfortably direct, reminding Jake once again that he didn't know the woman sitting across from him.

"I still want my marriage. I'll do whatever it takes to get you back, Tori."

"Including seeing a marriage counselor?" she asked.

Jake's stomach tightened as he stared at this woman he barely recognized. In spite of loving Tori with his whole soul, he knew it would never be the same between them ever again. Sheila was right. Tori would pray to her God and she would forgive him, but she could never forget. She would lord it over his head for the rest of his life.

He was sitting here feeling awkward and a little ill at ease. Hiding his hands beneath the gleaming cherry-wood table, Jake wiped his damp palms on his pants legs.

"Jake?" Tori prompted. "Did you hear me?"

"Huh?" He returned his attention to her. "I'm sorry, what did you say?"

"I said I thought we should consider seeing a marriage counselor. I need to know what you think."

He couldn't discuss the intimate details of his marriage with a complete stranger. "I . . . I can't, Tori."

"Why not?"

"We don't need someone else telling us how to make our marriage work. All those people do is confuse the issues."

"I don't agree, Jake. We could talk to Pastor Allen. He can counsel us. We need to see a counselor if we want to rebuild our relationship. I don't see our marriage having a chance otherwise."

"I'm not going to confess my sins to the world." Jake threw his hand up to his chest. He could feel it tightening, and he was having difficulty breathing. He rose quickly. "I've got to . . . get out of here. . . ."

Fighting his panic, Jake walked briskly out of the house. He practically fell against his car, still struggling to breathe. He heard Tori running toward him.

"Jake, are you okay?" she asked. "What happened back there?"

Humiliation washed over him as he turned around to face her. "I couldn't breathe," he panted. Putting a hand to his chest, he stated, "Panic attacks."

"You have them often?" Concern was etched all over Tori's face. He nodded.

"Are you taking anything for them?"

"I have some medication, but it makes me feel sluggish."

"How long has this been going on?"

"Since Tiffany died," he answered quietly. Jake opened the door to the driver's side of the car. "I'm sorry, Tori. I need to get out of here." Right now he was too embarrassed to face her.

"Jake . . ."

"No," he stated firmly. "I need to leave." Jake climbed inside and started the car. Without looking at Tori, he backed out of the driveway. He allowed himself one glance at his wife before driving away. Even from a distance, he could tell she was crying. Guilt spilled from his pores. He had broken her heart all over again.

Chapter Nineteen

Sheila was in her office when Jake arrived the next morning. She immediately dropped the project she'd been working on diligently when he summoned her to the conference room. She strolled into her private bathroom and quickly checked herself in the mirror. Sheila wanted to look her best for Jake.

"This is a pleasant surprise. I didn't expect you in the office today."

Jake watched her as if trying to discern whether or not she was sincere. Sheila warred with herself over whether to be upset. Jake often displayed his disbelief in certain situations, and it infuriated her. She had proven her loyalty to him more than once. "So, are you ready to come back to work in the office?" Sheila crossed her legs, revealing well-toned shapely thighs.

"After working via computer for the past year, I have to admit I'm not so sure. I'm not even sure I want to do this anymore. Matter of fact, I think it's time you took me up on my offer to sell you my share of Madison Moore."

"No," Sheila answered quickly. She forced the panic from her voice. "You don't have to leave, Jake. Charleston is your home, and your mother needs you." Standing up, she took him by the arm and led him over to one of the chairs. When Jake sat down, Sheila proceeded to gently massage his shoulders.

"Is this about Tori?" she asked. "What happened when you two talked?"

"Tori wants us to see a marriage counselor. Can you believe that? She wants us to tell our business to a complete stranger."

Sheila was afraid to breathe. "What do you want, Jake?" Her eyes grew wet with unshed tears, and she was glad he couldn't see her face. She couldn't bear the thought of losing him. His next words wounded her.

"I love my wife. I just don't know if we can get back what we used to have. Tori . . . I know she'll try her best to make things work, but . . ."

"But what?" Wiping her eyes, Sheila eased down into the chair next to his.

"I've cheated on her, and Tiffany's death—not many marriages can survive blows like that. Our marriage was already on shaky ground before that. Tori seems to think that a marriage counselor is the answer to all of our problems. I don't agree, so I guess there's no marriage."

Placing her hand on his knee, Sheila said, "Jake, listen to me. Running away is definitely not the answer. I think the best way to handle this situation is to stay here in Charleston and give yourself some time to think about things." Sheila was careful about the way she expressed her next comment. "Tori is testing you. She wants to control you, that's all this is about. Surely, she should remember one thing about you, and that's how private you are."

Jake was frowning. "I guess she doesn't care."

"I told you, Jake. Your wife is a very angry woman—only she's keeping it within. You have got to give her time to work through all that anger."

"I love Tori," Jake said a second time. "I just don't know if it's enough to save our marriage. On top of that, I'm not going to see some stranger who's going to blame me for everything that went wrong in my marriage."

"Tori has to share the blame," Sheila stated softly.

When Jake left the conference room, Sheila grinned. She had nothing to worry about. There was still a chance for her and Jake.

"You never said how things went with you and Jake yesterday?" Charlene inquired when Tori walked into the bookstore. After Jake left, Tori had decided that she would stay home. She didn't feel like going to work in her state of mind.

"Not well at all." Sighing in resignation, Tori dropped her purse in a nearby chair. "I don't think things are going to work out between us."

"Why? What did he say?"

"It wasn't anything he said. Jake wants to move home. At least that's what he says, but when I mentioned seeing a marriage counselor—he had a panic attack."

Charlene burst into laughter. "He did what?"

"He had a panic attack when I told him I wanted to see a marriage counselor before he moved back in the house."

"I'm sorry, Tori."

She gave a slight shrug. "Let's change the subject, Charlene. I'm not going to let Jake make me crazy."

Needing some time alone, Tori worked on the reference section of the bookstore. She took a deep calming breath before picking up a couple of dictionaries and arranging them neatly on the shelf.

The hair stood up on the back of her neck, causing Tori to glance around. "Jake," she whispered. She hadn't heard him come into the store. "What are you doing here?"

He came closer. "I want to apologize for the way I behaved yesterday."

"It's okay," she mumbled and picked up another stack of books.

Jake took them from her and promptly placed them on the shelf with the others.

"Do you have a minute?" he asked. "I want to talk to you."

Tori eyed him before she finally said, "Sure. We can go into my office, if you'd like."

"That's fine."

Tori led Jake to the back of the store, where the offices were located. She closed the door behind them.

When she was seated, Jake started to speak. "I was embarrassed yesterday. The panic attack, it came out of nowhere. I hadn't had one that bad in a while."

"Was it because of what I said?"

Jake shook his head no. "They just happen. Nothing in particular brings them on—at least that's what the doctor says." He took a deep breath and continued, "I'm going to be staying in Charleston with Mother and Shepard. For now."

"What does that have to do with me?"

"You were right, Tori. We shouldn't rush into anything."

"Is this your way of telling me that you want a divorce?" Tori held her breath as she waited for his answer.

"I'm not giving up on our marriage, Tori. I want to make that clear."

She let out a small sigh. "What about counseling?"

Jake shook his head no. "I still feel the same way. I'm not interested."

Tori's slender finger tapped a rhythm on her desk, her eyes fixed on Jake's face. "I see."

Jake raised his eyebrows in surprise. "Is that all you have to say?"

"What do you expect me to say, Jake? I told you what I wanted—"

"I'm not going to see a marriage counselor, Tori. That's final."

"I guess we have nothing more to say then." Tori pushed away from her desk. "I need to get back to the store. It's been heavy traffic all day and Charlene is going to need some help."

"Tori . . ." Jake began.

"Good-bye," she stated tersely. "Give your mother my best."

When Jake walked out of her office, Tori fought the urge to call him back. Pulling herself together, she returned to the area where she'd been working before his arrival and resumed her task.

That evening, Tori tried to finish Nicholas's novel, but she couldn't concentrate. Her mind strayed to her conversation with Jake. She didn't want to let negative thoughts overtake her, but it was so hard.

Jake hadn't given her much for which to hope. She believed he still cared for her, but she didn't care much for his attitude concerning the counselor.

Tori pressed both hands over her eyes, as if they burned from weariness. She was so tired her nerves throbbed. What she needed right now was a nap, she decided.

Her prayer before she fell asleep was for God to intervene and His will to prevail.

Tori slept about an hour. It was 6:30 when she woke up from her nap. She turned on the television to catch part of the news broadcast.

The phone rang. Tori answered it. "Hello."

"Hey, beautiful, it's Nicholas. I thought I'd call and check on you. See how things are going."

Tori stifled a yawn. "I'm doing okay. How about you? How's the research going?"

"Great." After a slight pause, Nicholas uttered, "It's fine, Tori."

"What?"

"If you want to talk about Jake, it's fine. When we were teens you used to talk about him all the time, remember?"

Tori laughed before replying, "Actually, Nicholas, I don't want to talk about Jake at all. What I would like to do is take in a movie. Would you go with me, because I don't want to be alone?"

"I'd love it. What time?"

Tori gave him the details and hung up. She got up off the sofa and strolled into her bedroom. She searched through her brand-new wardrobe and decided to wear the purple-and-cream-colored shirt with a pair of cream pants.

One hour and a half later, Tori met Nicholas at the local movie theater. They bought popcorn and sodas before sitting down so that they wouldn't miss any of the movie.

Tori couldn't remember ever laughing so much. She was having a wonderful time with Nicholas. Her thoughts filtered back to the day she'd met him. Two days after she and her family moved to Brunswick, he'd come over with his parents.

He had been extremely shy, but Tori had felt an eager affection for him. They'd instantly become close friends. When his parents were killed in a car accident, Tori had been the only one who could get Nicholas to leave his room.

They'd drifted apart during their senior year when she and Jake had started to become serious. Nicholas had gone off to Howard University while Tori had married Jake.

Years later, here they were on Edisto Island, enjoying a movie together. It reminded her of the old days. In their youth, Nicholas and Tori had spent most Saturdays at the theater. They'd prided themselves on watching all of the new movies within a few days of being released.

After the movie, Nicholas followed Tori back to her house. She'd invited him over for dessert. Over strawberry cheesecake, she told him what had transpired between Jake and her.

Nicholas captured her eyes with his. "You probably won't like what I'm about to say, but I kind of see his point about the marriage counselor."

"Why do most men freak out when someone mentions a marriage counselor or a therapist?" Tori asked with a vague hint of disapproval.

"I can't speak for most men, but I know for me, it's just not something I'd be comfortable with," Nicholas admitted. "I'm not very good at expressing my innermost feelings. Jake probably feels the same way."

"Maybe. I just figured he would at least give it a shot. Especially if he wanted the marriage bad enough." She chewed on her bottom lip.

"You shouldn't use that as a way to measure Jake's love, Tori. You're not being fair to the man."

Tori stared at him in astonishment. "Hey, whose side are you on, anyway? You're supposed to be my best friend."

When Nicholas spoke, his voice was tender, almost a murmur. "I am. That's why I'm being honest with you."

She looked at him with amused wonder. "I do appreciate it, Nicholas. I can always trust you to be completely honest with me— no matter how much it hurts."

"Sweetheart, I know how much you love Jake. If anybody knows, Lord knows I do." Amusement flickered in his eyes.

In spite of herself, Tori chuckled. "Loving Jake is not the issue, Nicholas. Living with him is."

"If you want your marriage, then I say let the man come home," he advised. "I didn't have that luxury with my wife. I wanted to work things out, but she just wasn't interested."

"What went wrong between you two?"

Nicholas gave a slight shrug. "I don't know. All I know is that I came home one day and she was gone. That's when I started working on *Deadly Secrets*."

"Your ex-wife inspired you to write a story involving a serial killer?" Seeing the amusement in his eyes, Tori laughed. "You're sick."

Chapter Twenty

Early Saturday morning, Jake knocked on his mother's door before entering. He found her sitting up in bed reading her Bible. He stood in the doorway, gazing at her in affection.

Gwendolyn smiled. "Come on in, son." Patting an empty spot beside her, she said, "Sit down here beside me. I want to talk to you."

Jake kissed her cheeks. A thread of sadness wound through him as he remembered how plump they used to be. "How are you feeling?"

"I'm feeling good today." Gwendolyn assessed his features. "What about you? How are you doing?"

Jake hesitated, measuring his mother for a moment. "I'm doing okay."

"Are you really? Tell me the truth, Jake."

"Mother, I'm doing the best I can. I've never felt so out of control in my life, and I'm at a loss as to what to do."

"Maybe it's time for you to let go and let God."

Shaking his head, Jake replied, "I don't know how to do that, Mother. God doesn't talk to me like He talks to you. Even Tori knows how to get through to Him, but I don't."

"Son, all you have to do is ask, and it shall be given."

"I don't know how to get God to listen to me, Mother. I've tried—" Jake stopped short. "All I want is peace of mind."

"What happened, son? When did you give up on God?"

He shrugged nonchalantly. "I don't know. Maybe it was when I asked Him to give me my father back. Mother, I prayed so hard back then, but I guess I didn't say the right words."

"Why do you say that?"

"God didn't answer my prayer. Father never came home," he said with detached inevitability. "He died in that plane crash. Father promised me he would come home and we would spend time together."

"Son—"

"I know Father couldn't help it," Jake said, cutting her off. "He died. I just felt that God could give him back to me. Mother, you can't change my mind. You may think prayer works, and maybe for you it does. I don't. God took my daughter from me. I tried to pray. . . . I've gotten more accomplished on my own and without the power of prayer."

Gwendolyn shook her head sadly. "My poor misguided son, when will you understand that you have nothing in your control? Everything you are—it's because God has allowed it. Everything you're not—it's because God has allowed it also."

"Mother, I went to God, and He closed the door in my face." Waving his hand in dismissal, Jake said, "I'm done."

"I don't agree, Jake. I think it was the other way around."

"Excuse me?"

"Son, I don't think you knocked hard, or maybe you just didn't wait long enough."

Her comment gave Jake something to consider.

"Honey, you have to welcome God into your heart. You don't just pray to Him when you want something out of the deal. His Word is a lifestyle—not a convenience."

"So, because I don't have a relationship with the Lord, my

prayers go unanswered. Is that what you're saying?" It actually made sense to Jake. God just wasn't listening to him, and now he understood why.

Gwendolyn shook her head. "No, that's not it at all."

"Then what are you saying, Mother?" Jake wanted to know.

"You can't set a time limit on God. And you have to understand that sometimes God says no."

"Well, that's all He's ever said to me." Jake got off the bed and walked toward the door. "But I think you're right, Mother. You have to have a certain kind of relationship with God for Him to answer your prayers. At least if you're expecting Him to say yes."

Sheila paced back and forth in her bedroom, wanting desperately to call Jake, but she resisted the urge. It wouldn't be wise to push at this point, she decided. If she intended to win Jake over, she was going to have to exercise patience. It had always been a challenge for her in dealing with personal restraint.

She strolled into her kitchen and poured herself a cup of steaming hot coffee. Something clicked in her mind and Sheila frowned. Even though Jake believed otherwise, Tori wasn't about to let her marriage end. She was playing with Jake's head.

Sheila wasn't fooled by Tori's little game. She would never play with Jake's mind like this, she vowed. It didn't matter that she was being manipulative and deceitful now, because she would change once Jake married her. She would become the woman he wanted her to be.

She and Jake belonged together. They were partners and made a great team in business. . . . A smile tugged at her lips. And in bed.

The image of them making love loomed in her mind, and Sheila could hardly wait to get Jake back into her bed. She muttered a string of curses as she thought of Tori and the night she'd shown up at the hotel uninvited. Sheila acknowledged she hated Tori because she had everything Sheila had ever wanted. Jake Madison.

Chapter Twenty-one

Tori peeked inside Charlene's office. "You have a minute? I really need to ask your advice on something."

"Sure. What is it?"

She dropped down into a nearby chair, her fingers tensed in her lap. Crossing her jean-clad legs, Tori stated, "It's about Jake. I was thinking about asking him out on a date. What do you think?"

Leaning back in her high-backed leather chair, Charlene answered, "I think it's a good idea."

Tori's face clouded with uncertainty. "Really?"

"Yeah. You and Jake need to start getting to know each other all over again. Especially if you want to have a marriage."

Tori rose to her feet. "Okay. I'm going to do it," she said happily. Tori strode with purpose into her office and picked up the phone. "Jake, hey. I'm calling to ask you to have dinner with me."

The voice on the other end was silent, prompting Tori to ask, "Are you still there, Jake?"

"I'm here."

Tori was consumed with hurt over his obvious rejection. It was a humiliating, deflated feeling. Tears welled up in her eyes. "You know what, you don't have to answer that. Just forget it—" She was about to hang up.

"No," Jake quickly interjected. "I think it's a good idea."

A tear slipped from her eye. Tori wiped it away.

"Honey, I would love to have dinner with you," he whispered. "I was just surprised. Things have been so strange between us. I just didn't expect you to call and ask me out on a date. This is a date, right?"

"So, you really want to do this?" Tori asked hopefully.

They talked a few minutes more before ending the call.

Charlene checked on her later and found Tori staring off into space.

"What's up, girl?"

Tori turned her attention to her cousin. "Huh?"

"Are you and Jake going out?"

Tori grinned. "We're going to have dinner tonight."

"Good. It's a great start."

Her smile disappeared. "Charlene, do you think that Jake and I will make it?"

"I do. If you both want it bad enough, Tori. All marriages have their slumps, but I do believe that they can be restored. Especially if both people want it."

"But how do I get past the lack of trust? Jake betrayed me, Charlene. I'm not sure I can ever trust him like before. I actually believed once that he loved only me and wouldn't even look at another woman. Then Sheila came along."

Her hands on her slender hips, Charlene questioned, "Tori, are you going to hand your husband over to that woman?"

"Excuse me?"

"You and Jake have a long history together. Are you just going to let Sheila win, or do you plan on fighting for your man?"

"I want my marriage. You know that."

"But you're keeping your husband at arm's length. What's up with that?"

Her arms folded across her chest, Tori said, "I can't just fall back into bed with Jake."

Charlene rolled her eyes heavenward. "I'm not talking just about sex. Although you do realize that if he's not getting any from you, and Miss Moore is doing nothing but throwing herself at him . . ."

"Thanks, Charlene. That's the last thing I needed. An image of Jake and Sheila having sex." Tori turned on her computer. "That's just great!"

Laughing, Charlene headed to the front of the store.

Muttering under her breath, Tori logged onto the Internet. She forced her mind to the task at hand—researching local African-American history. She didn't want to think about Jake or Sheila.

Jake spent the morning getting reacquainted with everyone at Madison Moore. Sheila had done a tremendous job holding down the fort during his hiatus. At eleven A.M., he sat in on a meeting between her and a potential client.

She quickly brought him up to speed. "Gemini, Inc. wants a Web site whose target audience is wide-ranging—sixteen- to thirty-five-year-olds who are looking for a big break into the entertainment business."

"So what you need is a design that's hip and cool. Something that will represent members of that diverse audience," Jake stated.

Smiling, Sheila asked, "Do you have any ideas, Jake?"

He leaned forward. "Well, something crossed my mind a few minutes ago. I'm thinking the best way to speak to the diverse members of Gemini's audience is through the use of hip and cool illustrated characters representing the different members. This way, each visitor coming to the site can identify with at least one of the characters."

Sheila's voice bubbled with excitement. "Yes! And we can make the site more engaging and entertaining by animating bubbles that can sequentially pop up over each character as if they were speaking to you. . . ."

"Telling you how the Big Break promotion works," Jake finished for her.

At the end of the meeting, Madison Moore had secured the Gemini, Inc. account.

"You were great!" Sheila acknowledged once she and Jake were alone. "I'm so glad you're back." Before he realized what was happening, she had thrown herself into his arms.

Jake took a step backward. "It's good being back. I didn't realize just how much I'd missed it."

"We make a wonderful team, don't you think?"

He nodded. "We do, Sheila. Thanks for letting me sit in on the meeting." Jake headed to the door.

"Why don't we have dinner tonight? We can celebrate both your return to Madison Moore and landing the Gemini account."

Standing in the doorway, he asked, "Can I have a rain check? I'm having dinner with Tori this evening."

Sheila's smile disappeared. "Sure."

"We'll do it another night," Jake stated. He could tell that she was upset. "Soon."

She nodded. "Whenever you want." Picking up a stack of pictures, Sheila uttered, "I have a meeting in about an hour. I need to go prepare for the presentation."

"Okay. I'll be in my office if you need me."

Sheila pasted on a smile that didn't quite reach her eyes. "Okay."

Jake eyed her for a moment before leaving the office. She was upset, but he wasn't worried. Sheila could never stay too angry with him for long. Once she was over her anger, she would move forward as if nothing had happened and she would never mention it again. He wished Tori were more like Sheila in that respect.

Chapter Twenty-two

Jake pulled out a chair for Tori. He then took a seat facing her. After they ordered drinks, Jake proudly announced, "I went back to work today." The day had gone well and his mood was buoyant.

Placing her napkin across her lap, Tori questioned, "How did it go?"

"Great. I even helped land a new contract. Sheila and I were in sync—it was just like old times."

Tori smiled tightly. "Congratulations."

Jake eyed her for a moment. Her expression put a damper on his mood. "You know that it's just business between Sheila and me, don't you?"

Their drinks arrived and Tori took a sip of her iced tea. She didn't respond to his question, just continued to watch him.

"There's nothing between us," he pressed. "I swear it."

She stared into his eyes. "I believe you, Jake." Signaling to the waiter, Tori ordered a bottle of champagne.

When the champagne arrived, Tori made a toast. "Here's to landing a new account. May it be the first of many more. Congratulations, honey."

Jake tapped his flute to hers, relieved that the night was off to a good start.

As they waited for their food to arrive, Jake told Tori more about the new project Madison Moore was about to undertake. ". . . looking to break into the entertainment business."

"It sounds interesting," Tori admitted. "I can't wait to see the finished project."

"It should be fun."

She smiled. "You're happy being back at work, aren't you?"

"I am," Jake confessed. "It feels good."

Covering his hand with hers, Tori said, "Then I'm happy for you."

"The company's doing well. Sheila did a good job holding down the fort." Jake played with his glass. He muttered a silent curse. He hadn't meant to bring up his partner's name again. Sheila was a sore subject between them.

"There's no denying that she loves the company as much as you do, Jake. I'm aware of that."

His eyes found hers once more. "You just don't like her much, do you?"

"No, I don't," Tori confessed. "Jake, how many women do you know who are friends with the women sleeping with their husbands?"

Jake's eyes darted around the room. "Maybe we should change the subject."

Tori burst into laughter, surprising him. "Something a little more safe, huh?"

"I want this night to be perfect. No arguments, nobody getting angry."

"I think we can manage that," Tori murmured softly. "Things are going well so far."

Jake wholeheartedly agreed.

When their entrées arrived, conversation was cut to a minimum. Every now and then Jake would steal a peek at Tori. He still couldn't get over how much she'd changed. The hair, the makeup, and the clothes . . . he sliced off a piece of steak and stuck it into his mouth. Jake chewed thoughtfully.

Tori stopped eating. "What is it?"

"I was just thinking about how much I'm enjoying this."

"I'm having a great time myself."

"I hope we'll be able to do this again."

"I don't see why not." Tori finished off her shrimp scampi. "We don't have to act like strangers, you know."

"There are times when I feel like that's exactly what we are. Strangers." His gaze met hers. "I don't think we had this much tension between us when we went on our first date."

She broke into a tender smile. "We didn't. But that was a very different time for us, Jake. We were young and there wasn't any pain or mistrust between us. Now we have to do damage control."

"Tell me the truth, Tori. Are we going to be able to move past this mess with Sheila? She is my business partner."

"I have to be honest with you. It won't be overnight, Jake. It's not going to be easy, but with God's help, I'm going to do the best I can."

"Sheila is my friend. That's all. You're going to have to trust me on this, honey."

Tori wanted to trust Jake. She really did. As much as she tried, she couldn't shake the feeling that as long as Sheila was a part of their lives, their marriage was in trouble.

Sheila sat in her rental car, watching as Jake walked Tori up the steps and into their house. She had followed them from the restaurant to their house. Her heart started to pound rapidly as she waited for him to come out.

Her imagination ran rampant as she sat in the parked car, wondering what was going on inside the house. Were they in each other's arms right now? Was that witch trying to seduce Jake?

Fury swept through her at the mere thought of Jake and Tori holding each other and kissing. She didn't even want to consider the fact that they could be in bed making love. A red haze surrounded her, almost choking Sheila. She felt nauseated and dizzy. "He c-can't . . ." she cried out.

Tears welled up and ran down her face. "Don't do it, Jake," she whispered. "Don't fall for her game. Tori's only trying to control you."

Sheila wanted to scream uncontrollably. Sticking her fist in her mouth smothered the sounds gurgling in her throat. She stifled the urge to march up to the front door and force her way inside. She wanted to plead with Jake to leave with her, but she knew to do so would only upset him. Sheila knew him well enough to know that Jake wasn't ready for her to declare her love for him.

She was eventually able to calm herself and she settled back to wait. Sheila had every intention of sitting there until Jake drove away. If he left at all.

Jake ran his tongue over Tori's lips. Clasping her body tightly to his, he whispered, "I've wanted to do this all night long."

She relaxed into his cushioning embrace, murmuring, "I love you so much, Jake."

He kissed her, the touch of his lips sending the pit of her stomach into a wild swirl. Tori pulled her lips away from his. She needed to come up for air. She needed to keep a clear head.

Jake captured her mouth once more, kissing her passionately while his hand traveled up and down her back.

Tori moaned in pleasure. Only Jake could make her feel this way. Her body was so tightly coiled that she ached for release. Her husband's fingers worked their magic, sending tremors of ecstasy shooting through her.

He pulled away from Tori reluctantly. She touched her lips, swollen from his kisses and aching for more.

Jake's voice was hoarse with desire. "I want you, sweetheart. I want to make love to you."

For an instant, Tori hesitated. "It's too soon," she murmured, a little surprised by her refusal. She didn't know where the words had come from. Especially with the way she was feeling right now. Tori held her head down to avoid Jake's questioning gaze.

"I know you want me just as much as I want you. What's holding you back?"

"Jake, we've been apart for a year. Falling into bed right now is not the smart thing to do. We still have some issues we need to work out." Desire rushed through her, causing her nearly to go weak in the knees. Tori felt the inexplicable pull of the past, which threatened to draw her in.

"Don't you think it would help if I move back here?"

Tori took a step back from him. "Jake, you said you wouldn't push."

"I'm sorry."

"This is a good start, don't you think?" Tori asked. "We should just stop here."

"I guess you're right." Jake put both hands to his face and sighed. "I have to confess that a cold shower is not how I thought this night would end."

Tori held back her smile. Jake looked downright pitiful, but she wasn't about to give in.

With a mischievous twinkle in his eye, Jake questioned, "Sure you don't want me to stay? I remember a time when you were afraid to stay in this big house alone."

"That was so long ago, Jake." Tori burst into laughter.

He chuckled. "You can't blame a man for trying."

Tori kissed him. "Good night, Jake."

Jake stood with his back pressed against the front door. "I hate leaving you, baby. I really do."

"You can sleep in one of the guest rooms," Tori offered.

Jake seemed to consider her offer, then shook his head. "No, I'd better go to Mother's. If I stay here, I may not be able to control myself."

"Yes, you will. I have faith in you, Jake. And a nice lock on the master bedroom door."

Throwing back his head, Jake burst into laughter. "You'd better not lock me out of my own bedroom."

"Don't give me a reason to do so and I won't."

Jake reached for her, pulling her into his arms. "Come here. Give me a real kiss good night."

Tori did as she was told. She thrilled over the idea of Jake spending the night.

As they headed up the stairs, Tori sent up a silent prayer of thanks. She and Jake had actually made it over the first hurdle. They were at least communicating for the moment.

Chapter Twenty-three

The week breezed by, bringing with it a new month. In exactly two weeks, it would be Mother's Day. Jake was trying to decide how best to handle that particular day. It was sure to be an emotional one for Tori. By the time he showered and dressed, he was still no closer to an answer.

When Jake came downstairs for breakfast, he found his brother sitting at the dining-room table alone. He joined him. "Where's Mother?"

"She's going to sleep in this morning."

"Is she feeling well? I knocked on her door but I didn't get an answer." Jake rose to his feet. "Maybe I'd better go up and check on her."

Della strode into the room carrying two plates laden with grits, sausage, bacon, and fluffy scrambled eggs. "Mrs. Madison is just resting. There's nothing to worry about. I was up there with her not too long ago, helping with her bath."

She placed a plate on the table in front of Jake and the other in front of Shepard. Della left and quickly returned with a pitcher of orange juice and a steaming coffeepot.

"You and Tori having a good time?" Shepard inquired. "Charlene told me you two have been out on a few dates."

Jake held out his cup for Della to pour coffee into it. "Things are going well," he answered.

"I really hope you two can work everything out, big brother. I really like Tori."

"We're trying, Shepard." Jake sliced off a piece of sausage and stuck it in his mouth. He stole a glance at his brother, who seemed to be concentrating heavily on his own plate.

Every now and then he would catch Shepard watching him. Jake gave him a tight smile and returned his attention to his food.

Shepard cleared his throat noisily. "We used to be close. What happened, Jake?"

"I felt we needed some space. We were arguing all of the time and we couldn't agree when it came to Sheila."

Shepard's eyes met his. "So, you chose to take sides with a woman you think you know over your own brother?"

"It wasn't like that, Shepard. You don't know Sheila."

"I know her well enough. It's you who don't know her like you think you do."

Jake finished off his coffee. "Let's drop it, Shepard. We're never going to agree on this subject."

"Sheila almost cost you your marriage once, Jake. Don't let her do it again. This time you could lose Tori for good."

"Sheila is my partner. That's all she can ever be. She knows that."

Shepard's smile was wary. "For your sake, man, I really hope so."

"What's up with you and Charlene? I thought you would've married her by now."

"That was the plan, but we have some issues that need to be resolved." Shepard finished off his eggs. "Now I don't know what's going to happen. I want to have children and Charlene doesn't."

"She doesn't want children? I'm surprised. I always thought she would want lots of children."

"Me, too. But I guess we were both wrong." Shepard sighed heavily. "Jake, I really want to have children. I want to be a father."

"What about adoption?"

Shepard gave a slight shrug. "I want my own."

Jake nodded in understanding. "Well, listen to your own advice. Charlene's a good woman. Don't mess around and lose her. I understand wanting your own blood, but there are so many children out there who need good parents. You're going to make a great father."

"Thank you for saying that, Jake. It means a lot to me." Shepard downed the last of his juice. "For the record, I feel the same way about you. Tiffany's death was not your fault."

Jake was spared from responding when Della strode into the room, asking, "Anybody want seconds?"

Both Shepard and Jake answered no.

Rising to his feet, Jake stated, "I need to get to the office. I have a meeting with the art department."

"I'll come by later. I want to discuss some ideas for a Web site for my law office."

Jake laughed. "You're finally joining us in the world of technology?"

"Might as well. It's a competitive world out there."

On his way to the office, Jake passed the church he'd grown up in. Every time he drove by, it reminded him of his father's funeral. After that day, he'd refused to set another foot into the church.

He recalled the day his father left on his business trip. Jake had stopped him at the door, begging him not to leave. His father had hugged him before promising to return in a few days. He'd promised they would spend some much-needed quality time together. Jake had lived for the day his father would return. Only he hadn't. He'd died in a plane crash on the way home.

Jake felt cheated. Just when he and his beloved father were going to spend time together—he was gone. He had always been closer to his dad than his mother, although he shared loving relationships with them both.

"Why didn't You ever care about me, God? Why weren't You here for me whenever I needed You?"

Jake heard a whisper on the wind, it seemed. It made the hair on the back of his neck stand up. He glanced up at the rearview mirror. He knew he was alone in his car, yet it was almost as if he'd heard a voice. The words *I am here* came as an audible sound.

Doubt crept through Jake and he suddenly felt foolish. There was no one with him inside the car, and the voice he'd heard was just his mind playing tricks on him.

Tori's first thought each morning was always Jake, it seemed. She climbed out of bed and did her stretches. It had been a while since she'd indulged in exercising, but since Jake's return, she had begun to feel motivated.

After her shower, Tori ate a bowl of cereal and headed out to Bible study. She sat down near the front of the church and opened her Bible to Psalms. Tori had always enjoyed reading the Book of Psalms and looked forward to the study.

"Psalm 42 talks about thirsting for God. Many things can cause us to long for the Lord. Perhaps you have a tragic history, suffering from alcohol abuse, being the victim of a crime, or perhaps losing a loved one. All those things can lead us to wanting a relationship with God. . . ."

Tori wrote furiously, trying to keep up with Pastor Allen. She had always enjoyed his teaching. When the session was over, she hung around a few minutes later to speak with her pastor.

"How are things going between you and Jake?"

"I still haven't been able to convince Jake to come to counseling. He's ready to come home, Pastor. I just don't know if I can go back to being his wife when he hasn't been a husband in a long time."

"Pray about it. But, Tori, you are going to have to forgive Jake.

There has to be forgiveness before you can have healing. You can't have one without the other."

"Thank you, Pastor Allen." Tori embraced him and headed out to her car, her mind clouded with thoughts.

"I'm starving. Why don't we have lunch?" Sheila asked.

Jake was surprised by her suggestion. For the past couple of weeks, she'd been acting a little distant with him. Ever since the day he'd turned down her offer for dinner.

"You're speaking to me again?" he teased.

"What do you mean by that?"

"You haven't said much to me this last couple of weeks. When I ask you something, you nearly bite my head off."

Sheila glanced at her watch. "I've been very busy. I had to have the Samsonite presentation ready and we had some last-minute glitches. I was a bit frustrated, I admit it."

"Well, I'm glad to see you back to your old self. I kinda missed you."

Sheila broke into a big smile. "That's so nice to hear."

"It's true. It felt lonely around here."

A few minutes later, they left the building and walked one block to a restaurant on the corner. Over lunch, Sheila rehearsed her presentation for Jake.

Two hours later, they returned to Madison Moore. As soon as Jake walked into the building, he spotted Tori in the lobby, talking to Selma. He strolled over to her and kissed her lightly on the lips. "Honey, what are you doing here?"

"I came to see you," she stated calmly. Staring pointedly at Sheila, Tori said, "Would you please excuse us?"

Casting Tori a nasty look, she uttered, "No problem." She took the elevator while Jake and Tori waited for the next one.

"Sheila and I went to lunch," he offered as an explanation. The elevator doors opened up and Jake ushered her into the car.

"I know. Selma told me."

He tried to gauge Tori's mood as he punched the button for his floor and the doors closed. She didn't look too happy seeing him with Sheila.

"I'm going to Brunswick for Mother's Day weekend. I want to visit Tiffany's grave. I was hoping you'd go with me."

Nodding, Jake murmured, "I'd like that. I was actually thinking about this exact same thing myself."

"Mama said you're welcome to stay at the house with us. It's up to you."

"That's fine. When do you want to leave?" Jake followed Tori off the elevator and into his office.

"Why don't we drive down early that Friday morning? Are you planning to stay the whole weekend?"

"Do you want me to?" Jake asked as he closed the door.

"It'll give us some time alone."

He smiled. "Thank you for inviting me, Tori. I'm looking forward to our weekend."

Sheila rapped on the door. "Am I interrupting something?" Her eyes issued a silent challenge.

"No," Tori answered. "In fact, I was just about to leave."

"Not on my account, I hope."

"Definitely not on your account, Sheila. I have some work to do." To Jake, she said, "I'll see you later." Standing on tiptoe, Tori pressed her lips to his.

On her way out, Tori uttered, "Bye, Sheila."

"What's she so happy about?"

Jake leaned over his desk, checking his appointment book. "Oh. Tori and I are going to Brunswick for Mother's Day weekend."

"Really? When did this come about?"

Jake looked over at his partner. "What's the problem, Sheila? I'm simply going away for the weekend with my wife."

Sheila sat down gracefully. "There's no problem. Have a good time. I was just surprised, that's all. I guess things are going well for you two."

His arms folded across his chest, he questioned, "Then what's the look for?"

"Jake, I just think this might be a mistake. Tori's trying to get you on her turf. Can't you see what's happening? She's trying to control you. This time around, she's planning on calling the shots. Remember that."

He laughed. "Tori's not like that. She's never been one to play games like that."

"Maybe the old Tori wasn't, but this one . . . I don't know, Jake. She's changed quite a bit. Look how sarcastic she's become to me. She wasn't like that before."

Jake had to agree with Sheila. Tori hadn't always been that way. She was different, but he still had trouble believing that his wife was trying to control him. Tori didn't have the guts to try to manipulate him.

Chapter Twenty-four

Tori put fresh flowers around Tiffany's grave. Tears slipped from her eyes as she pulled weeds from around the site. Wiping them, she just sat there, staring at the headstone. "I miss you so much, baby," she whispered. "Mommy really misses you."

She stole a peek across her shoulder. Jake was sitting in the car. He couldn't seem to bring himself actually to visit the grave. She returned her attention to the headstone. "Honey, Daddy is here. He's sitting in the car, but he wanted me to tell you that he loves you so much. He really does."

Tori stayed a few minutes longer. When she made her way down the hill to the car, she found Jake standing there, waiting for her. He held out his arms to her.

She rushed into his arms, needing him. "It hasn't gotten any easier," she murmured.

"I know. I don't think it ever really does. She was such a beautiful little girl."

Tori nodded sadly. "She looked just like you, Jake."

"But Tiffany had your smile." Jake's eyes grew bright. "If I could change that night . . ."

She shook her head sadly. They were both filled with regret. "We can't go back. We can only move forward."

"I think that is probably the hardest thing to do. Moving on."

Tori nodded in understanding. "I wished desperately that I'd just come home with you that night. Maybe things would've turned out differently."

Jake held open the car door for her. "I should have left her with you that night. If the accident had to happen, it only would have been me in the car."

"You could have died."

"At least you would still have Tiffany."

"This may sound selfish, but I would prefer to have both of you. I didn't want to trade one life for the other."

When they left Oak Grove Cemetery, Tori drove around Brunswick. "You once asked me why I kept running home to my mother. It wasn't so much that I wanted to see my mom. I wanted to come back for the history."

Frowning, Jake asked, "What history? You're always talking about Brunswick and its history. What's so special or historic about this small town?"

She grinned. "I'm going to show you. We're going to start with my high school, Glynn Academy." Tori drove along Albany Street. "Things look so different now," she murmured. "The houses along here seem so small now. I guess it's because I was a little girl."

"Things always look different through the eyes of a child."

Tori parked the car and they climbed out. Walking hand in hand, she gave him background information on Glynn Academy. Pointing to the science building, she said, "Nicholas and I used to hang right over there."

"When was the school built?"

"The first school was built in 1788, but the exact location is unknown. This particular building was built in 1923." Pointing, Tori said, "Each of the different buildings represents a history of architectural design, from the Georgian style to the Classical Revival to the Richardsonian Romanesque. The gym is new. I can't remember when it was built, but I think it was right after I graduated."

"You enjoyed your time here at this huge school?"

Tori nodded. "I did. I have great memories here."

"Why'd you keep coming to Charleston, then?"

"Because you were there."

Jake smiled. "Each summer, I would be so anxious until Charlene told me that you were on your way. I was always afraid you wouldn't show up. I thought you might meet some boy in Brunswick."

Tori stopped walking. "I only had eyes for you, Jake. You were the only person for me." She gave a small laugh. "I had those same fears where you were concerned, too. I was afraid you'd meet some girl in South Carolina and forget all about me."

"That could never happen," Jake confessed. "I was too wrapped up in you."

They headed back to the car, both caught up in their own memories.

Linda had dinner ready when they returned to the house.

Tori was surprised. "Mama, we were planning to take you out to dinner."

Waving a hand in dismissal, Linda replied, "It's all right. I wasn't sure y'all would be up to it after you visited Tiffany's grave."

With everyone seated around the table, Tori gave her mother a rundown of their day. "After we left the cemetery, I gave Jake a tour of Brunswick. Tomorrow, I'm going to show him the beauty of Jekyll Island and St. Simons." They'd decided to spend another night there and return home on Monday.

"I have a different view of this city now," he admitted. "It's an interesting town. Much more than I first thought. I'm glad I finally agreed to do some sightseeing. I've been here plenty of times but I admit that I've paid little or no attention to what the city was to offer."

After dinner, Tori helped her mother straighten up in the kitchen while Jake settled in the den, watching television. She joined him there half an hour later.

"Would you like to do something tonight? We could take in a movie or go dancing," Tori suggested. "Of course, we'd have to drive down to Jacksonville for that."

Jake shook his head. "I'd rather just stay in, if you don't mind. I'm not feeling up to being around people."

She dropped down onto the couch beside him. "Is something wrong?"

"Not really. I just miss Tiffany so much. I keep her on my mind."

"I understand. Sometimes, I'll see a toy or a book and I have to stop myself." Tori grabbed Jake's hand. "Mama told me about your coming to Brunswick."

"I figured she would eventually."

"Why didn't you tell me?"

Jake shrugged. "I don't know. I guess it just didn't seem important." He swung an arm around Tori. "Let's find something to watch on TV."

She knew this was Jake's way of saying the discussion was over. She let it drop for now to keep the peace. So far, they'd had a good time together, and Tori didn't want to spoil it.

Later, they retired to their bedrooms. Tori couldn't sleep, so she got out of bed and went to the room across the hall. She knocked on Jake's door. "Can I come in?"

"Sure."

Stepping into the room, she inquired, "Are you comfortable? Do you need anything?"

Jake was sitting on the edge of the bed, wearing a pair of black silk boxers. Tori pretended not to notice how sexy he looked.

"I'm fine, sweetheart," he answered.

She leaned against the bedroom door, her back straight, glancing around nervously.

Jake motioned for her to join him on the bed. "We are still married, Tori. I don't think your mother will mind."

She broke into laughter but didn't move.

"Come on," Jake urged. "We're just going to talk. That's all."

Tori eased into bed beside her husband. "This doesn't mean that anything more is going to happen." In her heart, she prayed for strength. It had been so long since she'd made love, and her body was reacting with a will of its own.

Jake kissed her. "I love you, Tori," he whispered in her ear.

"I love you, too."

Tori fell asleep in his arms. She woke up two hours later. Nudging Jake, she tried to wake him up.

"I'm going to my room. I'll see you in the morning."

"Don't leave," he pleaded sleepily.

"Jake, please."

"Okay. Can I at least have a kiss?"

Tori pressed her lips to his. "I'll see you in the morning. Go back to sleep."

"Yeah, right."

Jake sat up long after Tori had gone to her room. She still didn't trust him. It angered him, although he really couldn't blame her. All he wanted was a chance to make things right between them.

He knew he had to be patient and give Tori time, but Jake was getting tired of walking on egg shells around her. He was going to give her two more weeks, he decided. If Tori didn't come to her senses by then—Jake was moving back into his house whether she liked it or not.

Sheila's words haunted him. Maybe this was Tori's way of trying to control the situation between them. If he had his way, Jake would already be back at home.

Tori kept saying she wanted the marriage. . . .

JACQUELIN THOMAS

Jake punched his pillow as he sought to find a comfortable spot in the bed. He'd had no problem sleeping while Tori was lying next to him. But now, the bed seemed cold and lonely.

He tossed and turned for most of the night. Jake finally sat up in bed and grabbed the remote control off the bedside table. "Might as well watch some television," he muttered to himself.

Jake watched TV for nearly an hour before sleep overtook him.

Chapter Twenty-five

Nicholas stepped into the bookstore and looked around. Seeing Tori with a customer, he waved and headed over to the local history section.

Grinning, Tori strode over to him. "Looking for anything in particular?"

"I thought I'd come by and check on you. But I also came by to pick up a couple of books. I'm going to need you to order some titles for me as well." Nicholas stood there, scanning her face. "Are you really okay?"

Tori nodded. She greeted a customer who'd just walked in. "I'm doing okay. Just keeping busy with the store."

"Have you talked to Jake?"

Her smile was answer enough. "Yes, I have. We spent the weekend in Brunswick."

Before he could respond, Charlene walked over to where they were standing.

"Hello, Nicholas. Good to see you again."

"You, too," he replied with a bright smile. "Hey, can I take you two beautiful ladies to lunch?"

"I'm gonna have to have a rain check on lunch. I've just finished a huge salad and half a sandwich," Charlene explained.

"How about you, Tori?" Nicholas asked. "Mind having lunch with an old friend?"

She laughed. "Sure. Lunch is fine."

Nicholas selected a book from the shelf, then moved to another section while Tori assisted a customer with her purchases. She navigated back over to where he was standing. "Do you have a list of the titles you want ordered?"

He followed her to the register. Tori stepped behind the counter. Nicholas pulled out a piece of paper from his pocket and handed it to her.

After she ordered the books from his list, Tori went to grab her purse. She returned a few minutes later. "I'm ready."

Looking back over her shoulder, she announced to Charlene, "I'll be back in an hour."

Nicholas held the door open for her. Just as Tori was about to step outside, Jake appeared out of nowhere, startling her.

She pressed a hand to her chest and said, "Jake, my goodness! You scared me! What are you doing here?" Her heartbeat gradually returned to normal.

He looked from Tori to Nicholas, then returned his gaze to her. "I came to see you, but it looks like you're on your way out."

Tori thought she detected censure in his voice. "Nicholas and I are going to have lunch."

"We can do it another time," Nicholas interjected quickly. "Jake, it's good to see you again."

Jake ignored Nicholas. To Tori, he said, "You don't have to change your plans. It wasn't anything important. We can talk some other time."

Nicholas glanced down at Tori, who asked, "Can I have a rain check on lunch?"

He smiled. "Anytime. Just give me a call." Nicholas stepped

around her and Jake. "Thanks for ordering those books for me." The look he gave her assured her that everything was okay.

"No problem. I'll call you when they come in."

Nicholas left the store.

Tori glared at her husband. She itched to slap the smug look off his face. How could he treat her friend like that? Nicholas had always been very cordial to Jake.

"Why'd you give me that look?" he asked innocently.

"Could you have been more rude?" Charlene exclaimed.

Gazing at his wife, Jake questioned, "What's wrong with you two? What did I do?"

A couple entered the bookstore. Rolling her eyes at Jake, Charlene went over to assist them.

"We can talk in my office," Tori stated tersely. "Call me if you get busy out here," she whispered to Charlene.

Silent and brooding, Jake followed her to the back of the store.

"What's wrong with you?" he asked as soon as they were seated in her office.

"There's nothing wrong with me, Jake," Tori snapped. "Maybe you should ask yourself that question. After all, you were the one who was extremely rude to Nicholas, and you know it."

"I never cared for Nicholas Washington."

"He's done nothing to you," Tori defended.

"You don't care for Sheila, and you're not exactly very nice to her. This is kinda the same thing, don't you think?"

"What did you want to talk about?" Tori asked abruptly. She wasn't in the mood to have this discussion with Jake right now. The jerk was trying to turn this around on her.

"You could have gone to lunch with Nicholas if you wanted to, Tori. Especially if you're going to have an attitude."

Obviously, he wasn't just going to let it drop. "I'm aware of that," she responded tersely. "I'm sure that's not why you came all the way here. I assume you wanted to talk to me about something." Tori leaned back in her chair, watching him.

"I've been thinking about us. I think maybe we're going about this all wrong."

"How should we be going about this?"

"I think I should move back into the house."

Tori's eyes widened in her shock. She certainly hadn't expected Jake to say those words. Especially since they had already had this discussion.

"Well?" he prompted.

Confusion clouded her mind, prompting Tori to ask, "What's brought this on, Jake? And what about the counseling?" She intended to stand her ground on this issue.

"I don't think we need it. But look, let's just try it this way first. Then, if you still insist on seeing someone—we'll do it."

Tori clearly didn't believe him. "No, Jake."

His eyes registered his surprise. "Excuse me?"

"Jake, we don't have a chance without seeing a marriage counselor."

"Who's filling your head with this crap? Is it Nicholas?" Jake's voice was suddenly filled with anger.

"I have a mind of my own, Jake," Tori argued. "I don't need someone to make my decisions for me. *Not even you.*"

He shook his head in confusion. "What's gotten into you?"

"Nothing, Jake. I'm twenty-eight years old, and I know my own mind."

Jake stared at her as if she were a complete stranger.

Tori pointed to the door. "I should probably get back out there. It's usually busy during lunchtime."

He stood up. "You know, I have to wonder if you really think we need space, or if you're just trying to control me."

She rose to her feet. "I don't have time for this. I'll talk to you later, Jake." Tori stepped around her desk and walked briskly out of her office, leaving him staring after her in shock.

He was quickly on her heels. "Now you're walking out on me?"

"I have work to do, Jake," Tori shot back. "I don't have time for foolishness. Why don't you give me a call when you're ready to talk? Really talk."

Jake was angry, but for once, Tori really didn't care. She hadn't done anything to him. His bad attitude was his problem.

"I feel like you've been avoiding me," Charlene stated when Shepard entered the bookstore. Tori had already gone home for the evening, and she was working until closing.

"No, I haven't," he answered. "I've just been very busy."

Locking the door behind him, Charlene questioned, "You're still very angry with me, aren't you? You haven't said much to me since the night of the charity ball."

Shepard shook his head. He stood by, reading a magazine, while Charlene took a reading on the cash register. When she removed all of the money, they proceeded to the back.

Once they were in Charlene's office, she asked, "Then what is it, Shepard? Why are you still acting so distant? I thought you understood."

Sighing heavily, Shepard uttered, "Charlene, I want children. You don't. How am I supposed to act? I love you and I want to marry you, but I want to have a family. I can't just skip over that little fact."

"I realize that," she replied quietly.

He met her gaze. "Do you?"

"I love you so much, Shepard. I really do, but you misunderstood me. I never said I didn't want children. I said I couldn't have any children."

"Why not?"

"We've been together for seven years. I've never been on birth control in all that time, Shepard." She paused for a second and her eyes teared up. "I'm not able to have children."

"What?"

"I can't have children. There's scar tissue—" Charlene stopped short. She hadn't meant to say that much, because she wasn't ready to have this discussion with him. It was too painful.

Shepard's eyebrow rose in his surprise. "Scar tissue? Why would you have scar tissue?"

Charlene chewed on her bottom lip. "The doctors see some kind of mass, and they believe it's scar tissue, I guess."

Shepard was concerned. "Could it be cancerous?"

She shook her head no. Charlene didn't want to lie to Shepard, but if he continued pushing, then she would have no other choice. Bending her head, she pretended to be engrossed in working on the daily report.

He sat in the chair facing her, watching her in silence. When Charlene finished her report, Shepard offered to help her count the money.

When they were ready to leave, he escorted her to her car and followed Charlene to the bank to make the nightly deposit. Afterward, Shepard followed her home.

"I appreciate your looking out for Tori and me like this. Coming out here to make sure we're okay when we close."

"I care about you both."

"Your friend Ben is real nice. He arrives every night right on time." Charlene gave a short laugh. "You can pretty much set a clock by him."

"I know he'll take care of you ladies. This week he's working a different shift at the police station. That's why I came."

"You're not going to have to come out every night. Mall management has hired an off-duty cop for security. He's going to start day after tomorrow."

Chapter Twenty-six

Jake's two-week deadline had expired, and he hadn't made much headway with Tori. In fact, they hadn't said more than a few words to each other. He drove out to Edisto Island to see her. After parking his car in the driveway, he got out. He paced himself as he climbed the steps to the front porch. Although the keys were in Jake's pocket, he rang the doorbell. He felt like a guest at his own home, but he was going to put a stop to that immediately.

Tori answered the door wearing a beautiful sweater in a teal color with a pair of matching cropped pants. On her feet she wore a pair of silver strappy sandals. Running a hand through her short curls, she gave him a winning smile as she greeted him. "What are you doing here?"

"I came out to apologize. I was wrong."

Tori stared at him in amazement. "Really?"

Jake sat down in the living room. He and Tori sat in nervous silence, stealing furtive glances at each other.

Rising to his feet, Jake held out his hand. "Hello, I'm Jake Madison. And you are?"

Grinning, she stood up and shook the hand he offered. "I'm Tori Samuels-Madison." She burst into laughter. "This is so silly."

"It worked, though. I made you laugh." Jake settled back and relaxed.

He hoped they were finally on level ground. He was getting tired of going back and forth. It was time to jump-start their marriage.

"What made you decide to come back here?" Jake asked out of the blue.

Shrugging, Tori answered, "I don't know. I think it was my way of being close to you still. I just wanted to come home." She looked over at him. "Why did you come back, Jake?"

"Because of you," he stated quickly. "I came home because I missed you and I just wanted to see you again—even if it was from a distance."

"Why from a distance?"

"I didn't know how you felt about me. I had to consider the fact that you wouldn't want to see me, Tori."

She gave him a tender look. "Jake, I never blamed you for Tiffany's death. It was a terrible and most unfortunate accident."

"It means a lot to me to hear you say that."

"What about Sheila?"

Tori's question surprised Jake. "What are you talking about?"

"Are you still sleeping with her?"

Jake was quiet.

"Well, are you going to answer me?"

"Tori, it's over between me and Sheila."

Her body seemed to stiffen and she folded her arms across her chest. "So, you were involved with her, then?"

"I don't know if I'd call it being involved—we didn't have anything romantic going on."

"You're telling me it was just sex between you two?"

Jake felt uncomfortable talking about this with Tori. "There is nothing going on between us. Hasn't been for a long time."

"You didn't answer the question."

"I don't want to discuss this with you."

"Before anything sexual can happen between us, you will have to be tested for diseases."

"Excuse me?" Jake felt his chest tighten.

"I didn't stutter."

"I used condoms, Tori," he managed to get out.

"I still want you tested," she assisted. "You violated our marriage, and I'm not going to pay the price with my life."

Jake was offended by her words, although he had no right to be.

"Do you have a problem with it?"

He glanced over at his wife and shook his head. Jake had a change of heart about forcing his way back into the house today. Tori had suddenly knocked the fight out of him.

Gwendolyn broke into a big grin. "Tori, sweetheart. Come have a seat."

"You sure are looking good, Mother Madison. Jake told me you went shopping yesterday."

"I had a ball. Before you leave, I want to show you some of the lovely things I purchased."

"I can't wait to see them."

"Now, you can tell me to mind my own business, but I hope things are going well between you and Jake."

"I think so. Jake wants to move back into the house."

"I know. He told me you won't let him."

"Mother Madison, did he also tell you that I asked him to go to counseling with me, but he refused?" Lowering her voice, Tori added, "And I told him that he would have to have some tests done."

"What kind of tests?"

"For sexually transmitted diseases."

"Oh." Gwendolyn cleared her throat. "My son has never liked strangers in his business."

"Do you agree with him?" Tori inquired.

"It's not my place, dear. My personal feelings concerning marriage counselors is that they can sometimes make matters worse. Especially if they're not spiritual."

"I wanted Pastor Allen to counsel us."

Nodding her approval, Gwendolyn murmured, "He's a good man. A godly man."

Tori stayed and had lunch with her mother-in-law. Jake arrived just as she was about to leave. He greeted her with a kiss.

"I didn't know you were coming to Charleston. Would you like to have lunch?"

"You're too late. I just had lunch with your mother and Della." She admired the black pinstriped suit he was wearing. "Are you home for the rest of the day, or do you have a meeting?"

"I have a meeting scheduled later. I just left the doctor's office. I had the battery of tests done."

Tori was touched by Jake's sense of urgency. "I appreciate your efforts."

"If it'll ease your mind, then it's well worth the effort."

"It should also ease your mind, too."

"Okay. Let's not go back down that road."

She tried to hide her smile, but was unsuccessful. Tori checked her watch. "I'd better get back to the store. I'm closing tonight."

"You have to leave right now?"

"I'm afraid I do."

He sounded so disappointed.

"Tori, I want you to really give my moving home some serious thought. It's the only chance we'll have at saving our marriage."

"Jake, I've been thinking of nothing else."

"You know I've never been a very patient man."

She nodded in understanding. "Yes, I know." Tori hugged him. "I've got to get back to the island. I'll give you a call later."

Jake kissed her. "Drive safe. And, Tori, don't make me wait too long. I miss my wife."

Gazing at him, she responded, "I miss my husband, too."

Tori's drive back to Edisto Island was an uneventful one. She drove straight to the bookstore and parked in front, next to Charlene's Jeep.

Nicholas came up behind her.

Turning, she asked, "Hey, what are you doing here?"

"Charlene called and left a message that my books were in. I came to get them." Nicholas held the door open for her.

Tori joined her cousin behind the counter. "I'm so glad you came by. I feel so bad about lunch the other day, and I want to apologize for Jake's rudeness."

He waved away her apology. "There's no need. I completely understand."

"I want to make it up to you by taking you out to dinner tonight."

"Really?"

"Yes."

Smiling, Nicholas nodded. "What time?"

"How about eight?"

Nicholas made his purchases and left the store.

Charlene left shortly after to run errands, leaving Tori to close up the store alone at six P.M.

It was 6:45 when she arrived home. Tori ran into her house and rushed to the shower. She met Nicholas at Willow's promptly at eight. They were seated immediately and made small talk while they waited for their food to arrive.

"Jake wants to move back into the house." Tori said suddenly.

"What did you say?"

"I told him that I didn't want to rush things."

"How did he feel about that?"

"Well, he didn't like it, but I can't rush back into a life with Jake. We have to work out some things. Like Sheila."

"Excuse me?" Nicholas wiped his mouth with his napkin.

"His business partner, Sheila Moore. You met her, remember?"

Nicholas nodded. "Are they involved?"

"They were. I don't know about now. I asked Jake and he denied it."

"You don't believe him?"

Shrugging, Tori replied, "I guess. I don't know."

"So, where does that leave you and Jake?"

"I wish I knew," Tori answered honestly. "Jake keeps telling me that he loves me and he wants to come home."

"What do you want, Tori?"

There was no hesitation on her part. "I want my marriage, Nicholas. I still love Jake very much."

"I know you do."

Tori ate the last of her stuffed flounder. "Any words of wisdom? You were always so good at giving advice." She was feeling conflicted about her decision to pace herself with Jake. She still had to deal with her feelings about everything. But her feelings of loneliness threatened to overwhelm her. Tori was tired of living alone in that big house.

He laughed. "Tori, if you want your husband, then fight for him."

"And if it's a losing battle?" There was always that chance.

"Then I would say you have some decisions to make."

Tori made a face. "You're a lot of help."

Nicholas's laughter was rich and deep. "Follow your heart, Tori." He excused himself and headed to the men's room.

Girl, that is one handsome man, she thought to herself. And the fact that he was totally unaware of it made him so incredibly sexy.

Tori allowed her mind to jump back into the past. When they were fourteen years old, Nicholas had suddenly declared his love for her and kissed her. She smiled at the memory.

"Why are you grinning like that?" Nicholas asked when he returned.

"Just thinking about the past," she confessed.

"Sweetheart, the past is just that—the past. Live in the present. Stop looking back."

"I'm not looking back."

"Yes, you are. Tori, learn from the past, then leave it behind."

Uncomfortable beneath Nicholas's gaze, she glanced around, not looking for anything or anyone in particular. She just didn't want to look at him right now. Her eyes landed on a couple seated across the room.

Tori blinked twice. She could hardly believe her eyes. Jake was here with Sheila.

"What's wrong, Tori?" Nicholas asked.

"Jake's here. With Sheila."

"I see. It's probably a business dinner or something."

She nodded. "You're probably right." Tori's eyes assessed Sheila. The way she was dressed, that witch certainly didn't have business on the brain. Hurt slashed through Tori. How could Jake bring her here to the island? And to Willow's? This was their place, she thought jealously. It was now tainted with that blot of evil sitting with her husband.

The waiter arrived with their check. Tori insisted on paying. "This is my treat, Nicholas."

"Would you like to go over and say hello?" he offered. "We could stop by their table on the way out."

Tori shook her head sadly. "No. I just want to get out of here. Would you follow me home? I don't feel like being alone."

She took several deep calming breaths when she made it out of the restaurant. Tori wanted to get as far away from Jake and Sheila as she could. It hurt much too badly. The drive home became a blur.

Tori walked into her house, blinking back tears, Nicholas on her heels.

He pulled her into his arms, holding her while she cried. When she was done, Tori wiped her eyes. "I'm so sorry. I've got makeup all over your shirt."

Nicholas chuckled softly. "I'm not worried about it."

"I'll pay for the cleaning—"

"I'm not worried about it, Tori."

She looked up at him, staring into his penetrating gray eyes. Nicholas's head lowered and his mouth covered hers.

Tori matched him kiss for kiss. Images of Jake and Sheila dissipated as a wave of desire swept through her. "Make love to me, Nicholas," she murmured against his lips.

He pulled away from her. Stroking her face, he said, "As much as I would love to make love to you, I'm going to decline, Tori. I don't want you filled with regret when you wake up tomorrow morning."

Ashamed, Tori put her hands to her face. "I'm so embarrassed."

"Honey, there's no need for you to be embarrassed," Nicholas tried to reassure her.

"I . . . would you please leave? I just need to be alone right now."

He nodded. "Tori, don't be too hard on yourself, okay?"

She nodded, still unable to look him in the eye.

Nicholas left and Tori made her way upstairs. It was getting harder and harder to believe that her marriage to Jake was going to work. Tears stung her eyes. Tonight, she'd almost broken her marriage vows. As she thought of what could've happened tonight, another wave of humiliation swept through her. Thank God, Nicholas was such a good friend.

Chapter Twenty-seven

It had taken some doing, but Sheila had successfully talked Jake into having dinner with her tonight. It was her intent to take his mind off of Tori. She didn't relish the idea of having dinner on Edisto Island, but Jake wanted to have dinner at Willow's.

Three hours later, Sheila met Jake at the restaurant wearing a strapless black dress. He did a double take when he saw her. "Wow. You must have a date later."

Smiling, she shook her head. "No."

Picking up the menu, Jake uttered, "Well, that'll soon change. Every man in this restaurant is looking at you."

Sheila didn't care about the other men. She only wanted the attention of Jake Madison. She picked up her menu and skimmed it.

Jake ordered a bottle of wine for them.

Sheila surveyed the restaurant. Willow's was her favorite because this was the place where Jake had brought her the first time they'd had dinner together.

From her vantage point, Sheila glimpsed Tori and Nicholas sitting over in a dimly lit part of the restaurant. She smiled to herself. This couldn't have been any better than if she'd planned it herself. This was going to be so much fun.

* * *

"What is it, Jake?" Sheila questioned. Although she'd pretended not to notice, she knew the exact moment he'd seen his wife leaving with Nicholas.

"Nothing. I just can't believe that Tori's seeing that writer."

She decided to twist the knife a little. "She's been seeing a lot of him. I see them everywhere."

"Why didn't you ever say anything?"

"I didn't want to hurt you, Jake. Besides, I don't really know how close they are. They seem awfully close to me, though. Closer than a married woman should be."

Jake was burning with anger. Sheila could almost smell it seeping from his body. She laid her hand over his. "I'm sorry. I didn't mean to upset you."

"You didn't. I needed to know the truth."

"Ready to leave?" she asked softly.

"Yeah," Jake grumbled. "Let's get out of here. I want to get the hell off this island."

"We can drive by your house, if you'd like," Sheila suggested.

"No. I want to head back to Charleston."

"We can go back to my place. You need a friend right now."

Jake nodded in resignation. They rode in silence. He was grateful that Sheila knew him so well. She had always been able to read his moods. She understood when he just needed time to think.

He still wasn't good company by the time they arrived at her town house. Jake was always astonished at how sterile the place looked. The house was lavishly decorated in ivory with splashes of vivid purple thrown throughout. Sheila had spared no expense for her dwelling. The place was spotless.

"Why don't you stay with me tonight, Jake?" Sheila pressed her body seductively against his. "Let me ease your pain," she murmured.

Lust rose up in Jake. It had been a few months since his last sexual encounter with Sheila. He accepted the kiss placed on his lips and hugged her to him.

Jake followed her upstairs. Sheila closed her bedroom door and was about to undress. He stopped her.

"I should leave."

"Why?"

"This isn't right, Sheila." Jake limped toward the door. "I'm sorry about all this."

"You don't have anything to be sorry about." She blocked his exit. "You're hurting, Jake. You shouldn't be alone tonight."

He disagreed. "I want to be alone. I'll see you in the morning, Sheila." Jake navigated around her. "Good night."

Chapter Twenty-eight

"Looks like you had a good time last night," Tori uttered. She'd brought flowers from her garden for her mother-in-law, and ran into Jake as he was coming down the stairs. "In fact, I'm surprised to find you home this morning."

"Is that why you came here so early? To see if I slept here last night?"

"You can wipe the smug expression right off your face. I admit it. I was checking up on you."

"Tori, I want to know something. Are you seeing Nicholas?"

"No. He and I are just friends. You and Sheila, on the other hand, looked awfully cozy. Anything you need to tell me?"

"You know my relationship with her is strictly platonic."

"Does she know it?" Tori countered.

"Yes."

"I'm not so sure, Jake. Sheila has an agenda where you're concerned."

Jake clearly didn't agree. "I think you're wrong. She's been there for me in ways no other person has."

"I bet. That's part of the problem, isn't it?" Tori fingered her hair, drawing Jake's attention.

"Did you have to cut it so short? I loved it long."

"Jake, you weren't here. I didn't even know if you were ever coming back. I was moving on with my life."

"So I see."

"I'm happy with my hair. I think I look better with it short."

"I like it long," Jake insisted.

"It's going to be this way for a while." Tori refused to back down. "Until I decide to change it. We've had this discussion before."

"Why have you changed in the way you're dressing? And now you even wear makeup. You doing all this for Nicholas?"

Glaring at him, she said, "This is for me, Jake."

"You never even liked to wear makeup."

"*You* never wanted me to wear it." Tori moved around Jake. "I'm taking these flowers to your mother's room." She started to climb the stairs. Pausing halfway up the staircase, she glanced down at him, asking, "Are you coming?"

Grinning, Jake followed her to the second floor.

After Tori left her mother-in-law's house, she drove to the bookstore. Just before walking into the store, she took a minute to soak in the beauty of her surroundings. It was a breathtaking June day. Tori wanted to photograph it in her mind.

She strode into the store, heading straight to her office.

Charlene stuck her head in Tori's doorway a few seconds later. "You have a minute?"

"Sure. Come on in."

"I'm going to stand here to see if anyone comes in. I need to talk to you about something."

"What is it?"

"Tori, I'm going to lose Shepard, and it's all my fault."

She frowned. "What are you talking about?"

"Shepard wants children. I can't give him any."

"Why not?"

Charlene grew quiet.

"What's wrong?" Tori put down her pen. "Honey, talk to me."

"When I was nineteen, I did something stupid. It seemed my only alternative at the time, but now . . ." Charlene's eyes filled with tears.

Tori stood up and walked around her desk. She handed her cousin a tissue. "What is it, honey?"

"It was the first time Shepard and I ever made love." Charlene took a deep breath and exhaled. "I got pregnant."

Tori was shocked. "*What?*" She'd had no idea. Charlene was the one who was always bad at keeping secrets. How'd she managed to keep this one?

"I tried to tell Shepard, but I couldn't. Whenever I mentioned the word *baby*, he made it clear he wasn't looking to be a father. I was in college and I didn't know what else to do, so I had an abortion." A lone tear rolled down her cheek. "It was a horrible experience for me, Tori. I wanted my baby, but I was so scared."

"Why didn't you come to me, Charlene? You shouldn't have gone through this alone." She felt a little hurt that as close as they were, Charlene hadn't trusted her enough to tell her about the pregnancy. "You never said a word."

"I was ashamed. I knew if I'd told you, then Shepard would've found out, and I didn't want to lose him."

Tori hugged her. "I'm so sorry."

"I feel like God's punishing me now. He trusted me with one of his own and . . . that's why I can't have a child. He's not going to give me another child." Charlene took a step and wiped her face.

Tori handed her another tissue. "Honey, God's not like that. I truly believe that if you ask God for His forgiveness, He'll give it to you. It's in the Bible."

"I know. . . ."

"Charlene, you've got to forgive yourself. God loves you. Honey,

He loves us in spite of our mistakes, our choices—God loves us unconditionally." Pausing for a heartbeat, Tori advised, "You should tell Shepard the truth, Charlene."

"He'll hate me. I can't do it, Tori. I love him too much."

"Honey, you're going to have to tell Shepard. Especially if you two are thinking about getting married."

"Tell me what?" he asked from behind Charlene.

They exchanged startled glances. Although Charlene had been keeping watch on the selling area, neither one of them had heard him come in.

"We're going to have to get a bell or something for the door," Charlene mouthed. Turning to face Shepard, she said, "Let's talk in my office."

"I'll cover the front," Tori stated. She felt bad for the pain her cousin was going through. She hoped Shepard would understand and not harbor any harsh feelings toward Charlene.

Thinking about her own situation, Tori decided she would drive to Brunswick for the weekend. She wanted to talk to her mother about Jake. She needed some perspective on her relationship with him.

Between customers, Tori made her phone calls to her mother and to Jake.

"Jake Madison speaking."

"Hey. I'm calling to let you know I'm going home for the weekend. I'm leaving tomorrow around noon."

"If you wait until Saturday, I'll drive down with you."

"You don't have to. I'm going to hang out with my mother. You know, spend some quality mother-daughter time together."

"Okay. When will you be back?"

"On Monday morning."

"Sure you don't want me to go with you?"

Tori smiled. "I'll be fine, Jake. I'm going to miss you."

"Me, too. Call me when you get back."

"I will. Gotta go. The store's getting busy." Tori hung up. She was looking forward to seeing her mother. Her feelings were all over the place, and she needed someone to help her make sense of it all.

Jake turned his attention to Sheila. "Sorry about that. What were you saying?"

"I was talking about adding interactive video to the Web site. . . ."

He nodded, but Jake was hardly listening. His mind was on Tori. Jake was a little surprised by his wife's refusal to let him travel with her. Maybe she really wanted some quality time with her mother, he decided.

Yet Jake could recall all the times in the past when Tori would throw a fit when he didn't want to go with her. For some inexplicable reason, it bothered him that she didn't want him with her this time.

Chapter Twenty-nine

Jake hadn't heard a word she'd said, Sheila fumed. He was probably thinking about that plain-faced cow he'd married. What in the world could he possibly see in that woman? It was way beyond Sheila's comprehension.

She was so upset that she stormed past Selma, who was practically yelling out her name. Sheila didn't feel like being bothered right now. She wanted to shake some sense into Jake, but doubted it would do any good.

Sheila's mood brightened when she spotted Nicholas across the street, walking out of the bank. She waved to get his attention.

"It's interesting running into you like this. I just spoke to Tori," she lied.

"You did? Is she here in Charleston?"

"No, she called the office." Although Sheila hadn't spoken to Tori, she decided to embellish the truth. "She was just telling me that she's looking forward to going to Brunswick tomorrow." In a conspiratorial whisper, she added, "She seemed real excited about the weekend, actually."

"Really? Why is that?"

JACQUELIN THOMAS

Sheila continued her lie. "Well, I was under the impression that Tori was leaving town to be with you. That's why I was so surprised to see you."

"Tori and Jake are still married."

"Just barely."

"What do you mean by that?"

"Jake's confided in me that their marriage is over. I imagine he's told Tori the same thing."

Nicholas eyed her suspiciously. "What's your interest in all this?"

"I don't have any reason to lie to you, Nicholas. Tori and Jake are my closest friends."

"But I suspect you're closer to Jake."

"Jake and I are partners. Of course we're close."

"Let me get this straight. Jake told you that his marriage to Tori is over?"

She nodded. "Yes, he did. He told me that he was going to tell her as soon as possible. That was a couple of days ago."

"Sheila, I know about you and Jake. Is he leaving his wife for you?"

"Jake didn't want to hurt Tori, but we're in love. Neither of us planned for this to happen."

Nicholas muttered a curse. "You two are a piece of work. You deserve each other."

"I've seen the way you look at Tori. You're in love with her. Have been for a long time, I would assume. Nicholas, she's going to need you."

"I doubt you're as concerned as you're trying to make me believe."

"I do care about Tori. I also think you two belong together. You could make her very happy, Nicholas."

He laughed harshly. "You've got it all figured out, don't you?"

Sheila stared into his gray eyes. "This is a chance for you. Don't tell me you don't want it."

"I'm not telling you anything," Nicholas stated flatly. "If you will excuse me . . ."

"You don't have to," Sheila murmured softly. "I can see it on your face."

"So, are you going to tell me what you and Tori were talking about earlier?" Shepard questioned. "And don't give me that same crap as before, because I'm not falling for it. You've stalled all day long. Now we're here at your place. Talk to me."

"It was nothing."

"Don't do this, Charlene. I know you better than that."

She was quiet.

"Charlene?" he prompted. "Something's been bothering you for a while now. Especially whenever I mention children. What is it you're not telling me?"

Leaning back in her chair, her arms folded across her chest, Charlene stared him straight in the eye. "You think you know me so well. You don't know me at all."

"What are you talking about?"

She rose to her feet. "I can't do this. Just forget it, Shepard."

"Honey, will you please talk to me?" Shepard reached out and took her hand into his. "Don't run off, please."

Charlene sat back down. "There's something I should have told you a long time ago."

"What is it?"

"I got pregnant."

"What?"

"I found out I was pregnant shortly after we made love for the first time. The baby was yours, in case you're wondering."

"What happened?"

She swallowed hard. "I had an abortion."

Shepard was stunned into silence.

Charlene started to explain. "Do you remember the way you were back then?" She didn't wait for a response. "Shepard, you told me flat out that my getting pregnant wouldn't ever make you marry me, that if I told you I was pregnant, you wouldn't even acknowledge the child without a paternity test."

"I—"

"Those words hurt me deeply, Shepard," Charlene interrupted. "I couldn't believe you were being so cold. And that was before I even knew I was pregnant."

"So many girls were tricking guys into marriage back then—" he began.

Charlene interrupted him a second time. "And you thought that I was just like them?"

"No, that's not what I was saying. Why didn't you tell me about the baby?"

"Because of the things you said back then. I was scared and I felt like I didn't have any choice."

"I had a right to know about the baby."

"So that you could refuse to claim it?"

"I wouldn't have done that."

"You would have wanted a paternity test. I know it."

"If the child was mine, why would you have had such a problem with it?"

"I didn't want to be humiliated."

"Carrying my child would have been humiliating for you?"

"Don't try to twist this around on me," Charlene argued. "You were so mean back then, and I was young. I wasn't ready to be a single parent. I was scared to death, Shepard. Can't you understand?"

He stood up. "What I understand is that you didn't want my child, Charlene, and you don't want me!"

"That's not true."

"Then why did you murder our child?"

Without waiting for an answer, Shepard stalked out of the room, never once looking back. His exit left Charlene wounded, but not as much as his hurtful words. She dropped to the floor, sobbing hysterically.

Chapter Thirty

Early Saturday morning, Tori and her mother drove down to Jacksonville, Florida, to go shopping. Around three o'clock, they headed back to Brunswick. They hadn't been home an hour when Linda entered Tori's bedroom, saying, "Nicholas Washington is here to see you."

Surprised, Tori sat up and swung her legs off the bed. "Nicholas is here?"

Her mother nodded. "I guess he decided to come home this weekend, too."

She quickly changed into another shirt and strolled out of the room. When Tori saw Nicholas, she said, "I didn't know you were coming home. Why didn't you tell me?"

"It was spur of the moment. Besides, you didn't tell me you were coming to Brunswick, either."

"I guess it was an impulsive decision as well." Tori pointed to the sofa. "Have a seat."

Nicholas was watching her intently.

"What is it? Is there something on my face?"

"No. I was just wondering how you were doing."

"I'm fine."

"Have you spoken to Jake?"

Tori eyed him warily. "Not since I left South Carolina. Nicholas, what is this about?"

"Have you given any more thought to where you and Jake are headed?"

"I've given it nothing but thought. I'm just not any closer to real answers."

Leaning forward, Nicholas rested his arms on his knees. "What will you do if Jake doesn't want this marriage?"

She was beginning to feel uneasy about his line of questioning. "Has he said something to you? Nicholas, please tell me the truth." Tori forced herself to remain calm. She silently prayed for strength.

"I haven't spoken to Jake. I'm not exactly one of his favorite people."

"Why would you say that?"

"Jake knows how I feel about you, Tori. And he's not happy about it. I guess I wouldn't be if the shoe were on the other foot."

"What are you talking about, Nicholas? Jake knows that you and I are friends."

"Tori, I love you. I've always loved you."

She was taken aback by his admission.

"Nicholas, I still love my husband. In spite of all that's happened, I still love Jake."

He gave her a sad smile. "I can respect that."

"If this were a different time or situation . . ."

He nodded in understanding. "You don't have to explain," he said softly.

"We will always be good friends, Nicholas."

"I know that. I really hope Jake knows what a wonderful wife he has."

Tori laughed. "Me, too."

Nicholas stood up. "I guess I'll be going."

"Do you have to leave right now?" she asked. "I was thinking about going to MoJo's. I love their hot wings. Would you like to go with me?"

"I'd love to."

After dining on a bucket of wings, Nicholas talked Tori into going to the movies with him. Her mother was in the den when she returned home three hours later.

"Mama, you nearly scared me to death. I didn't think you were still up."

When she sat down, her mother stated, "Nicholas is in love with you, Tori."

"I know. He told me tonight."

"What did you say?"

"I told him we could only be friends. My heart has always belonged to Jake."

"I haven't wanted to pry, but I'd like to know where things stand between you and Jake."

"Mama, I love Jake. Do I trust him? I'd have to say I don't know. Do we communicate? Throughout our marriage, Jake made all of the decisions. There was no compromise."

"And now?" Linda inquired.

"I have a mind of my own. Jake can't just decide to walk out of my life and then turn around and walk right back in."

"Sugar, what do you want to do, then?"

"I need to know that I can trust my husband, for one thing. We need to learn how to communicate, for another."

"He needs to get rid of that partner of his," Linda threw in.

Tori glanced at her mother. "He's not going to do that."

"Not even to save his marriage?"

"We're at a standstill. Jake won't go to counseling. He won't get away from Sheila. . . . I don't know what to do."

"Pray about it, hon. Give this situation over to the good Lord." Linda rose to her feet. "I'm going to bed. You going to church with me in the morning?"

Tori nodded. "I'll see you in the morning." She leaned back against the plump overstuffed pillows on the sectional sofa and closed her eyes. Taking her mother's advice, she gave her marriage over to God.

Sheila and Jake were the only ones working in the Madison Moore building on Sunday afternoon. Jake had no plans, so he'd allowed Sheila to persuade him to meet her at the office. They were finishing up on the Gemini project. She sat on the sofa with the laptop while Jake sat at her desk, using the desktop computer.

"Have you spoken to Tori lately?" Sheila asked casually.

"A few days ago," Jake answered without taking his eyes off the monitor.

Pretending to be interested in the document on her computer screen, Sheila inquired, "How are things between you two?"

Jake gave a slight shrug. "I'm not sure where her head's at. She's changed so much in the last year."

"She's been through a lot, Jake."

"I know that."

"I didn't mean anything behind it. Besides, I don't think the change in Tori has anything to do with you."

Jake gave her his full attention then. "What are you talking about, Sheila?"

"Surely you know," she replied cunningly. "She's been seeing a lot of that author, Nicholas Washington."

"They're just friends, Sheila," he snapped.

"I'm not implying anything. I'm just going by what I've seen and heard. Since she's been back on Edisto Island, Tori's been spending a lot of time with Nicholas. As a matter of fact, I think her return was around the same time as his appearance."

"You think my wife came back to the island to spend time with Nicholas?"

"It's quite a coincidence, don't you think? I heard that Nicholas went home to Brunswick this weekend. *Where is Tori?*"

"She said she wanted to visit her mother."

"So, she's in Brunswick, too. Another coincidence?"

Jake couldn't believe Tori had lied to him. Rising to his feet, Jake turned to stare out the window. He didn't want Sheila to see his pain. So that's why Tori hadn't wanted him to go with her, he mused. She was with Nicholas.

"Are you okay?" Sheila asked. She came up behind him, placing a comforting hand on his arm.

Without bothering to face her, Jake nodded.

"I wouldn't have said anything about this, but I care too much for you to just stand back and watch Tori make a fool of you. I don't want to see you get hurt."

Jake turned to face her then. "Sheila, my wife has every right—"

"No, she doesn't," she quickly interjected. "If Tori doesn't want your marriage, then she needs to be honest with you."

"Have you forgotten that I was unfaithful, Sheila? All of this started because I slept with you."

"What happened between us was wrong, but, Jake, we can't undo the past. Tori doesn't have the right to pay you back with an affair of her own."

"You think she's having an affair with Nicholas?"

It was almost as if he hadn't even considered the idea.

"I can see the attraction between the two of them. What do you think is going on between them, Jake?"

"I don't know," he replied honestly. "I've tried not to think about Tori and Nicholas as anything other than friends."

"Then you're being naive, Jake."

"I don't want to discuss this any further with you. We have a lot to do, Sheila. Let's get back to work." He pushed aside all thoughts of Tori and Nicholas. He would deal with his wife when she returned.

Chapter Thirty-one

Charlene came over shortly after Tori arrived home from her trip to Brunswick. Tori sensed the sadness in her cousin's spirit. She didn't want to pry, but desperately wanted to know what had happened.

While she made a pitcher of iced tea, Charlene made herself comfortable in the den. Tori poured two glasses and carried them over to where her cousin sat. Putting them down on the coffee table, she dropped down beside Charlene. Curiosity got the better of her and she asked, "How did things go with Shepard?"

When Charlene lifted her eyes, pain flickered in their depths. "Not too well. He's furious with me."

"You told him everything?" Tori questioned.

Charlene took a sip of her tea, then nodded. "I can't believe he's so angry. I'm the one being punished."

Wrapping an arm around her cousin, Tori murmured, "I wish there was something I could do. I really didn't think Shepard would be this angry."

"It's over between me and Shepard. He wants nothing else to do with me." Her eyes grew bright with tears.

Tori was shocked. "Did he tell you that?" This was all her fault. If she hadn't pushed her cousin to tell him in the first place . . .

"He said that since I didn't want our child, then I didn't want him."

Her heart went out to Charlene. Rubbing her back, Tori tried to comfort her cousin. "Give him some time. Shepard just needs time to get used to the news."

"He hates me, Tori. He asked me why I murdered his child." She started to cry.

"Shepard didn't mean that. He loves you, Charlene. You know he does. I'm so sorry I told you to tell him. I should've minded my own business."

"It's not your fault."

"He still loves you," Tori insisted. "He's just angry right now. When he calms down, he'll come to you."

Charlene was in better spirits by the time Tori had prepared a huge chef's salad. They sat down to eat dinner. Afterward, they navigated back to the den to watch a video.

Before they started the movie, they heard a car in the driveway. Charlene jumped up to see who their visitor could be.

"Jake's here," Charlene announced.

Tori couldn't hide her surprise. "I didn't know he was planning to come by tonight."

"Guess he couldn't wait to see you."

She heard the sadness in Charlene's voice. Tori ran to answer the front door. She embraced Jake. "Hey. I was going to call you later."

He assessed her from head to toe. "Really?"

Tori was a little taken aback by the tone in his voice. "Yes, I was. I missed you."

She waited for him to touch her, pull her into his arms, but he didn't. Instead, Jake stood stiffly in place.

"I'm surprised you thought of me at all. I'm sure Nicholas commanded most of your attention, if not all."

Tori gasped. "How did you know that he was in Brunswick?"

"I have my ways," was his response. He stood with his arms folded across his chest, as if waiting for an explanation.

His attitude was beginning to irk Tori. "It's not what you're thinking, Jake."

"How do you know what I'm thinking? Feeling a little guilty?" He had a hard cold-eyed smile.

She tried to keep her frustration out of her voice. As calmly as she could manage, she stated, "I don't have any reason to feel guilty. I've done nothing wrong."

"Why didn't you tell me he was going to Brunswick? Did he drive with you?"

Tori didn't like the accusation she heard in Jake's tone. "No. I didn't know Nicholas was going home. It was a surprise to me as well."

"I bet."

She swallowed hard, trying not to reveal her anger. "It's true. Look, Jake, I have company. If you came all the way out here to start a fight, we're going to have to reschedule."

"Who's here?" he demanded.

"I am," Charlene announced. "But I'm on my way out. It sounds like you two need to have a long talk." She gathered up her keys and her purse.

Tori grabbed her cousin by the arm. "*You* don't have to leave. We were going to watch a movie."

"I wasn't really in the mood for the movie," Charlene confessed. "I'd rather be home alone in my room with a good book."

Tori surveyed her face. "Are you sure? I can come over there, if you want." She walked her out to her car. "You really don't have to leave, Charlene. Jake's being a jerk. He can leave."

"Girl, he's your husband. Y'all need to talk."

She waved as Charlene drove off. When Tori returned to the house, she found Jake in the den. "Let's get this over with," she whispered.

*   *   *

Jake started up as soon as she walked into the room. "If you want to be with Nicholas, then just say it, Tori. I don't have any right to try and hold you back."

"Where is all this coming from?"

"When I walked out on you, it was wrong. I understand that you needed someone and I wasn't there for you. Tori, I'm not blaming you for anything. I want to know the truth. Hell, I think I'm entitled to know the truth."

"What are you talking about, Jake?" She ripped out the words impatiently.

"Just tell me if you want to be with Nicholas Washington. Isn't he the reason you moved back home? No one would blame you. I just want to know where I stand."

Tori was confused. "You think I came back here because Nicholas was here?"

He sat down, asking, "Didn't you?"

"*No.* When I moved back to the island, I had no idea that Nicholas was here. The last time I saw him was when we attended his book signing. He was here two weeks before I came back."

"You didn't know he was on Edisto Island? You had no idea?"

Tori was offended. "I already told you that I didn't. I didn't know he was here until the night Charlene and I saw him at Willow's."

"Are you telling me that you didn't see Nicholas in Brunswick?"

Tori was beginning to feel as if she were being interrogated, and she didn't like it. It reminded her of all those times as a teenager when her mother and stepfather would sit side by side while she stood in the middle of the room fielding their questions. "I saw him, but it wasn't planned, Jake. How many times do I have to tell you that I didn't know he was in Brunswick? I have no reason to lie to you."

Realization washed over her, causing her to break out into loud laughter. "You're jealous. That's what this is all about."

"What?"

"You're jealous of Nicholas."

"The man's in love with you, Tori. Haven't you noticed?"

She dropped down onto his lap, throwing her arms around him. "Nicholas knows there's only one man in my life, and that's you." Eyeing him lovingly, she continued. "Jake, you don't have any reason to be jealous. I love you."

Tori pressed her lips to his, kissing him with a hunger that belied her outward calm. She wanted to erase any doubts he was having about her feelings for him.

"I love you, too. I felt like a dying man when I'd heard that you were in Brunswick with Nicholas." Jake held her snugly against him. "I thought I'd lost you."

Sitting up, Tori asked, "Who told you? I'm just curious. How did they know we were both going to be there?" Gazing at him, Tori snapped her finger. "It was Sheila, wasn't it?"

"Yeah. She must have run into Nicholas or something, because I know you didn't tell her about your plans."

"Jake, do me a favor. Don't listen to Sheila when it comes to me. If you have any questions, just come to me. I have nothing to hide." Kissing him again, she said, "I don't want to spend this evening fighting or even talking about your partner. I would rather do this. . . ." Tori kissed him on his earlobe. "And this . . ." This time she kissed each eyelid. "And this . . ." She covered his mouth with hers.

"These just came for you," Charlene announced as she strode into the office carrying a beautiful bouquet of roses. "You two must have had some night. . . ."

Tori read the note that was enclosed. "We had a good time." She sniffed a delicate rosebud. "But it isn't what you're thinking. Jake went home and I slept alone."

Charlene raised an eyebrow. "Whose fault is that? Girl, what are you saving yourself for? You made the man take a bunch of tests and they all came out negative. Jake is your husband. Give the man some sex. If you don't, he might end up falling into Sheila's bed. I know you don't want that."

Tori thought about everything Charlene said as she stared at her flowers. She picked up the telephone. "Hi, Jake," she said when he answered his phone.

"Did you get the roses?"

She was grinning from ear to ear. "I did. Thank you so much. I love them."

"I'm glad. I know how much you love them. What did I do to deserve this?"

"I wanted to thank you for last night."

Frowning, Tori asked, "For what?" She searched her memory, but had no idea what he was thanking her for.

"You made me feel loved. Really loved."

"Jake . . ." Her feelings defied words. "I miss you so much."

"Then let me come home, Tori. It's obvious we want to be together. We're married and it's time we start acting like it."

"Can we have dinner together tonight?" she asked. "I'll let you know my decision then." Tori already knew what her answer would be, but she wanted to contemplate and pray on it a little while longer. "I'll make all of your favorites."

"Sure. I'll see you tonight."

Tori was still smiling when she hung up the phone. Picking up her pen, she made a grocery list. Tonight was going to be special, and she didn't want to risk forgetting even one item. As an afterthought, she made a mental note to pick up a bottle of champagne.

Chapter Thirty-two

Sheila closed her laptop and suggested, "Let's do something fun tonight, Jake. I'm tired of all work and no play. We could—"

He interrupted her. "Not tonight, Sheila."

"Aren't you tired of just going home to your mother's house every night?" She didn't want to appear pushy, but Sheila was getting tired of waiting on Jake.

"I am," Jake admitted. "In fact, I might be changing my situation real soon."

She drew a quick breath. "In what way?" Sheila reached for her water and took a sip. This was it. Jake was finally coming to his senses.

"Tori's going to let me know if I can move back into our home tonight. If we're ever going to get our marriage back on track, we need to be in the same house."

Sheila almost choked on her water. "Are you sure this is what you want to do? It's still so soon."

"I love Tori and I want a life with her. It's time I do something about it."

"Does Tori want the same thing, Jake? Maybe she's feeling guilty after spending the weekend with Nicholas."

"Yes, she does. For the record, nothing happened between her and Nicholas. They are just friends. By the way, how did you know that they were both going to be in Brunswick at the same time?"

"Nicholas told me. I ran into him at the bank across the street. The way he was talking—it sounded like they were involved to me." Sheila swallowed hard. "Just be careful, Jake. You know I wish you much happiness. I don't want to see you get hurt."

"Thank you. It means a lot to me to hear you say that. You're a wonderful friend, Sheila." He stood up. "I'm going to my own office to make a few calls before I leave for the day."

No sooner had Jake walked out of her office than Sheila burst into tears. "You're a wonderful friend, Sheila," she mimicked. "How could you be so blind, Jake? Tori can never be the kind of woman you need. *Why can't you see that?*"

She paced back and forth, trying to figure out a way to put another wedge between them. Smiling, Sheila picked up the phone. "Hello. I'd like to order some flowers." She silently congratulated herself on this new plan.

"Yes, they're from Nicholas Washington, and he'd like to include this message . . ."

After a romantic dinner, Jake and Tori moved to the den to finish their discussion.

"I know we still have a lot of problems to work out, Tori, but I don't see why we can't do it in the same house. We don't have to sleep in the same room. At least not right away." He took her hand in his. "Honey, I love you and I want to be with you. Only you."

"But you're still not willing to see a marriage counselor. Jake, you can't even visit Tiffany's grave with me. I want to have another child one day. Do you?"

Jake couldn't respond. The thought of having another child scared him. When Tiffany was born, he'd had no idea he could love another person as much as he loved his daughter. He didn't realize he was capable of that much love. But everybody he loved ended up leaving him. His father. His mother was dying, and he feared Tori would wake up one morning and decide she didn't want to be married anymore.

"Are you going to answer me?"

Jake returned his attention to her. "It's too soon to even talk about having a child, don't you think? I can't seem to really make any headway with our marriage. As far as the counseling goes, I don't think we need it. Tori, I don't believe in it. I just don't."

She sighed heavily. "Unfortunately, I do believe in it."

"Please, Tori. Let me come home."

"You know that I love you, Jake. But is love enough?"

The doorbell rang, interrupting their conversation. She stood up. "I'll be right back."

"Are you expecting anyone?" Jake asked.

She shook her head. "No. It's probably Charlene."

Tori came back into the den carrying an elaborate and romantic bouquet of flowers. "These are beautiful, Jake. You're spoiling me."

He was dumbfounded. "Who are they from?"

Her smile disappeared. "They're not from you?"

Jake shook his head. "No." He rose to his feet and snatched the card before Tori could get to it. Opening the envelope, he read the card enclosed. "These are from Nicholas," he stated coldly. "He wants to thank you for the memorable weekend in Brunswick. It also says that you will always own his heart."

"What?" Tori snatched the card from him. "I don't believe this." Why would Nicholas send flowers and a card like that? she wondered. Was he trying to cause problems in her marriage? This was not the man she knew—maybe she didn't know him at all.

Sheila's words came back to haunt Jake, prompting him to ask, "Did something happen between you and Nicholas in Brunswick? Is that why you're being so nice to me now?"

"No. One doesn't have anything to do with the other," Tori answered distractedly. She was still having a hard time digesting Nicholas's callous actions.

"You're still my wife, Tori."

"How kind of you to remember," she snapped in anger. "It's only taken a year or so for you to recall that fact—" Tori stopped short. The night was taking off in a totally different direction than originally planned.

"I see." Jake pulled out his car keys. "Maybe I should leave."

Putting the flowers on the counter, Tori rushed to his side. "I don't want you to leave. I'm sorry for what I said. I didn't mean it." She took his hand in hers. "Jake, I don't have anything going on with Nicholas. When I saw him in Brunswick, I told him that I loved you. I told him that in spite of everything that's happened between us, I still wanted my marriage. I want to be with you, Jake."

"You told him that?"

Tori nodded. "Yes. Honey, I love you so much, and I'm not ready to give up on our marriage." Placing a hand on his cheek, she asked, "Do you really want to move back in the house?"

"Yes, I do."

Stepping away from him, she said, "Jake, if you do, it has to be for good. I won't accept a revolving door in our relationship."

"If you let me come home, I promise that you will never regret it, Tori. You're stuck with me till death do us part."

"It's all I've ever wanted, Jake."

Tori gave her customer back her credit card. "Thank you for shopping with us. I hope you found everything you were looking for."

"Oh, I did. I love your store. I didn't realize there were so many black authors out there."

"There are, and more emerging every day."

"This puts me in mind of the Harlem renaissance."

Tori agreed. When the woman left, Tori resumed her conversation with Charlene. "Jake's moving back into the house when he gets back from New York. He's been staying with me for the last four nights anyway."

"This business trip of his sure came up rather quick, don't you think?"

"Not really. He expected it."

"I wonder how Sheila's taking this bit of news. I'm sure she's having fits over at Madison Moore."

Shrugging, Tori said, "I really don't care how she feels. Sheila's a big girl."

The rest of the week breezed by for Tori as she prepared for the store's grand opening. She was putting out a box of new releases when Jake walked into the store on that Friday. Squealing with joy, she threw herself into his arms.

"Down, girl," Charlene whispered. "We have customers in the store."

"When did you get back?"

"Not too long ago. I went by the house to check on Mother and then I came straight out here."

She kissed him. "I missed you, too."

While Tori was in her office, grabbing her purse, Charlene embraced Jake. "I'm happy you two are finally getting it together."

"Me, too. Maybe now I'll finally have the peace I've been searching for."

"I hope so."

Tori joined them. "Thanks, Charlene."

"No problem. Have fun."

Taking Jake by the hand, Tori left the store. "I'm so glad you're home." She embraced him. "I've planned a very special homecoming for you."

Inclining his head, Jake uttered, "Really? What is it?"

"You'll just have to wait and see."

Chapter Thirty-three

The next morning, Tori woke up seeing the world in a different light. The leaves on the trees looked greener, the sky bluer and the yard in full bloom and in vivid colors. She stood on the balcony giving thanks to the good Lord for blessing her with the beautiful vision before her.

This day she had a lot for which to be thankful. Last night, when she and Jake had made love, it had been perfect. Before he'd left this morning, Tori had felt like they were finally on track. They still loved each other, and they both still wanted the marriage. It was definitely worth fighting for. In the back of her mind, Tori was firm in her belief that counseling could help, but for now it was on hold.

After breakfast, Tori called Madison Moore. She was at first a little surprised when a female voice answered Jake's direct line.

"Hi, Tori. This is Sheila. Jake had to step out of the office for a while."

"Any idea when he'll be back?" She kept her tone pleasant, despite her true feelings.

"In about two hours. Do you want him to call you back?"

Sheila's voice was syrupy sweet, and it grated on Tori's nerves. Never had she felt such an intense dislike for a person. If her marriage was to be a success, she was really going to have to work through her feelings for this woman.

"Yes, I do. Ask him to call me at the store. I'm going to be there for the rest of the day. I'm working late tonight."

"How are things at the store?" Sheila asked. "I've heard nothing but good things about it."

"Business is good. Charlene and I feel very blessed."

"That's wonderful. I'm glad to hear it."

Tori kept her true thoughts to herself. "We're starting to get busy again, so I'd better get off this phone. You won't forget to tell Jake to call me, will you?"

"I won't forget. I'll tell him as soon as he gets back."

Hanging up, Tori had a strong suspicion that Jake would never know about this call. Jake was always telling her that she was wrong about Sheila. Well, this was a chance to prove it. She strongly hoped she *was* wrong. If Sheila proved to be the witch Tori believed she was, Jake was going to have to choose.

Sheila hung up the phone. "This is one message Jake won't get," she stated flatly. "I'm not about to make this easy for you, Tori."

"Who are you talking to?" Jake asked from behind her.

Turning swiftly, Sheila put on a smile. "Just brainstorming to myself."

Today, he was wearing the tie she'd given him for his birthday. She was touched by his thoughtfulness.

After setting his briefcase on the floor beside his desk, Jake picked up a small stack of messages. "I see. Come up with any new and innovative ideas?"

Sheila eyed him hungrily. "Nothing concrete."

"Any new messages? I went through these this morning."

She shook her head. "No. Nobody called. Guess you're not very popular today."

He looked over at her. "Tori didn't call?"

Sheila didn't hesitate with her lie. "Haven't heard from Tori. She didn't call you on your cell phone?"

Jake shook his head. "Guess I'll try and give her a call later on." He sat down at his desk and immediately started to work on his computer. It was a moment before he realized she was still in the room. "You need to talk to me, Sheila?"

"No. Actually, I need to go down to accounting." Pulling on her jacket, she stole a glance at Jake. He was staring at his monitor. Fuming, she walked briskly out of the room.

Jake strolled through his house, looking for Tori. He saw her car in the garage, but she was nowhere in sight. He checked the family room and kitchen, the patio, and then upstairs in the master bedroom.

He bumped into Tori, coming out of one of the guest rooms. "Hey. I was wondering where you were."

She kissed him. "Why didn't you call me back? I called you earlier because I wanted you to pick up something for me from your mother."

"When?" He'd been in his office all day long except for that one meeting. Sheila had told him that Tori hadn't called.

"Earlier, I left a message at your office. Sheila didn't tell you I called?"

"No." Had Sheila deliberately lied to him?

Tori gave a frustrated sigh. "How can you work with that woman? I keep telling you she's not to be trusted."

"Maybe she forgot, Tori. It happens." Jake didn't want to consider that Sheila had meant anything malicious. It was possible that she'd forgotten about the call, but deep down, even he seriously doubted that. He would confront her on Monday.

"Jake, you're always defending her."

Tori was gearing up, and he wanted to put a halt to it. The last thing on his mind tonight was arguing. "Let's not talk about Sheila.

Every time we do, we always end up arguing." He took the linens from her and dropped them to the floor in a heap. Embracing her, Jake pulled her closer to him.

"You're right," Tori agreed. "I don't want to waste any more time on Sheila."

For the first time in their married life, Jake helped her with laundry. Seeing the surprised look on Tori's face brought a smile to his lips. He knew she didn't quite know what to make of it because, in the past, he'd never shown any interest in helping her with any of the household tasks. When she'd complained in the past, Jake's response had always been "hire a maid."

Since moving home, he took out the trash without being nagged and helped her in the kitchen whenever he was home—he had even vacuumed a room or two. This time around, he decided to try and be a much better husband.

Long after they had gone to bed, Jake woke up in the middle of the night, unable to breathe. Drenched in a cold sweat, he eased out of bed and made his way downstairs. He stood with the patio door open, letting the warm June night air drift inside. Jake needed to feel the fresh air blowing on his face. He slowly breathed in and out.

The panic attack subsided and Jake slid the door closed. He sank down on the sofa, holding his hands to his face. Why were they starting up again? He was home with Tori. That's where he wanted to be. He hated going through these attacks. They made him feel as if he were about to die. They made him feel weak—less than a man. *Why am I being punished?* he screamed in his mind. *I didn't mean to hurt Tiffany.* Tears streamed down his face. "God, why won't You help me? Am I that horrible a person?"

Jake suddenly felt emotionally exhausted. It was as if his mind had simply shut down. He stretched out on the sofa and closed his eyes. He hurt. God's rejection hurt worse than anything he'd ever known. It was a feeling that went beyond the scope of words.

Chapter Thirty-four

Charlene ran to get the telephone. "TC's Books and Gifts."

"Hello, Charlene. It's Shepard."

"What do you want?" she asked coolly.

"It's Mother," he announced. "She's in the hospital. This time it doesn't look as if she's going to make it."

Charlene's tone changed immediately. "Oh, I'm so sorry. Tori and I will be there shortly." She hung up the phone.

"What's wrong?" Tori asked. "You look upset."

"It's Mrs. Madison. She's back in the hospital. Shepard says it doesn't look good. Get your purse, Tori. We need to get to the hospital."

They closed the store and rushed off, en route to Charleston Memorial Hospital. The entire time Charlene drove, Tori prayed. She knew Mother Madison hadn't been feeling well over the past day or so. She'd been meaning to go by and visit, but hadn't made it. Now her mother-in-law was in the hospital.

"I'm scared, Tori. Mrs. Madison is the glue that holds that family together. What will Shepard and Jake do if something happens to her? You know how much they both adore her."

Shrugging, Tori answered, "I don't know. Maybe they will go

back to being close. I hate seeing them act so distant with each other."

"You know why, don't you? It's because of Sheila. Shepard has been trying to get Jake to see the type of person Sheila really is."

"And Jake refuses to hear anything he says, I'm sure. He wears blinders where that woman is concerned."

"Girl, you'd better find a way to get them off. I think Sheila uses roots or something."

"Prayer is powerful. Even more powerful than witchcraft." Taking Charlene's right hand, Tori said, "Honey, we're going to believe that Mother Madison will get better. We want her free of pain and well." She wiped away a tear that slipped down her cheek.

Jake's eyes were wet when Tori arrived. They embraced.

"Honey, your mother's a fighter. She'll pull through like she always does." Reaching up, she wiped away his tears. "She's going to be okay."

Hanging his head in resignation, Jake muttered, "I don't think she can do it. Not this time. Earlier she didn't even know who we are. . . ." His voice broke. "Now sh-she's in a coma."

Tori held on to him as he cried. She glanced over his shoulder and saw her cousin comforting Shepard. When the doctor came out to speak with them, she held on to Jake's hand, lending him her strength.

She and Jake went into his mother's room first. Tori prayed as she sat beside Gwendolyn Madison's hospital bed. This woman was like a mother to her, and she loved her dearly. "You can't leave us, Mother," she whispered. "We need you so much. We all do."

Jake placed a hand on her shoulder. "She looks so peaceful lying there, doesn't she?"

Tori nodded.

"I wish she would just open her eyes. There's so much I need to say to her. She can't die, Tori. I can't lose my mother. Not now."

"Honey, sit next to me. Why don't we pray together?"

He wore a strange expression on his face. "I . . ."

"Come on. I'll pray."

Jake dropped down into the chair beside her. Taking her hand, he closed his eyes.

"Heavenly Father, we praise Your holy name and we come before You this evening to ask Your help. . . ."

As Tori prayed, Jake tried to take in everything she was saying. Maybe there was a special way one had to pray in order for God to hear you. He wanted to pray for his mother's life. Jake wasn't ready to let her go. His mother's words came back to him. "Let go and let God. . . ."

He heard her voice so clear—almost as if she'd just said the words.

Tori was shaking his hand. "Jake . . ."

"Huh?" He glanced over at his mother and, to his amazement, he saw her looking at him. "Mother . . ."

He was vaguely aware of Tori jumping up and leaving the room. She returned a few minutes later with Shepard and Charlene in tow. Jake held on to his mother's hand. When she squeezed his hand, he returned his gaze to her face.

Her mouth was moving. Although he couldn't hear the words, he knew what she was saying.

"Let go and let God," she mouthed. Gwendolyn turned to face Shepard.

Jake had no idea what she was trying to tell his brother. He was still a little unnerved by what she'd said to him. He was beginning to wonder if he was losing his mind.

Gwendolyn Madison died half an hour later. She wasn't in any pain, or so it seemed. She'd awarded each of them a smile, closed her eyes, and was gone.

"I can't believe she's gone," Jake cried.

Tori held on to him as he sobbed. She stroked his back as she murmured words of support and encouragement. He composed himself and left to make a couple of phone calls and the necessary arrangements. She'd offered to do it for him, but Jake had refused.

"Shepard, I want you to come with me and Jake to Edisto Island. I don't think you should stay in the house alone tonight."

"You don't have to—"

Tori cut Shepard off. "I want you to come home with me. I won't take no for an answer."

He nodded in resignation. "Thank you."

It was after eight P.M. by the time they made it to Edisto Island. After seeing that Shepard was comfortable in one of the guest rooms, Tori went back downstairs to check on Jake. She found him staring off into space.

"Jake, are you okay?"

He nodded.

"Why don't you go to bed? You look tired."

"I don't think I can sleep. I feel too numb to sleep."

Tori sat down next to him. "I wish I had some words of wisdom for you, but I don't. I've never really known what to say during times like this. When Tiffany died, I got so tired of people coming up to me, telling me how sorry they were. Or they would tell me how in time, things get better. It got on my nerves."

"Just having you beside me is enough. I just need to know that I still have somebody I love. I've lost everybody else."

It was well after midnight before Tori was finally able to coax Jake up to bed. He tossed and turned until pure exhaustion took over. She fell to the floor on her knees, praying for strength. Not only for herself, but for Jake and Shepard, too.

The next morning, Tori eased out of bed and made her way to the bathroom. She hoped Jake wouldn't wake until much later. He needed his rest. Taking off her clothes, she jumped into the shower.

When she came out, Tori heard Jake moving around in the bedroom. She heard the television come on and smiled. A few minutes later, Jake joined her in the bathroom. She'd just slipped into her robe.

Grabbing his toothbrush, he greeted her. "Morning. Hope I didn't keep you up last night."

"You didn't." Tori wrapped both arms around him. "We were both so tired that I don't think either one of us moved the whole night."

Tori had breakfast ready when Jake emerged out of the bedroom. He came down the stairs in a pair of linen shorts and a linen shirt.

"I called Sheila and told her that I was going to be out for the next couple of weeks. She's going to handle all of my meetings and appointments."

She handed him a cup of coffee. "That's good. You really need her now."

"Where's Shepard? I stopped by his room but it was empty."

"He left already," Tori announced. "He's going to meet us later at the funeral home."

After breakfast, Tori and her husband left to meet Shepard. It broke her heart seeing these two handsome men standing there, looking so lost. She had never seen them look so vulnerable.

Shepard broke down when it came time to pick out the coffin. Big brother Jake reached over to comfort him. Tori hastily wiped away a lone tear. Mother Madison's death made them both realize how much they loved and needed each other.

Chapter Thirty-five

Gwendolyn Madison was laid to rest four days later. After leaving the cemetery, everyone gathered at the house in Charleston.

"What on earth is Sheila doing here?" Kate complained. "That woman has no morals whatsoever. Gwendolyn's not been dead a week and here she is, sniffing after your husband. The poor man can't even grieve for his mother in peace."

"Maybe Jake invited her," Tori answered. "She is his business partner."

"She wants to be his bed partner, too," Kate huffed.

A couple of people standing nearby glanced their way.

"Aunt Kate!" Tori said in a loud whisper. "Please keep your voice down."

Charlene had been silent until now. "Keep your thoughts to yourself, Mama. Tori doesn't need to hear talk like that. She and Jake are trying to work things out."

"Tori, honey, are you sure Jake's worth the trouble? Seems to me if you want to keep your marriage, then you need to make him choose. He needs to either buy out that witch or sell his share to her. Mark my words, Sheila means him nothing good. The woman is a snake."

"Jake can't see it, Aunt Kate. Until he does, there's nothing I can say or do." Tori stole a peek at her husband. He was sitting by the window, staring off into space. Out of the corner of her eye, she spotted Sheila heading in his direction with a plate.

"Jake, why don't you eat something?" Sheila handed him a plate and coaxed, "Come on. Just try some of the greens and maybe some ham."

He shook his head no, but she continued to push.

Tori excused herself and crossed the room. "My husband will eat when he's hungry, Sheila."

Meeting her gaze, Sheila responded, "He needs his strength. This has been a grueling time for Jake."

Taking the plate from Sheila, Tori was firm in her response. "Jake is a grown man. He'll eat when he's hungry."

She immediately backed down. "You're right, of course. I was just trying to be helpful."

"Thank you."

The two women stared at each other until Sheila finally looked away. With a look of concession, she turned on her heel and disappeared around a corner.

Looking up at her, Jake uttered, "She was just being nice, Tori. Why don't you give her a chance?"

Turning her attention to Jake, she replied, "She's your friend— not mine. I don't have to give her anything." She hadn't meant to be so short with him, especially when he was grieving for his mother, but Tori didn't care for his defending Sheila at the moment.

In a low voice, he said, "She didn't betray you alone, Tori. I betrayed you, too."

"I haven't forgotten, Jake. Not for a minute," she snapped. "This is not the time or the place for this discussion."

After taking the plate back to the kitchen, Tori strode into the den to spend a few moments alone. Everyone was in the living room and on the front porch. Feeling anxious, Tori ran her fingers through her hair. Every time Sheila was around, she and Jake argued. When would he see the light?

Hearing footsteps, she turned around. It was her husband.

They stood there, staring at each other.

"I'm sorry, sweetheart."

Hearing those words, Tori held her arms out. Jake eased into them.

"I love you," he whispered as he held her close.

"I love you, too, Jake."

Bending his head, he lowered his mouth to hers. A truce had been declared for now.

Watching Jake kiss his wife like that sent a knifelike pain ripping through Sheila. She almost felt like doubling over in agony, but managed to keep her facade. For a wild moment, she wished that it had been Tori's funeral instead of Jake's mother's.

She should have been the one comforting him, not Tori. It didn't matter to her that the woman was his wife. Sheila was tired of having to stand by, playing the caring friend while hiding her true feelings.

She wanted to wear her love for Jake like a banner. Sheila wanted nothing more than to be the lady on his arm and by his side always. At home and at work. That had always been her dream. To have her life mate working alongside her.

If only Jake had noticed her in college. While she was in school, Sheila couldn't afford to have any of the cosmetic surgery she desired. By the time she could afford it, Jake had already married Tori. Hate flowed through Sheila. If it was the last thing she did, she vowed, by this time next year, she and Jake would be man and wife.

Chapter Thirty-six

Everyone had already gone home. Before Charlene could get away, Shepard grabbed her hand and pulled her off to the side. "Can we go somewhere and talk?"

She was very distant with him. They hadn't spoken since his mother's death. "I have to take Mama home. Besides, we have nothing to talk about."

"You're wrong."

She refused to look at him. "Shepard, you've just buried your mother. You're upset right now and not thinking clearly." Charlene stepped around him. "I've got to go."

Shepard blocked her path. "Losing my mother has made me realize how much I don't want to lose you, Charlene."

This time she gazed into his eyes.

Taking both hands into his, Shepard kissed them. Staring into her eyes, he said, "I love you, baby, and I really don't want to lose you. I've been a jerk for so long. It's time I tried to make things right."

Charlene shook her head sadly. "It's too late, Shepard."

"I don't believe that. Charlene, you love me, and I know I love you. It's not over between us."

She pulled her hands away. "Shepard, I can't forget what you said to me. It hurt deeply."

"I'm sorry, Charlene. Honey, I was angry. And hurt. I was wrong."

"Mama's waiting for me in the car. I have to go." She made her way to the door.

"Can I call you?" Shepard asked.

"I would prefer you didn't. It just wasn't meant to be. I see that now." Charlene strode out onto the porch. She glanced back briefly to say, "I'm going to miss your mother. She was a wonderful lady."

"She loved you like a daughter, Charlene."

Charlene gave a slight nod, then walked away. She loved Shepard with her whole heart, but he'd hurt her deeply. She'd forgiven him once, but she wasn't sure she could do it again.

"Jake," Tori said, "I've been playing with an idea for a few months now. I'm thinking of starting an African-American heritage tour. We could take groups up and down the coast and other points of interest."

Jake glanced up from the book he was reading. "It sounds like an interesting project."

"You really think so?"

"I do. Like Georgia, the Carolina coast is filled with so much of our history, and we're not going to get it in traditional history books."

"I'm thinking of starting the tour in Charleston and ending up back on the island."

Putting the book on the coffee table, Jake inquired, "Have you already selected sites to visit?"

"Yes. I'm doing some research for other areas. There's so much history to uncover. Eventually, I'd like to extend the tour from a few hours to a full weekend."

"What would you do in a weekend?"

"We could go all the way down to Brunswick. Did you know that the slave ship, the *Wanderer*, made its last stop on Jekyll Island? Then there's Sapelo Island. The inhabitants there are direct descendants from African slaves. The island's full of history and tales from the homeland."

Jake listened with interest.

The more she talked, the more animated she became. ". . . We have the Sea Islands and the Gullah people. . . ."

Every now and then he would give a suggestion as to how she could promote the event. She was touched by Jake's show of support.

Tori made dinner for them. Afterward, she cleaned the kitchen while Jake worked in his office. She joined him there when she was done.

"How long are you planning to work?"

"Not too much longer. " Jake glanced over at her. "What do you have in mind?"

Grinning, Tori crooked her finger. "Follow me and I'll show you."

Sheila picked up the yellow legal pad. "Is this what you're talking about, Jake?"

"Yes."

She read over his notes. "What is this?" It didn't look like Madison Moore business.

Jake looked up. "Oh, those are some marketing notes I made for Tori's project."

Frowning, Sheila asked, "What project?"

He gave her a rundown of what he and Tori had discussed for the heritage trail. "So, what do you think?"

"If you really want to know the truth, I think it's a silly idea, Jake. Who wants to go up and down the highway looking at plantations? I know I wouldn't be interested."

"But there are people who love history, Sheila. Just because you don't, doesn't mean we won't find others that will."

"We? Are you in this with Tori?"

"She's my wife," he stated almost defiantly.

"I know that, Jake," Sheila snapped. "Lord knows you don't have to say it over and over again."

He looked up at her. "What's gotten into you?"

It was time to put her cards on the table. "I care too much to see you made a fool of. Tori's not good for you. Why can't you see that? You two do nothing but argue."

Jake's expression was one of surprise. "What is it with you, Sheila? I thought you liked Tori."

"I do," she lied. "I just don't think she's the woman for you."

"Well, you're wrong. Tori's the only woman for me, Sheila. I have always loved her and always will."

"You say that over and over again. Are you trying to convince me or yourself?" she questioned.

Jake's gaze hardened.

"I'm sorry, but it's just that you complain about your wife, yet you stay with her. If she's keeping you confused, why do you want to be with her?"

"I love my wife," he insisted.

"Yet you seduced me."

His eyes dropped. Jake looked away. "Sheila, I've apologized for that."

"I know. We were drinking that first night. But what about all those times after that?"

"Tori and I were separated. You and I have been there for each other, so we've grown closer, right?"

"Right," she uttered. Sheila rose to her feet. "Look, it doesn't matter what I think about Tori's latest venture. That's between you and your wife."

"Is that why you lied to me that day?"

Sheila froze. "What are you talking about, Jake?"

"You lied to me when I asked you about Tori calling. Remember?"

"I don't have a clue as to what you're talking about." Sheila wasn't about to confess to her deed. She decided pleading ignorance was the best defense. "If I told you something like that, I must have been so busy that I didn't realize what I was saying. We've all been guilty of doing that."

Jake's phone started ringing. He answered it.

Sheila chose that moment to make her escape.

Chapter Thirty-seven

Tori's car was in the shop, so she arranged for Jake to pick her up from Bible study at the church. She'd invited him to attend with her, but he'd refused. Pastor Allen was getting something out of his car when he pulled up.

"Hello, Pastor," Jake called out.

Pastor Allen did a double take, sparking laughter from Jake. He walked over to the car.

"Jake Madison. How are you?"

"Doing okay. How's Mrs. Allen? I haven't seen her in a while."

"She's doing good. Still working at the hospital. I was so sorry to hear about your mother. I was in Georgia the week of the funeral."

"Mother lived a full life. She used to always say how she had no regrets."

Pastor Allen agreed. "She was always optimistic. Full of faith." He stole a quick peek at his watch. "Why don't you come inside?" he suggested. "Bible study is over."

Jake shook his head. "Not this time."

Tori came out five minutes later. She embraced Pastor Allen before getting into the car with her husband.

"How did it go?" he asked.

"Good. We're studying the Book of Matthew. I wish you'd come with me sometime."

"I'll think about it." That was about all he could commit to at the moment.

More and more, Jake thought about his mother's last words. How did one go about letting go and letting God? Let go of what? he wondered.

Jake considered asking Tori, but changed his mind. He didn't want her to think he was crazy. He stole a quick peek at her. She was sitting there, looking happy and content. He envied her peaceful expression.

Charlene was surprised to find Shepard standing on her doorstep. She hadn't heard from him since the day of the funeral, and that had been three weeks ago. "What are you doing here?"

"I thought maybe we could have dinner."

"Shepard . . ."

"Honey, I'm not giving up on you, so you might as well give in." She suddenly burst into laughter.

"What is it? What's so funny?"

Leaning against the front door, she said, "That's exactly what you said to me the first time you asked me out and I refused."

Shepard broke into a grin. "Does it still work?" he asked hopefully.

She nodded. "A girl's gotta eat." Charlene stepped aside to let him enter the house. "Give me a moment to get ready."

Kate passed through the living room. When she saw Shepard, her face twisted into a frown. "Didn't expect to see you here."

"Miss Kate, how are you?"

"I'm fine. I hope my little girl don't come home crying like she did before. I don't want to have to come after you with a rifle."

Biting back his laughter, Shepard simply nodded. "You won't have to do that, I assure you. I love Charlene."

"Humph. I heard that before. Still came home with a broken heart, though."

"Miss Kate, I give you my word that I will never willingly hurt your daughter again. I hope to one day convince her to marry me. With your blessing, of course."

"Humph," was all Kate would say.

Shepard shook with laughter when she walked out of the room. He vowed to win her over one day. Miss Kate had always been feisty, but she was a good woman with a good heart. Charlene was just like her.

Chapter Thirty-eight

Jake's office was a source of pride for Sheila. She'd spent hours browsing through upholstery and carpet samples, and she'd traveled all the way to London to purchase his dark mahogany furnishings and leather accessories. The two huge Boston ferns were Tori's contributions to the decor.

Everything about this office reminded her of Jake. When he was away, Sheila spent a lot of time in his office. It was her way of being close to him.

Out of the corner of her eye, she caught sight of Jake putting some papers into his briefcase. "You're leaving work early?" Sheila asked.

Her heart sank. She wasn't ready for him to leave yet. Leaving meant he would be going home to Tori. Sheila gritted her teeth to keep from giving sound to her rage.

Jake nodded. "I need to go home and pack up some things. I'm moving all my stuff over to Tori's. We've been living together for weeks now, but I feel like I'm between two houses."

"Need some help?" she offered.

He shook his head. "I've got it all under control. Call the house if you need me. I'm going to be there for a while."

She nodded. "I guess I'll see you tomorrow, then."

"Bright and early," Jake responded on his way out. Trembling, Sheila muttered a string of curses. They were getting closer. She had to find a way to come between Jake and Tori. Her face broke into a wide grin. "I know just what to do."

Jake walked into the house in which he'd grown up. With his mother gone, the house seemed different now. He walked past the room that used to house his father's collection of books. Now the floor-to-ceiling shelves were filled with Shepard's law books. Since Jake had his own home, he agreed that his brother should have the family home. He moved to stand in front of the fireplace, staring at the huge oil painting of his mother.

His father had commissioned a local artist to do the painting from a photograph for his mother's birthday. He'd then hung it in his library, because this was where he'd spent most of his time. Jake's father had adored his mother.

Both his parents were gone now, and he missed them both. Gazing up at his mother's picture, he recalled her last words to him. *Let go and let God.*

Jake left the library and went into the storage room beneath the stairs. He pulled out several empty cardboard boxes. He took two upstairs with him.

He cleared out the drawers in his bedroom, dropping his clothes into one of the boxes. When the two boxes were filled, he took them back downstairs one at a time, leaving them in the foyer.

Jake took two more boxes upstairs with him. The doorbell sounded. He descended the stairs.

"Sheila, what are you doing here?"

She was holding a folder in her hand. "These arrived a few minutes ago and they need your signature. Since you were here, I thought I'd just bring them over. These are the contracts we've been waiting for."

Jake took them from her. Sheila followed him into the library. Sitting down at his father's desk, he began to read through the contract.

"Mind if I use your bathroom?" she asked.

"No. Go ahead." Jake didn't even lift his head. He was too busy reading the contract. Sheila decided she hadn't seen him look so happy in over a year. Sadly, she knew whatever he was feeling right now had nothing to do with her.

Sheila glanced stealthily over her shoulder. Opening her purse, she pulled out a sheer teddy and a pair of lacy panties and quickly hid them in one of the open boxes sitting on the floor. *You and I are supposed to be together, Jake.* If not, it wouldn't have been so easy to do it. Her mother always used to say, "When something's for you, it comes easy."

She returned to the library. Jake signed the contracts, then handed them back to her.

"Thanks for bringing them over. I appreciate it."

"No problem." She backed toward the door. "I'll see you later. Have a good evening."

Smiling, he muttered, "I plan to."

Sheila returned his smile with one of her own. She hoped and prayed Tori would be the one to find her "little gifts."

Chapter Thirty-nine

Tori waited for the wave of nausea to pass before getting out of her car. She stopped briefly at the reception desk to speak with Selma before making her way toward the elevators.

Just as she walked past Sheila's office, she heard someone call her name. Tori stepped backward. "Did you just call me?"

"Yes, I did. Do you have a minute?" Sheila asked.

She wasn't in the mood for Sheila's antics. "Not really. I'm on my way to see my husband."

"Jake stepped out, but he should be back shortly. Anyway, this won't take long." She closed the door to her office, then gestured for Tori to sit down.

Eyeing her suspiciously, Tori questioned, "What is it, Sheila? I can't imagine what we'd have to discuss."

"Jake told me about this idea of yours."

"And?"

"Tori, I thought you were running a bookstore—not a tour service."

"What I do is none of your business."

"I'm only trying to give you sound advice."

"I don't need your advice, Sheila. When I need advice, I go to Jake."

"He had his own misgivings, Tori. That's why he came to me. He wanted to know what I thought."

Tori was furious, but she kept her true feelings undercover. Jake would not be as fortunate, however. He would feel her full wrath. He had no right discussing her business with Sheila. How could he do this to her? "Jake shouldn't have bothered you with this."

"Oh, it wasn't a bother," Sheila quickly interjected.

"Regardless, I would have preferred it kept just between me and my husband. This has nothing to do with Madison Moore."

"I understand."

"I'm sure you do. Now, if you will excuse me, I need to see if Jake's back." Tori rose to her feet and swayed. She reached out, blinded by dizziness.

"Are you okay?"

Tori leaned against the desk for support. "I'm fine. Just got a little dizzy, that's all."

"I'll go see if Jake's in his office."

"I'll be fine in just a few minutes," Tori snapped.

"I was just trying to help."

"I'm sorry. I shouldn't have snapped at you like that. I just don't want you to scare Jake."

"It could be something serious."

"I'm okay. I just need to get something to eat." Tori made a move toward the door. She swayed as dizziness tried to overtake her once more.

"Why don't you stop trying to be so stubborn and let me help you, Tori?"

She allowed Sheila to lead her over to a nearby chair. Tori sat down and held her head between her legs. She couldn't ever recall feeling so bad.

Sheila disappeared for a few minutes. When she returned, she handed Tori a damp cloth. "Here, press this to your forehead."

Tori did as she was told. The cool cotton felt good against her skin. She gave a soft sigh of relief as her dizzy spell evaporated. A short while later, she felt strong enough to stand.

"Are you feeling any better?" Sheila asked. "I checked Jake's office, and he's not back yet."

Tori nodded. "Thank you."

"Why don't you go lie down on the couch in Jake's office until he gets back? I'm sure he's not going to mind."

"No. I'm feeling much better now." Tori handed the cloth back to Sheila. "I appreciate your help."

"I don't want anything to happen to you."

Tori didn't respond. She rose to her feet slowly. Feeling much stronger now, she navigated toward the door. She moved as fast as her body would allow. Tori waited another ten minutes in Jake's office.

When he still hadn't arrived, she hastily wrote him a note and left it on his desk.

From her car, Tori called her doctor and made an appointment. She had an idea of what was wrong, but until she confirmed it, she wasn't going to say a word.

Could Tori be pregnant? Sheila wondered. If it was true, then she would lose Jake. He would feel honor-bound to stay with his wife. Her heart started to pound faster at the thought of losing Jake again.

She'd come too far to lose him now. But even if Tori was pregnant, there still had to be a way to get her out of his life once and for all. Sheila was just going to have to work harder to get him back into her bed. She knew that Tori would not forgive him a second time. She would divorce Jake and raise her child alone.

Sheila didn't like the idea of a child being involved in this situation. Her own father had walked out on her mother when she was five years old. She wasn't a bad person. She was a woman in love and fighting to spend her life with her soul mate.

As she pondered the possibility of a child, an idea formed in Sheila's mind. But the timing had to be perfect, because the next time she and Jake made love, she planned to become pregnant. Jake would never abandon his child.

And Tori's love for him would quickly turn to hatred. Meanwhile, Sheila would be there to pick up the pieces.

Chapter Forty

After her doctor's appointment, Tori went straight to the bookstore.

"You okay?" Kate asked when her niece strode through the front door. "Charlene said you went to see the doctor this morning."

"I'm fine. I'm pregnant," Tori announced softly.

"What? How in the world did this . . ." Kate looked embarrassed. "Humph!"

"Mama, don't be mean."

"I'm not being mean. I'm just surprised, that's all." Shaking her head, Kate muttered, "Girl, I sure hope you know what you're doing."

Charlene glanced over at her cousin. "You okay, Tori?"

She nodded. "Still in shock." Tori was overjoyed at the news, but also a little fearful. She recalled how he'd reacted when she'd told him the first time. "I was just thinking about Jake's reaction when I told him I was pregnant with Tiffany. He was a little thrown in the beginning. It was as if I'd broken some sort of rule."

"You don't think he'll be happy about the baby?" Charlene questioned.

"This little one certainly hadn't been in mine or Jake's plan."

"What are you going to do?"

"Tell Jake, of course."

Kate sighed loudly. "I sure hope he don't act like he did the first time. Remember how upset he was? You would've thought Tori had been sleeping around or something."

"Mama—" Charlene tried to interrupt.

"Don't try to shush me, girl! I'm gonna have my say. Jake Madison is not gonna do right by you, Tori. Mark my words, I don't blame him much, though. It's that Sheila Moore. She got roots on him. And if you look at her good—she's got these two spots on her face, right above her eyebrows. It looks like there used to be horns there."

Tori and Charlene burst into laughter.

"This is no laughing matter. That woman is the spawn of Satan, I tell you. I wouldn't trust her and I certainly wouldn't eat her food."

Embracing her, Tori whispered, "I'm not worried about Sheila, Aunt Kate. God's got my back. His Word says that what He puts together, no man—or woman, for that matter—can come between."

"It takes two to make a marriage work," Kate reminded her. "I hope Jake's as devoted to you as you are to him."

"Aunt Kate, Jake is a good man. When he and I first got married, we'd planned on having children in five years. Tiffany came in three, and Jake wasn't quite prepared for fatherhood. Initially, he was a little resentful, but even you have to admit—once he laid eyes on his daughter, he was in love."

Kate mumbled in agreement. "Yeah, he loved Tiffany. Plumb crazy about her."

Hands on her hips, Charlene asked, "Mama, why do you hate them so much? Were they that terrible to you as children?"

Tori was just as curious. She'd been wondering herself what was behind her aunt's intense dislike for the Madison men.

"I don't hate Shepard and Jake," Kate mumbled. "I just know how men can be, and I want you two to be careful."

"But you only have a problem with the Madison men, it seems," Tori interjected.

"It's because I know them so well. Now, look, I don't want to discuss this any longer. If you two want to hinge your hopes and dreams on Shepard and Jake, then it's your own business. I'll see y'all later." Muttering to herself, Kate stormed out of the store.

Turning to her cousin, Tori asked, "What just happened here?"

Shrugging, Charlene replied, "I don't have a clue. I was just about to ask you the same thing."

"Something must have happened between your mother and some man in the Madison family."

Inclining her head, Charlene questioned, "You think?"

"I wonder if my mom knows."

"Ask her. I'd like to know the answer to that myself."

"I think I will. She's coming up for the tour this weekend, so I'll ask her about it then." They were having the first heritage trail tour for the Fourth of July weekend. Tori was starting to feel anxious about the whole thing. Scanning through the list of people who'd already signed up, she sent up a silent prayer, asking for God's blessing.

Jake raced home and up the stairs as much as his bad leg would allow him. Tori was standing in front of the floor-to-ceiling windows in their bedroom. Her back was to him.

He walked cautiously toward her. "Honey?"

Tori turned around, facing him.

"You sounded so strange on the phone. What did the doctor say?"

She moved closer to him. "Jake, there's something I have to tell you."

The tone of her voice unnerved him. "What is it?"

Tori took a deep breath. There was no other way to say it than, "I'm going to have a baby. We're going to have a baby."

Jake couldn't seem to think straight. He was speechless.

Tori broke into nervous laughter. "Will you say something, please?"

"I . . ." He put a hand to his mouth. "We're going to have a baby. Another child. Wow."

"Are you happy?" Tori asked softly.

"Am I . . ." Jake couldn't contain his joy. "Honey, I'm ecstatic."

She and Jake stared at each other for a long time before Tori took hold of his hand and placed it on her stomach.

Smiling, she said, "God's blessed us with another little baby."

"I'm going to do right by you and this baby. I give you my word. We're a family, sweetheart."

"The flowers and candy—all this is real nice, but we haven't really talked." Charlene led Shepard over to the couch. "Before we go any further, I think we should talk now."

He nodded. "I was wrong about the way I reacted."

"You had every right to be angry, and I expected that. I just didn't expect to be called a murderer."

"I never called you that."

"You said I killed our child." Charlene's voice broke. "You don't kn-know how many t-times I said that about myself. I wanted my b-baby, I really did. But I was young and afraid. I didn't want to go through the pregnancy alone or knowing that you didn't want the child."

"I don't know how I would've reacted, hon. Back then I was young and stupid. Only thinking of myself."

"I wanted to tell you. So many times I tried, but I would always chicken out. I didn't want to hurt you."

"I love you, Charlene. After tonight, we will never talk about this again. Let's concentrate on the future."

"Can you forgive me, Shepard?"

Staring into her eyes, he nodded. "I already have. I must ask the same of you, too. Can you find it in your heart to forgive me?"

"Yes. That's the easy part. Forgiving myself is the hard part."

Chapter Forty-one

Sheila eyed her partner. Jake was practically bouncing off the walls. He just couldn't seem to keep still. "You certainly look very happy today. What's going on with you?"

"I have some good news, Sheila. It's incredible."

"Well, don't keep me in suspense. Share. . . ."

"Tori's pregnant." Jake pulled a cigar out of his pocket and handed it to her.

"Wh-what?" Although she'd already suspected it, his words still managed to stun her.

"Tori and I are having another child. Isn't that great?"

Sheila swallowed hard. "Y-yes. Congratulations."

"I never thought it would happen. I never thought that Tori and I would have another chance."

He was going on and on about his impending fatherhood. One would think the man hadn't fathered a child before. She wondered if he would be this happy when she conceived.

*   *   *

Tori's excitement grew as the number of people showing up for her first tour increased. By nine A.M., there were more than forty people in attendance.

"Wow, girlfriend," Charlene exclaimed. "I think you've got something here. This is your first tour, and look how many people are coming along."

"I feel very blessed. Thank you so much for supporting me in this venture, Charlene. Just think . . . if this is a success, this will be another facet of our business."

"You know how much I love history. I think it's probably the only class I got A's in when I was in high school. Well, that and literature."

Tori glanced around. "I thought Jake would be here by now."

"Shepard's coming, too." Gesturing to her left, Charlene whispered, "Here comes Nicholas."

Following her cousin's line of vision, Tori watched as her friend got out of his car and headed over to the line. She returned his wave. She wasn't as happy to see him as she normally would've been. She didn't appreciate the flowers or the card that had accompanied them. It was so unlike Nicholas.

"Jake just got here," Charlene announced. "Shepard's with him."

"He must have driven to our house and parked his car there."

"Probably," Charlene agreed.

Jake greeted her with a kiss. "I had to wait for Shepard."

"You made it in time, that's all I care about."

"It's time to board the bus," Charlene announced to the group. "Please form a single line."

Tori, Jake, and Shepard stood off to the side as people started to get on the bus. Linda gave her a thumbs-up and she blew her mother a kiss.

"This is a great showing for the inaugural tour. Congratulations, Tori." Jake awarded her with another kiss. "I'm proud of you."

"I couldn't have gotten it off the ground if it hadn't been for you and Charlene. I should be the one thanking you guys."

When everyone was on the bus and seated, Tori, Jake, and Shepard climbed in behind Charlene and took their seats near the front. The driver was about to close the door when they heard a woman calling out.

"Someone's coming," Charlene stated. "Wait."

Sheila stepped up onto the bus, panting. "Thanks so much for waiting. I ran into a bit of traffic leaving Charleston this morning."

Jake glanced over at Tori, who smiled and said, "I'm glad you made it, Sheila. As soon as you take a seat, we'll be on our way."

"I had no idea she was planning to come," he whispered.

"It's okay. We're still going to have a good time. Nothing is going to spoil this day for me."

Tori stood up with microphone in hand. "I would like to thank all of you for joining us for the first African-American Heritage Trail. For those of you who don't know me, my name is Tori Madison, and this is my partner, Charlene Daniels."

She talked a little about her reasons for starting the tour. ". . . The tour will begin near the historic town of McClellanville. We are going to the Hampton Plantation State Historic Site."

Her eyes met Sheila's. Tori smiled sweetly and continued. There was nothing Sheila could do to spoil this event for her. "The Hampton Plantation was home to more than three hundred and twenty enslaved Africans. . . ."

The bus took them along Highway 17 to see Boone Hall Plantation and the Charles Pinckney National Historic Site.

Even Jake seemed awed by it all. "You can certainly see the contrasts between the lives of slaves and their owners. It is a blatant reminder of just how fortunate we are."

Tori agreed.

"Well, it's very depressing," Sheila announced. "I think a lot of our problem is that we dwell on the past far too much."

Just off Highway 17, they were taken to Sullivan's Island, where Fort Moultrie stood guard over the Charleston Harbor. There they viewed the historic marker commemorating the point of entry of countless enslaved Africans. They also learned more about the history of the legendary 54th Massachusetts Volunteer Infantry Regiment.

The tour continued on to Fort Sumter National Monument, then to Bull Street in Charleston, where they stopped at the Avery Research Center for African American History and Culture.

Sheila looked completely bored by the time they toured the Emanuel AME Church and the old Slave Mart. Tori pointed out the Denmark Vesey House, which was now a private residence.

After a picnic lunch of fried chicken, potato salad, fresh baked rolls, and iced tea, generously donated by Willow's restaurant, they toured the McLeod Plantation on James Island.

"You won't want to miss the lovely avenue of oaks, so make sure you have your cameras ready. . . ." Tori also gave a short history of the plantation's unique wooden slave cabins.

Just past Johns Island, they stopped at the site of the Stono River Slave Rebellion. "This rebellion took place in 1739, when Spanish Florida offered lands to Africans and African-Americans. . . ." Tori explained.

They headed back to Edisto Island, where they stopped to visit Zion Baptist Church and Hepzibah Townsend's grave.

When they returned to the bookstore, everyone disembarked, murmuring how much they enjoyed the tour.

Nicholas embraced her. "Congratulations, sweetheart. I really enjoyed myself. It even gave me some ideas for my book."

"I'm glad," Tori stated with a grin.

"You look so happy, Tori. Things must be working out."

"They are. But there's another reason, too. Nicholas, I'm going to have a baby."

"Really?"

She nodded.

He embraced her a second time. "I'm very happy for you, Tori. Maybe you'll even consider making me godfather."

She broke into laughter. "I'll certainly give it some serious thought."

Jake joined them.

Nicholas shook his hand enthusiastically. "I hear you're about to become a father. Congratulations, man."

"Thanks."

"You are a lucky man, Jake. A very lucky man."

"I think so, Nicholas. Tori is the only woman for me. It's always been that way."

"Well, I enjoyed myself, but it's time I get back to my book. My deadline is looming right before my eyes."

"Thank you for coming, Nicholas. Oh, can you come by the store one day this week? I need to talk to you."

"Sure. I'll give you a call."

"He's a good friend to you," Jake acknowledged for the first time ever.

Tori glanced up at her husband. "Yes, he is. Nicholas has been a wonderful friend to me." The more she thought about it, the more unlikely it seemed that he could've been the one to send those flowers.

Sheila intruded upon their moment.

"Well, I have to admit it was quite an interesting event. I certainly hope you'll get others to come for the next one."

"I'm sure I will. Some people embrace their history, while others tend to make up theirs."

Stiffening, Sheila asked, "What do you mean by that?"

"What's wrong? Did I strike a nerve or something?"

"Jake, you need to better control your wife."

He laughed. "Sheila, calm down. You and Tori have always been like this with each other. I'm going to do what I always do—stay out of it."

Glaring at them both, Sheila muttered, "You both can go straight to hell!"

"What's going on with her?" Tori asked before bursting into laughter.

Jake shrugged and answered, "I don't know. She's been kinda moody a lot lately. I just leave her alone."

"Does she know that I'm pregnant?"

Jake nodded. "I told her. Why? You think that's why she's acting this way?"

"It could be. Although you refuse to believe me, Sheila's in love with you, Jake."

Embracing her, he replied, "She knows how I feel about you. I've never lied to her or misled her in any way."

"But you slept with her," Tori pointed out.

"That's all it was, sex."

"Maybe for you, Jake. For Sheila, it was something more. Most women get emotionally involved with the person they're sleeping with. It's not just about sex."

"What's this all about?"

"All I'm saying is that I think it was more than that for Sheila."

"It's in the past, Tori. I made a big mistake and I just want to move on. My life is with you, and I've made that very clear."

Chapter Forty-two

"Where are you going?" Jake asked from where he lay in bed.

Buttoning up her blouse, Tori replied, "I was just about to leave you a note. I have a hair appointment this morning. Denika's going to give me a much-needed cut." She sat down on the edge of the bed and proceeded to put her shoes on.

Jake jumped out of bed. "I thought you were going to let your hair grow out."

She looked up at him. "What made you think that?"

"You know how much I love your hair long."

"I cut my hair because I love having it short. I'll let it grow out when I'm ready, Jake. I intend to live my life for me—not for you anymore."

He stiffened. "I'm not sure I even know you anymore, Tori. Look at the way you're dressed."

She glanced down at the purple-and-teal two-piece short set she was wearing. "What's wrong with this outfit?"

"Since when did you start wearing shorts like that? And that top, there's not a whole lot of material there. You're pregnant."

"I like what I'm wearing. I was tired of walking around looking years older than I am. Jake, I'm twenty-eight. I'm still a young woman. And as far as my being pregnant, I'm not showing yet. I think I look great."

"I don't want my wife walking around showing her body to the world."

"I'm not. Even my mother used to dress more stylish than I did. My body is covered up. This is a halter top—just my back is out. What's so ironic about all this is that Sheila's clothes are even skimpier than this, and you have no problem with anything she wears."

"She's not my wife. *You are.*"

"I'm also my own person, Jake. Being your wife is just an extension of who I am."

Tensions ran high when Tori returned to the house two hours later. Jake took one look at her hair, then turned away. She pretended that his action hadn't affected her. Tori made her way to the kitchen and proceeded to make a chef salad.

"Lunch is ready, if you're hungry," she announced from the doorway of his office.

"I'll be there."

Tori eyed him for a moment longer. "Jake, I can't believe you're acting so childish. It's my hair."

"You've made that very clear, Tori. My feelings don't come into play here. It's all about Victoria Samuels-Madison these days."

Jake had never called her Victoria. The name sounded almost foreign coming from him.

"I have always put your needs before my own, Jake. You know it. Before I die, I would like to do something for me. Is that okay?"

Jake rose to his feet and walked around the desk. "Do what you want, Tori."

She followed him to the dining room. Jake sat at one end of the table and she sat at the other. "I can't believe you're acting like this."

"And I can't believe you're being so selfish. You never used to be this way before. What ever happened to the woman I fell in love with?"

"Excuse me?"

"You've changed so much, Tori. I have to really step back at times and ask myself if you're the same person."

"If you have to ask that question, then maybe it's not meant for us to be married."

Jake dropped his fork. "You want a divorce?"

"That's not what I said. Don't try to twist my words around on me." Laying her fork down, Tori looked across the table at him. "I don't want to fight with you. All I want is for you to let me be me. You can't make me into your dream woman."

"You are my dream woman, Tori."

"Only if I wear my hair long and dress the way you want me to. At least, that's the way I'm interpreting this conversation."

Leaning back in his chair, Jake eyed her. "I don't know if I'll ever really like your hair so short. Can't we compromise and let it grow out a little longer?"

Tori smiled. "I can do that."

"Thank you. One more thing. Everything you wear looks beautiful on you. I'm just not used to seeing you dress this way." Jake sipped his wine. "However, I don't want you dressing even remotely close to the way Sheila does."

"You don't have to worry about that," Tori assured him. "I want to keep certain things just between you and me."

"There's something I've been meaning to ask you about, Nicholas. Why did you send me those flowers?"

He frowned. "What flowers?"

"You didn't send me flowers? It was about two months ago. Right after we got back from Brunswick."

"No."

"Well, somebody did. They put your name on the card and a

message that said, 'Thanks for the memorable weekend in Brunswick.' It also said that I would always own your heart."

"I never ordered any flowers or any note like that. In fact, that's why you haven't heard from me. I was trying to stay out of the way. I didn't want to disrespect your husband."

Tori glanced up at him. "Nicholas, have you by any chance talked to Sheila?"

"She was the one who told me you were going to Brunswick for the weekend."

"What else did she say?"

"She led me to believe that Jake was leaving you for her."

Tori's mouth dropped open. "What?"

"Sheila told me that Jake was in love with her and he was going to leave you. That's why I went after you in the first place."

"That . . ." Tori shook her head in disbelief. "She is something else."

"Jake had better watch his back."

Tori wrapped her arms around Nicholas. "I'm so sorry. You never should have been caught up in all this mess."

"It's okay. At least we know who the players are now."

"I've just got to let Jake in on it. I don't think he knows."

"Be careful, Tori. Sheila is dangerous."

"So am I."

Nicholas laughed. "I'm going to be leaving here in a few weeks. It's been so good seeing you and spending time together. It was like old times."

"I had a good time, too."

"I will always be here for you, Tori. If you ever need anything, I'm only a phone call away."

"Same here. I wish you much success, Nicholas. And a lifetime of happiness. Oh, and don't you forget, I'm hosting a book signing for you when your next book comes out."

"We'll be in touch." Nicholas kissed her cheek and then disappeared.

Tori arrived home to flowers and candles everywhere. She looked around in amazement. "Jake," she called out.

"I'm up here," he answered.

She rushed up the stairs and into her bedroom. There were rose petals all over the bed. "What's going on?"

"This is my way of saying I'm sorry. I . . . I guess I haven't quite gotten used to the new you."

"Jake, I haven't changed that much. I'm still very much the woman you fell in love with and married. I'm just more at peace with myself. I'm more secure and self-assured. If you want to know the truth—I think I'm a much better woman now."

He smiled. "You've become a little spitfire, but I believe I can handle you."

Tori's eyes issued a challenge. "We'll just have to see about that, won't we?"

Jake picked her up and carried her over to the bed.

From her position at the bar, Sheila spotted Nicholas when he walked in. She smiled and waved.

He waved back and took a seat at one of the tables. She watched him a minute before getting off the stool and strolling over toward him. "Hey, can I sit down?"

His gray eyes roamed over her body slowly. "Sure. It's a free country."

Sheila leaned forward, giving him a great view of her breasts. She was tired of going to bed alone. "Tell me something, Nicholas. You're a very handsome man. You're famous. Why are you here drinking alone?"

"What are you doing here by yourself? Jake's not available tonight?" He leaned forward. "I know you must be hurting with him choosing Tori over you."

Sitting back in her chair, Sheila replied, "Tori managed to get herself pregnant and he feels obligated."

"You need to get over this little fantasy about Jake," Nicholas warned. "The man loves his wife."

"Their marriage is not going to last, I assure you."

"You sent those flowers in my name, didn't you?"

Sheila gave him a tiny smile. "I was merely trying to give you some help."

"I don't need your help."

She finished her drink, then ordered another.

"Don't you think you've had enough?"

"Not nearly enough," Sheila responded. Staring at him, she broke into a sexy smile.

"Why don't you come back to my place with me, Nicholas? We could get to know each other better. Maybe even have some fun."

He shook his head. "No, thanks."

"What is it? You don't think I'm good enough for you?"

"That's not it at all, Sheila."

"Then what is it?"

Throwing two twenties on the table, Nicholas rose to his feet. "I don't think I'm good enough for you." Taking her by the hand, he said, "Come on, I'm putting you in a cab before you really get into trouble."

Chapter Forty-three

Tori hit her toe on the corner of a cardboard box. "I'm so tired of these boxes just sitting here." Jake had brought them from his mother's house and had just left them sitting in one corner of their bedroom. She decided to unpack his clothes and break down the boxes. Tori wanted them gone.

Holding up a lace thong, Tori asked, "Jake, who does this belong to?"

He strode into the room. Surprise registered in his face. "Where did it come from? I know I didn't pack it."

"Well, they were in your box. Are they Sheila's?" She pulled out another piece of women's lingerie. Holding up a see-through teddy, she asked, "And what about this?"

"I don't know anything about them, Tori."

"Have you slept with anyone besides Sheila?" Deep down, she wasn't sure she really wanted to know the answer to that question, but she couldn't stop herself from asking.

"Tori, please don't do this."

"Answer me, Jake. How many women have there been? We already know you were sleeping with Sheila."

"There was no one else."

"Then these must be hers." Tori threw the items on the floor. "Remind me to wash my hands in bleach."

"I'll get them out of here." Sighing heavily, Jake bent to pick them up. "They can go out with the trash."

Tori suddenly stopped him. "No. We're not going to throw them in the trash. I'll give them back to Sheila personally."

His eyes met hers. "You don't have to do that, Tori."

"Yes, I do. If I want to have peace in my marriage, then I'm going to have to set this woman straight once and for all."

Sighing heavily, Jake took Tori by the hand. "I wish you and Sheila would at least make an attempt to get along."

"You have some nerve, Jake. You're lucky I even acknowledge the woman after all she's done to me."

"Tori, you can't just blame Sheila for what happened."

"I don't," she stated sharply. "I blame you even more because you should have known better."

Sighing in resignation, Jake murmured, "I deserve that."

"And much, much more."

Jake's eyes rose to meet hers. "Are we about to have a fight?"

"Only if that's what you want. I'm tired of Sheila's games, and I intend to put a stop to them. I talked to Nicholas. He never sent those flowers. I'm pretty sure Sheila did. This lingerie—Sheila."

"She did come by the house when I was packing my things."

"Sheila was up in your room?"

"No, Tori. I'd already carried them downstairs. They were in the foyer."

"Sheila is not your friend. If she was, she would be happy for you and not trying to tear your marriage apart. She's in love with you. I suspect it goes as far back as your college days."

He looked surprised by her words, but remained silent.

Tori was grateful for his silence. It meant he was thinking about what she was saying.

"What do you want me to do? Sheila's my partner. We've even been talking about branching out."

"I can't tell you what to do, Jake. I know what I would like to happen."

"You want me to sell my share to her or buy her out of Madison Moore, right?"

Tori gazed up at him. "I won't deny it. It's exactly what I would love to see happen." She made her way over to the bed with an armload of Jake's shirts and tossed them on top of the comforter. She sat down and started to fold them neatly. He had just thrown them in the boxes.

Glancing over at him, she asked, "What do you think you should do?"

Jake moved to sit down beside her. "I guess you're right. I don't have much of a choice. Sheila shouldn't have interfered with our marriage. If I hadn't come on to her that night . . ."

"I don't think you did. Honey, the more I think about it, the more I believe you were the one seduced. Not the other way around. I really believe Sheila tricked you. I told you the woman was a snake."

During dessert, Shepard pulled out a gray ring box and asked, "Charlene, will you marry me? I know you gave this back to me, but it's time you put it back on your finger. I love you and I want you to be my wife."

She gasped. "Oh, my goodness." Tears filled her eyes. "I've waited so long to hear you say that." Using her napkin, she dried her eyes.

"I didn't mean to make you cry."

"These are tears of joy, silly. Yes. *Yes*, I'll marry you." Charlene jumped up out of her chair and rushed around the table, throwing her arms around Shepard. "I love you so much."

He pulled her onto his lap. "I love you, too." Shepard covered her mouth with his, kissing her passionately. "I was so scared you were going to say no."

"No. There's no way I'd make it that easy for you. I've been waiting for months for you to come to your senses."

Shepard burst into laughter.

Charlene stared down at her hand as he slipped the diamond solitaire on her finger. "It's beautiful."

"So are you," Shepard murmured. "What do you think your mother is going to say?"

"Who knows?" Charlene kissed him. "Who cares? I certainly don't. I'm marrying the man of my dreams, and there's nothing she can do about it."

Chapter Forty-four

Sheila was surprised to see Tori. "Jake's not here."

Stepping all the way into Sheila's corner office, Tori closed the door behind her. "I didn't come to see Jake. I came to see you."

"I can't imagine why," Sheila murmured.

"I came to return these to you," Tori said as she held out a small gift bag. "It's your teddy and panties. They mysteriously ended up in one of Jake's boxes."

"Excuse me?"

"Don't play innocent with me, Sheila. There are a few things I need to say to you. First of all, you might as well give it up. You can't come between me and Jake. Our marriage is stronger than ever."

Folding her arms across her chest, Sheila asked, "Do you really believe that?"

"Yes, I do. It's time you moved on."

"Tori, your husband and I are business partners. *We are a team.* There is nothing you can do about that. You're just going to have to deal with it. The long nights . . . the endless dinner meetings. I hope for Jake's sake you're not as insecure as before."

She smiled. "I'm not."

"I know Jake thinks you've made this big change, but I don't. I think you're still scared of losing your husband. If you weren't, you wouldn't be here."

Dropping the bag on Sheila's desk, Tori added, "I just wanted to return your stuff. I'm not worried about losing Jake."

Sheila's lips twisted into a cynical smile. "That remains to be seen."

The door opened and Jake stuck his head inside. "Hello, ladies. Selma told me I could find my wife in here."

"Jake, I didn't know you were back," Sheila acknowledged as he walked all the way into the office.

"Just got here." He kissed his wife. "I just tried to reach you on your cell phone."

"What did you want?"

"Nothing. Just wanted to hear your voice."

Sheila wore a look of disgust. "Eh . . . I would like to get back to work. You two can get all mushy in Jake's office."

"She's throwing us out of her office," he whispered.

Looking over her shoulder, Tori said, "I hope you remember what I said, Sheila. I meant every word."

Sheila didn't respond.

"I need to talk to you, so don't go anywhere," Jake said to her.

"I'll be here," Sheila replied. "I don't have any meetings until after two."

When they were alone, Tori turned to her husband. "She's cool. She wouldn't deny or confirm that they were hers."

"They have to be hers. There wasn't anybody else."

"I know this is tearing you apart. I just don't see any other way around it."

They stood in the middle of the room, holding each other. Tori could hear Jake's heart racing. She knew this was going to be extremely hard for him, but they had no other choice. Sheila was poison.

* * *

Jake made another visit to Sheila's office. He was not looking forward to this conversation, but Tori was right. It was necessary. She was on the telephone when he arrived. She waved him in and gestured for him to take a seat.

He watched her as she conducted her sales pitch. Sheila was beautiful, intelligent, and very aggressive. She was also a master manipulator. It was a shame that their business relationship had to come to an end. Madison Moore would not be the same without her.

But what if she decided she wanted to stay? Could Jake walk away from his dream? He had to, for Tori's sake.

Sheila ended her call. "What did you want to see me about, Jake?"

"I can't go on refereeing you and Tori. She's my wife, and I intend to make my marriage work."

"Is it because of the baby?"

"No. I love Tori."

"What are you trying to tell me, Jake? Surely you didn't come in here to tell me how much you love your wife." She leaned back in her chair. "What is this really about?"

"Making my marriage work. I've been trying to figure out the best way to handle this situation. Maybe the best thing to do is for me to buy you out."

Sheila jumped to her feet. "You don't want me to be your partner anymore? I've been nothing but a friend to you, Jake. *How can you do this to me?*"

Her eyes filled with tears.

"I'm not trying to do anything to you, Sheila. I should be asking you that question."

"What are you talking about?"

Jake picked up the gift bag off her desk. "When did you put this stuff in my box?"

"I must have left them during one of my trips to see you."

"You're lying, Sheila. When I packed my bags to come home, those things weren't in any of them. Believe me, I would've remembered."

"Jake—"

"Please don't insult my intelligence, Sheila. You put them in my boxes the day you came by with the contracts, didn't you?"

She stared at him defiantly, but did not respond.

"You sent those flowers, too. You wanted me to believe that Nicholas and Tori were having an affair."

"How can you be so sure they weren't? They seem awfully close to me."

"They grew up together, Sheila. They are best friends."

"You thought the same thing I did. That is, until you and Tori got back together. Now you're trying to act all high and mighty. I have been there for you from day one." Tears were running down her face, leaving black streaks of mascara. "You came to me because you were having problems at home. I listened to you and I . . ." Sheila couldn't continue.

Jake was beginning to feel terrible. "I appreciate all you've done, I really do."

"I suppose you blame me for that night, too. But I hope you remember that it was you who kept ordering the champagne. It was you who started kissing me. Don't get me wrong—I'm not blaming you for what happened." She sighed loudly. "Jake, the only thing I'm guilty of is caring about you. Wanting you to be happy."

"I understand that, Sheila. I feel the same way. I want Tori to be happy."

"And what about you? Don't you deserve to be happy, too?"

"What do you suggest, Sheila? You and Tori are like oil and vinegar. She's my wife, and she doesn't trust you. I'm not exactly sure she trusts me, but I'm working hard to change that. I betrayed her, and so did you. When you do all the sneaky things you've done, it doesn't help matters."

"So, you think buying me out is the answer. Do you think you can run the company all by yourself? I don't."

Jake stiffened.

"I only mean that it's the same for me. I can't run this company without you, either. We are a team, Jake."

"Sheila, I'm so sorry. I wish there was another way. I really do."

"There is. You can tell your wife to mind her own business. She has nothing to do with Madison Moore."

"I defended you all those times, Sheila. I have to be honest with you. I feel a little betrayed myself. I'm not sure we can get past this."

"We can," she assured him. "All you have to do is keep your wife under control."

Shaking his head, Jake met her eyes with his. "It's not going to work, Sheila. I'm sorry. If you won't buy me out, then I'm going to sell you my share of the company. One of us will have to go."

Devastated, Sheila ran out of the office.

Three hours passed, and Jake still hadn't seen or heard from her. She'd even missed her afternoon meeting. That was so unlike her. Sheila would never let her personal life interfere with business.

He had no luck in reaching her when he called her cell phone. When Jake left for home, he stopped by her town house, but there was no answer. He was really starting to worry about her.

After Jake had his shower, he told Tori what happened.

"Honey, I don't think you have anything to worry about. Sheila's a grown woman. She can take care of herself."

"This is so out of character for her. Tori, you didn't see her face. She was really hurt."

Tori touched his shoulder. "Jake, please don't let her act fool you. Sheila didn't get her way, and she's having a temper tantrum right now."

"I don't agree. She wasn't acting. Her pain was real." Jake squeezed his eyes shut, trying to block out the memory of Sheila crying. It never should have come to this.

The telephone rang shortly after eight.

"It's Sheila," Tori stated and handed the phone to him.

Jake watched her, trying to discern whether or not she was angry. The last thing he needed was two hysterical females carrying on around him. "Hello."

"I'm sorry to bother you at home like this."

"It's okay." He glanced over at his wife. "What is it, Sheila?"

"I thought about everything you said earlier. You're right. I'm in the way, so I'm going to get out of your life."

"Sheila . . ." Jake began.

"No, it's okay," she interjected sadly. "I just wanted to let you know that I don't want to cause any problems for you. Since you want me gone, I'll go."

She sounded sluggish. He wondered if she'd been drinking.

"Are you selling your share of the company to me? Is that what you're trying to say?" Jake glanced over at his wife. She was steaming a pot of broccoli, and it didn't look as if she was listening to his end of the conversation. However, he really couldn't be sure. He returned his attention to Sheila.

"You'll get the company, Jake. All of it. Anyway, I just want to say good-bye."

"Are you leaving town?"

His question was met with silence.

"Sheila?"

The line went dead. Jake navigated into the kitchen, where Tori was preparing dinner.

"That was quick."

Leaning against the counter, he stated, "That was real strange."

She looked over at him. "How so?"

"Sheila didn't sound like herself."

Tori stopped what she was doing. "Don't tell me you're worried about her?" she asked in amazement. "The woman's playing you, Jake."

"I don't think so. Tori, you didn't hear her voice. Sheila told me she called to say good-bye." A horrifying thought crossed his mind. Jake stared at his wife. "Do you think she's capable of trying to kill herself?"

"I think she'd try to make you believe that. Sheila is a very manipulative woman, Jake. When are you going to see that?"

He still wasn't convinced. Jake couldn't shake the uneasy feeling fluttering through him. Something wasn't quite right about all this. "Right now, I want to make sure she's okay."

Walking back into the den, he picked up the phone and dialed Sheila's number. There was no answer. He tried three more times. Still no answer.

"I'm going over there," Jake announced.

"No, you're not. Can't you see that's what Sheila wants you to do?"

He heard the frustration in Tori's voice. Holding his hands up in resignation, Jake said, "Fine. I'll stay here. Let's not argue over this."

"I don't want to fight with you, Jake. But it's time to get Sheila out of our lives once and for all."

Shortly after midnight, the phone rang, waking them up. It was the hospital. Jake jumped out of bed and scrambled into a pair of jeans and a sweatshirt.

"Where are you going?" Tori questioned. She sat up and glanced over at the clock. "Do you see what time it is?"

"Sheila's in the hospital. She tried to kill herself."

"Who called and told you? Sheila?"

"No. Someone from the hospital. My name was listed as her emergency contact."

"What about her mother? Doesn't she have a mother living somewhere close by?"

Jake dropped down on the bed and bent to put on his shoes. "I don't know. She never mentioned her much."

Tori got out of bed. "I'm going with you, Jake."

She dressed quickly and rushed out behind him. They rode to Charleston in silence.

As soon as they arrived at the hospital, Jake and Tori rushed to the emergency room. His bad leg was bothering him, and Jake started to hurt badly. Since the accident, he now had a permanent limp, and it would hurt whenever he tried to hurry.

"You okay?" Tori asked softly. "Is your leg hurting?"

"I'm fine," he lied.

A doctor came out to see them.

"Can I see her?" Jake questioned before the man could utter a word.

"I'm afraid Miss Moore doesn't want to see either one of you. Why don't you go home and come back tomorrow?" he suggested.

"How is she doing?"

"She's still a little agitated. I've prescribed a sedative for her, so that she can sleep. I'm going to keep her under observation for a few days. . . ."

When the doctor moved on, Tori said, "He's right, Jake. We should go home."

"I'm not leaving."

Tori's eyes grew wide in her surprise. "Excuse me? What did you just say?"

"I said I wasn't leaving. Not until I know Sheila's going to be okay." Jake saw the fire in Tori's eyes and knew she was furious. Why couldn't she understand? Even though Sheila had recently tried to sabotage his marriage, she'd been a good friend to him. She had never let him down. Jake wasn't about to abandon her now.

Chapter Forty-five

"There's nothing you can do here, Jake."

"You heard me, Tori," he snapped impatiently. "I'm not going to abandon Sheila right now. She is my partner and my friend."

"*And what am I?*" she demanded. "Oh, now I remember. I'm just the wife you abandoned the night our daughter died." Tori waved her hand in resignation and said, "I'm getting out of here."

Angry, Jake grabbed her roughly by the arm. "Tori, how could you bring up that night? I was in pain and I was confused—"

"You were a coward!"

Removing his hand, Jake let her go. "So, the truth finally comes out, huh?"

She regretted the words as soon as they left her mouth. "Jake . . ."

"Just leave, Tori. Please." Jake turned his back to her and walked away.

She tried to blink her tears away, but was unsuccessful. Tori walked briskly down the corridor and through the exit doors. Aunt Kate didn't live too far from the hospital, so Tori decided just to spend the night there. Tomorrow morning, she would have Charlene follow her back to the hospital so that she could leave the car for Jake.

Thoughts of her husband brought on a fresh batch of tears. Jake had once again abandoned her.

Sheila still refused to see Jake the next morning. After his all-night vigil, his body ached and craved a good night's sleep. Finally, he decided to leave the hospital.

Tori was in the den reading when Jake arrived home. When he entered the room, she didn't bother to acknowledge him.

"Are you not talking to me now?" he asked. Jake was tired and irritable. If Tori was looking for a fight, that's exactly what she was about to get. A thread of hurt wound through him as he recalled her words of the night before.

"I don't see where we have anything to talk about."

She sounded hurt and defeated.

"If you don't want to talk, fine." He limped up the stairs to the bedroom.

As tired as he was, Jake couldn't sleep. He kept thinking about everything Tori had said to him. She'd actually called him a coward. . . .

For the first time, Jake truly understood what he'd done to her. In his arrogant selfishness, he hadn't really given much thought about what he'd put her through. The night Tiffany died, he'd walked away from her. He'd walked out of her life . . . with Sheila. Anytime he had a fight with Tori, Jake always ran to Sheila. He'd betrayed her in so many ways, he had just begun to understand.

He climbed out of bed and slipped on a pair of shorts. Jake went downstairs. Tori was still in the den. Her eyes were wet. He felt an intense sickness inside. He was always making her cry, it seemed.

"I think we should talk, Tori."

"I told you we have nothing to talk about," she replied quietly.

"I disagree." Jake sat down beside her. "Tori, I handled this thing with Sheila all wrong. I realize that now."

He saw a flash of pain in her eyes.

"You don't know how much you hurt me, Jake. You chose to stay and comfort Sheila in her hour of need, yet when our daughter died—you walked out on me. I'm sorry, but it seems to me as if you've got your priorities mixed up." She wiped away a tear that escaped.

"The night Tiffany died, I was scared, grieving, and heartbroken. I thought I'd lost you for good, and I couldn't handle seeing the look of hatred on your face. You were right, Tori. I was a coward that night, I admit it."

"I shouldn't have said that."

"You said what you felt, Tori. I can't get angry for that." Jake placed an arm around his wife. "We're going to get through this, Tori. Our marriage is going to work. I'm not going to abandon you again."

"If you're not abandoning me, you're trying to control me. Jake, I just don't know if we have what it takes to make this work."

He'd never heard Tori sound so resigned. Jake felt his chest tighten, and it was getting hard to breathe. "It can get better."

"I'm not so sure. Our relationship has always been this way. You decided we would date for two years before we got married. Then it was five years before we could have a child—"

"Only you got pregnant before then," Jake interjected.

"It wasn't something I could control. Do you remember the night I told you about the baby? You got so angry because it didn't fit in your neat little plan. Jake, you were so mean that night. It really hurt my feelings."

Rubbing his chest, Jake asked, "Why are you telling me this now?"

"Because I've grown up. You don't scare me anymore, and I don't need you as much as I thought I did in the beginning. I thought I couldn't live without you, Jake, but when you left—it showed me that I could."

"What are you saying, Tori?"

"I love you. I just don't know if we are equally yoked. After what happened last night, it made me think. I—"

"I love you, Tori," Jake cut in. "I have always loved you and I loved our daughter. I love this baby that you're carrying now."

"I know that. I never doubted your love for me or Tiffany. Jake, I only question where we fit into your plan. You dictated everything throughout our marriage."

"That's not true."

"Yes, it is. You decided the way I would wear my hair, the way I dressed. Everything. I wanted to go to college, but you decided I didn't need to since I was going to be your wife. I had no identity, Jake. I was your wife and Tiffany's mother, that's all. When you and Sheila went into business together, it was like she replaced me."

"How can you say that?"

"Because it's true, Jake. You never took time out to get to know me. The real me. Look how you've acted over my hair and the way I dress."

"Are you saying this is the real you? Then who was the woman I married?"

"The one you created. Jake, you married a part of me. It's not your fault. I allowed you to make me into what you wanted me to be. However, it made me so unhappy and I didn't know how to express it. In my unhappiness with myself, I started to resent you, I think."

"You resented me?"

Tori nodded. "It's only now that I've come to really realize what it was. I projected my own feelings of low self-worth onto you. I wasn't very nice to you back then." She looked up at him. "I realized that I drove you into Sheila's arms. I wanted so much to win you back—"

"Honey, you don't have to win me back. *You have me.*"

"Do I?" she cried.

Jake wrapped his arms around her. "Tori, you've always had me.

I don't want anybody else. Even in our worst arguments, I still wanted you. I could never get you to see that. We had a long talk before Sheila and I went into business together. You said you were okay with it."

"I was until I started getting signals that she had a hidden agenda. It hurt me that you always defended her."

"I guess I felt responsible for your anger toward her. When we . . ." Jake cleared his throat. "That's why I wanted to stay at the hospital. Because this is my fault. I lose everybody I love and I seem to keep hurting the people I care about. . . ."

For the rest of the evening, Jake and Tori discussed their marriage. This was the first time they'd ever sat down to communicate openly and honest. He felt his anxiety ease as the night wore on. Maybe now he would find his peace.

Two days later, Jake brought flowers to Sheila. He strode into the hospital room without knocking. "Hey, partner. How are you feeling today?"

"I'm fine." She looked down at her hands. "I didn't expect to see you."

Jake caught a glimpse of the pain lingering in Sheila's eyes. Although Tori had tried to reassure him that what had happened was not his fault, he still thought otherwise. He felt responsible for Sheila's unhappiness.

"Why are you here?"

"I care what happens to you. You really had me worried."

"You? Care? Yeah, right." Sheila's eyes suddenly filled with tears. "You already made yourself clear."

"I'm sorry, Sheila. I never meant to hurt you."

She wouldn't look at him. "I understand. Tori means a lot to you, Jake. She hates me, and she made you choose. You chose your wife."

"I care for you, too, Sheila. I want you to know that."

Sighing in resignation, she said, "I know that, Jake. I've always known it. You don't have to worry about me."

Jake couldn't continue to destroy Sheila. He couldn't stand to see her hurting like this. Covering her hand with his, he said, "Please get better, Sheila. You are my friend and I need you. I want you to hurry up and get better, because we've got a company to run."

She suddenly brightened. "Do you mean that, Jake? Are we going to stay partners?"

Smiling, Jake nodded. "We're partners."

"What does Tori have to say about it? Or does she know?"

"She knows and we've already discussed it. Tori doesn't have a problem with our working together."

"Why the change of heart?"

"Tori and I trust each other. Our marriage is finally on the right track."

Phase one of her plan had worked.

Sheila was in heaven after Jake's visit. She had him eating right out of her hands. She knew him well enough that her faked suicide attempt would keep him by her side. Picking up the phone, Sheila made a quick phone call.

She would be getting out of this psycho ward in a few days, and then Sheila decided she'd spend a few days at home "recuperating." Jake would be a constant visitor, she knew, but that was just to gain his trust. She would be the perfect friend. A real friend. The final phase would take place on their trip to Los Angeles. She'd secretly arranged for her and Jake to meet with Knight Electronics representatives in L.A. Sheila needed this time alone with him. The timing couldn't be more perfect, because it coincided with her most fertile period.

Chapter Forty-six

Jake came home and found the note Tori had left for him. She'd gone to Bible study and wouldn't be home until later. She also noted that she'd left a casserole in the oven for dinner.

He was somewhat relieved she wasn't home right now. Jake needed time to rehearse what he was going to say to her. He and Sheila had been summoned to Los Angeles to do a formal presentation to a potential client. They would be there for a week. He had a feeling that Tori wasn't going to like this situation, but there wasn't anything he could do about it. Knight Electronics, Inc. was as large as Sony, and landing the account would put Madison Moore on the map.

Tori had always supported him in his business, so this time shouldn't be any different, Jake reasoned. It wouldn't bother her if he were going on this trip alone. Tori wouldn't like the fact that Sheila was coming along. Knight representatives wanted to meet them both.

He heard her coming in and limped toward the door. Jake greeted his wife with a kiss.

Putting her purse on a nearby sofa table, Tori asked, "Have you eaten yet?"

He shook his head. "I decided to wait for you."

Smiling, she said, "Let me wash up and I'll warm up the casserole." Every now and then, she would glance up at him. "Are you okay?"

"I'm fine, sweetheart."

The telephone rang.

Tori eyed him curiously for a moment before answering the phone. She was soon engrossed in a conversation with her mother.

Jake's thoughts returned to his present dilemma. How was he going to tell his wife about the business trip? Sheila suggested he lie to Tori, but Jake refused. He wanted to regain the trust of his wife.

She came up behind Jake, hugging him. "How did your day go?"

He felt like he'd been punched in the gut. "It was good."

Tori stepped around him. "Land any new accounts?" she asked as she headed into the kitchen.

"Actually, that's what I want to talk to you about." Jake strolled after her. When he entered the kitchen, Tori was pulling a bowl of salad out of the refrigerator. He turned on the microwave oven to heat up the lukewarm chicken casserole.

Tori eyed him, a smile forming on her lips. "You're helping in the kitchen! Oh, I know what this is about. You have to go out of town, don't you? That's when you're the most helpful around the house."

"Yes. I have to go to Los Angeles."

"When do you have to leave?"

"Day after tomorrow. I'll be gone a week." Jake paused for a moment before continuing, "Tori, there's something else. . . ."

She looked up at him. "What is it, Jake?"

"Sheila's going with me. Knight Electronics wants us both to come to California for the presentation."

"I see." Tori walked over to the microwave and turned it off. Pulling it open, she took out the casserole and placed it on the Formica countertop.

"Honey, let's talk about this."

She glanced up at him then. "What's to talk about? It sounds to me as if the decision has already been made. You and Sheila are going on a business trip."

"That's all it is, Tori. Business."

"Uh-huh."

"What's that supposed to mean?"

She acted as if he hadn't asked a question. Throughout dinner, Tori was quiet. Jake tried to get her to talk but didn't have much success, so he finally gave up. She would talk to him whenever she was ready. He thought they had gotten past Tori's jealousy of Sheila, but obviously not.

In bed later, Jake tried to hold Tori, but any contact with him caused her body to stiffen.

"I need you to trust me, Tori," he whispered.

"It's not that I don't trust you, Jake. That's not it at all. I just have a bad feeling about this trip. I don't know what it is—"

"It's going to be fine," he assured her. "I have everything under control."

Just before Jake closed his eyes, he could have sworn he heard the words, "Let go and let God. . . ."

The next day, Tori told her cousin about Jake's business trip. "Girl, if I were you, I'd be on the first plane to Los Angeles," Charlene advised. "Join your husband and have a second honeymoon."

"You really think I should go?" Tori walked around her desk, rubbing the tiny mound that was her stomach. "I don't think it's just my insecurities. Not this time. I have this strange feeling in the pit of my stomach."

"If you feel that strongly, then you should go. If you don't, you may regret it for the rest of your life."

Pacing back and forth in her office, Tori chewed on her bottom lip. "Maybe I should call Jake and tell him I'm coming. The last time I planned to surprise him—I was the one surprised."

"I really don't think you should tell anyone that you're coming. Jake's not going to be upset."

"You really don't think so?"

Charlene picked up the phone. "Which airline would you prefer?"

Tori laughed. Maybe flying out to Los Angeles would rid her of the uneasy feeling she was experiencing. She trusted her husband, but Sheila . . . there was no way. While Charlene was talking to the airline rep, Tori closed her eyes and murmured a quick prayer. "Dear Lord, protect my husband. Guide him. Give him the strength to resist temptation. . . . My marriage is in Your hands, Lord. It was Your gift to me. With Your help and Your healing, it can be made better. I thank You in advance."

Hanging up the phone, Charlene announced, "It's all set. They're faxing over your confirmation."

"I'll be there soon, Jake. Just hold on," she whispered.

Jake eyed Sheila with suspicion. There was a strange little gleam in her eye and she seemed unusually giddy. She was definitely up to something.

"Come on. Have some more champagne, Jake." Sheila held out a crystal flute.

He moved out of her grasp. "I think I've had enough for tonight."

She started to pout. "Jake, don't be such a bore! We have just landed a major account and we should be celebrating." Sheila sat down on the sofa and crossed her legs, causing the split in her knee-length skirt to rise even higher.

Staring pointedly at her face, Jake shook his head. "Sheila, I'm going to call it a night. You should, too."

"But we have all this champagne. Surely you're not going to let it go to waste." Sheila rose to her feet. "I guess I'll just have to celebrate all by myself." She swayed to the music playing in the background.

Giving Jake a seductive look, she murmured, "Sure you don't want to join me?"

She'd definitely had enough to drink, he decided. "Sheila, you shouldn't drink anymore."

She looked surprised. "Why?"

"Because I think you might be a little drunk."

Sheila laughed. "I'm not d-drunk." She removed her jacket, revealing a white blouse made of lace. The strapless bra she wore beneath was clearly visible.

Jake was grateful she'd kept her jacket buttoned during their presentation. He'd cautioned her to dress a little more conservatively when it came to business. The majority of their clients were men, and he didn't want to risk Sheila sending out the wrong messages.

A knock sounded on the door, surprising them both.

Sheila turned to Jake. "Are you expecting anyone?"

Shaking his head no, Jake headed to the door and opened it. "Tori." His face broke into a wide smile. "What are you doing here?"

"I came to spend some time with my husband." She strolled into the room. "Hello, Sheila."

"Well, isn't this a surprise. I certainly didn't expect to see you."

Looking around the hotel suite, Tori replied, "I'm sure."

Jake embraced her. "I'm very happy to see you, sweetheart."

They heard the sound of glass breaking. Turning, they found Sheila bending down and trying to pick up the shreds of glass with her hand.

"The g-glass just fell," she mumbled.

"You don't have to worry about that. Housekeeping can get it up in the morning." Jake strode over to her. "Why don't you go to your room and rest? We've got a busy day tomorrow."

Sheila didn't look happy at all with the turn of events. "Good night, Jake. Tori."

"Night, Sheila," Tori replied. "We'll see you in the morning."

When they were alone, Jake pulled his wife back into his arms. "I'm so glad you're here. I almost called you earlier today to ask you to fly out here."

"I'd like to freshen up, if you don't mind."

"Would you like me to order something from room service for you? You must be hungry."

"I ate on the plane," Tori replied as she carried her overnight bag with her to the bathroom. "I'm fine."

When she came out twenty minutes later, she was wearing a delicate sheer nightgown in white. Jake couldn't ever remember seeing her more beautiful. She was letting her hair grow out some, and even he had to admit that she looked more sophisticated.

"What's this?" Tori bent down and retrieved a tiny packet off the floor.

Jake glanced in her direction. "Probably something that missed the trash."

She made her way to his side. Holding out her hand, she said, "I don't think so. You should take a look."

It was a condom. Jake's eyes widened. "It has to belong to Sheila. I've seen her with that particular brand. I guess she carries them around in her purse."

"I see."

"Honey, I wasn't—"

"I know you weren't planning anything," Tori interrupted. "But your partner definitely had something planned for this evening." She examined the packet. Staring at it, Tori ran a finger across the top.

Puzzled, he asked, "What are you doing?"

"I felt something. Like a tiny hole . . ." Tori ripped it open. "There's a hole in it."

"What?"

She looked squarely at him. "Are you surprised?"

Jake looked stunned. "Do you think Sheila did this?"

Tori nodded. "I think it was her intent to try and get pregnant tonight. By you."

Jake shook his head in disbelief. "No. She wouldn't do something this underhanded."

"I think so. Honey, what is it going to take to get you to see that this woman is trying to destroy our marriage?"

He stared down at the condom in his hand. Sticking his finger in it, he found there was indeed a hole in the tip.

"If I hadn't come—" Tori began.

"Nothing would've happened," Jake interjected. "I was about to send Sheila off to her room when you arrived."

Tori gestured all around the suite. "Look at all this champagne. Did you order this?"

"No. Sheila did."

"She was trying to get you to party?"

"She wanted to celebrate," Jake admitted. "Things went real well today."

"Jake, she was trying to get you drunk. Then she was going to get you into bed, and if things went her way, she would've ended up pregnant."

Jake was too stunned for words.

Later, while Tori slept in his arms, Jake lay in bed, thinking about Sheila and her plan. How could she have thought something like that would've worked? Once again, she'd made a fool of him. Tori had been right about her all along. Once again, when Jake thought he'd had everything under control—he was never more wrong.

Sheila was furious. Why did Tori have to show up again? In her anger, she threw a pillow toward the door of her hotel room.

She tossed the condoms she'd cleverly hidden in her bra. When she'd bought them earlier, she'd stuck a tiny pinhole in each of them. Her plan was to put one on Jake in the dark so he'd be none the wiser—if things had gone according to plan, Sheila would have gotten pregnant before their return to South Carolina. Now it was all ruined because of that witch, Tori.

She punched one of the remaining pillows on her bed. *Give up*, her heart reasoned. *Jake will never be yours.* Sheila had never been one to give up, however.

Chapter Forty-seven

"So, how was California?"

"You were so right, Charlene. It was a second honeymoon for me and Jake. We had such a wonderful time. It just went by much too fast. One week isn't enough to see L.A." Tori hugged her cousin. "I'm so glad you advised me to go."

"Did the snake behave herself?"

"You're not going to believe this, Charlene." Tori proceeded to tell her cousin about the condom.

Charlene was astonished. "I can't believe Sheila was actually trying to trick Jake into getting her pregnant. What did he say?"

"He hasn't said a whole lot," Tori answered. "I think he's really hurt. You know how much he trusted Sheila." Holding up Charlene's hand, she asked, "Have you two finally set a date?"

"Yes. We're getting married next June."

Tori hugged her a second time. "It's about time. I'm so happy for you, Charlene."

"I keep pinching myself just to make sure I'm not dreaming."

"It's no dream. And we've got to get busy. Weddings have a way of sneaking up on you."

Kate walked up to them. "All I have to say is that Charlene had better do a whole lot of praying before she marries Shepard Madison."

"Mama, it's my life, and I'll live it with the man of my choosing. I love Shepard and I always will."

"You should never marry somebody you love—you should marry a man who loves you." Her hands on her hips, Kate rambled on. "Charlene, you're my daughter, but I don't know where your senses are."

"If you don't want to come to the wedding, Mama, then don't. I'm marrying Shepard."

Kate stomped out of the room in a huff, mumbling to herself as always.

A tear slipped from Charlene's eye.

"I'm sorry."

"I just wish Mama wasn't so against Shepard and Jake. It's almost as if she hates them."

Tori was shaking her head. "I know. I can't figure it out. Why does she hate them so much?"

"I don't know, but I wish I did."

"I forgot to ask my mom, but she's coming down in a couple of weeks. I'll ask her then," Tori promised. "Well, I'd better get going. I'm meeting Jake for dinner; then we're going home, locking ourselves in the house, turning the ringer off on the phone, and we're going to relax."

Charlene broke into laughter. "Yeah, right. Is that what they're calling it these days?"

Tori sent one of the pillows on the sofa flying her cousin's way.

"What do you think about putting little-known history facts on the Web site?" Tori opened a can of cashews and popped one into her mouth. "By the way, I really appreciate you doing this for me. Designing the site and everything."

"We're partners. Besides, I love doing stuff like this," he acknowledged. Jake scribbled down notes as they talked. He really enjoyed their time together and working with her on the heritage trail tours. They were becoming more and more popular. He reached over and took a handful of cashews. He ate them one by one.

Tori was now on the Internet, checking out some site she'd discovered earlier, while Jake finished off the last of his beer. He got up and took another out of the refrigerator, then came back to the table, where they'd set up shop.

While Tori worked, Jake leaned back in his chair and closed his eyes. He struggled to find out why he couldn't shake that lost feeling. It was so strange. After everything he and Tori had gone through, Jake still hadn't achieved that sense of peace he desperately sought. Would he ever feel free? he wondered.

His eyes raked over his wife's body. Right now, he didn't want to think. He just wanted to lose himself in Tori. Jake got up out of his seat and walked around the table to her side.

Pulling her up, he murmured huskily, "That's enough business for one night."

The following Friday, Linda Samuels-Dawson drove up to spend the weekend with them. The next morning, they all got up and spent the day in Beaufort.

When they returned, Linda freshened up and went into the kitchen to cook dinner. Tori and Jake took a shower together. After they were dressed, Tori followed Jake downstairs. They'd made it halfway down when the phone started ringing.

"Mama, could you get that, please?"

Linda did as she was asked. "Hello."

"Yes, he is," Linda responded sweetly. She turned to Tori. Covering the mouthpiece, she whispered, "It's Sheila."

"Jake doesn't want to talk to her." The woman just wouldn't give up. According to the caller ID, this was the tenth time she'd called today. When Tori played back the messages, six of them had been from Sheila.

Plumping up a pillow, Tori sat down beside Jake. "You're going to have to talk to her sooner or later."

"I know. It's gonna have to be later. If I talk to her right now, I won't be able to take back what I say."

There was a slight pause before Linda said impatiently, "No, you can't, dear. He's busy with his wife."

A few minutes later she hung up. "That woman has some serious problems. I think she needs therapy."

Tori glanced over at Jake. He was furious with Sheila. Since the nearly disastrous episode in Los Angeles, he hadn't mentioned Sheila's name. Jake had been working from home since then, too. She realized it was best that he keep his distance for now. There was no telling what he would do to her if he was forced to deal with Sheila at this time.

She didn't push Jake. Tori had no idea how he was going to handle the company moving forward. She certainly didn't envy his position. This was probably one of the hardest decisions in his life. Jake loved Madison Moore. If he had to be the one to walk away, it could kill him.

He had fallen asleep. Tori eased off the couch and joined her mother in the kitchen.

"Mama, what are you doing?" she asked with a smile. "We didn't invite you to spend the weekend with us so that you could cook."

"Now, you know how much I love cooking." Closing the oven, Linda pleaded with her. "Honey, let me do this for you and Jake."

"Those muffins sure smell good. Mine never come out like yours." Tori leaned over the counter. "Mama, I need to ask you something."

"What is it, honey?" Linda came around the counter and sat on one of the chairs.

"It's about Aunt Kate. She's giving Charlene such a hard time about Shepard. And you know how she feels about Jake."

"My sister," Linda moaned. "I keep telling her forgiveness is the answer."

Tori frowned. "What are you talking about? Forgive who?"

Linda looked uncomfortable. "I don't know that I should be discussing this with you, Tori. Kate's entitled to her privacy."

"I just want to know why she hates the Madison men so much. What happened?"

"Randolph Madison. Have you heard of him?"

Nodding, Tori answered, "Yes. He's Jake's uncle."

"That's right. Well, that was the love of my sister's life."

Tori gasped. "Aunt Kate? But he was married to Miss Maybelle."

Linda nodded in agreement. "He wasn't married when he and Kate were involved. She was working as a housekeeper and Randolph chased her until he finally caught her. He wooed her with flowers, candy, and lots of promises. He was Kate's first."

"I suppose he dumped her right after that."

"Not exactly." Linda rose to her feet and went back into the kitchen. She stole a peek into the huge black pot on top of the stove.

She returned to where they were sitting. "Now, where was I? Oh, yeah. Randolph didn't dump Kate immediately. It was only after he found out she was pregnant."

Tori's mouth dropped wide open. "Charlene's not . . ."

"Goodness, no. Kate's first child was a little boy."

She was almost afraid to ask, "What happened to him?"

"He died a few days after he was born."

"Poor Aunt Kate. That's why she's so bitter, I guess." This revelation gave Tori more insight into her aunt. She didn't want what happened to her to happen to Tori and Charlene. In her own gruff way, she'd been trying to protect them.

Her mother's voice intruded upon her thoughts. "Tori, do not repeat this. Kate would have a fit."

"Don't worry, Mama. I'll never say a word."

Tori followed her mother into the kitchen. While Linda stirred the red beans, she cooked a pot of rice. Stealing a peek into the den, she checked on Jake. He was still sound asleep on the couch.

"I'm happy to see you two together in this house. This is where you both belong."

She turned to face her mother. "It seems a lifetime ago. We've been through so much in the past three years."

"But you made it through." Linda put an arm around her. "Honey, marriage is hard work, but it's worth every effort."

Leaning on her mother's shoulder, Tori agreed. "I can't blame Jake for everything. A lot of it was my fault, too. I've matured a lot in the last year or so. I grew up."

"Better late than never, sugar."

Tori took plates down from one of the oak cabinets and laid them on the counter. "I thank God that we're at least on the right path."

"Welcome home, newlyweds," Tori exclaimed. She and Jake embraced Charlene and Shepard. "I can't believe you two just ran off and got married like that. What was the big rush?"

"We decided we'd waited long enough." Wrapping his arms around his new wife, Shepard said, "I didn't want to wait any longer."

Charlene laughed. "We sure didn't expect to see you two here."

Giving her a knowing smile, Tori murmured, "I'm sure. Don't worry. We're not going to stay long. Jake and I just wanted to let you know that the kitchen's stocked with all types of groceries. Della's made a couple of casseroles and they're in the freezer, so you don't have to worry about starving. Aunt Kate even left you a pie."

"You two are going to need your strength," Jake teased.

Tori elbowed him. "We're going to leave now. Oh, Della's taking the rest of the week off, so you two have this big old house all to yourself. Jake's already paid her, so you don't have to worry about that, either."

"Sounds like you two have taken care of everything." Shepard embraced his brother once more. "Thank you, Jake. It means a lot to me."

Wrapping his arms around Tori, he said, "We'll be leaving now. We'll see you in a week or two."

Charlene laughed. "I'll be at the store tomorrow, Tori."

"Oh, no. That's not necessary. Aunt Kate's been helping me out, and she's doing great. She wants to come in and help us on the weekends. Especially on the days we do our heritage tours."

"That's wonderful. I never thought she'd be interested. I'm glad though."

Shepard gestured to the sofa. "Why don't we take a seat and visit for a while?"

Tori shook her head. "No, thank you. You two just got home, and I know you must be tired—"

"Lack of sleep and all . . ." Jake threw in, bringing a round of laughter.

"We'll see you guys later on in the week."

Shepard kissed his wife. "Maybe . . ."

Jake embraced Tori as they headed to their car. "They look real happy, don't they?"

"Yes, they do." Looking up at him, she asked. "Do they remind you of anyone?"

"Us."

"I was thinking the same thing. Do you remember how happy we were back then?"

"Yeah, I do. I feel it every time I look at you, Tori."

She put a hand to his cheek. "You are such a wonderful man. I love you." He held the car door open for her. Tori climbed into the passenger side. When Jake got in on the other side, she said,

"Honey, I've been trying not to bring this up, but I am dying to know what you've decided."

"I still don't know."

"Have you thought about praying about it?"

"I've thought about it," Jake admitted. "Just don't know if it would help."

"Prayer always helps."

"For you maybe. God doesn't listen to me."

Tori couldn't believe she'd heard Jake correctly. "Honey, God listens to everyone. He does." Taking him by the hand, she asked, "Would you like for me to pray with you when we get home?"

He nodded.

As soon as they reached their house, Tori wasted no time in leading Jake over to the couch in the living room. Facing the chair, they fell to their knees side by side.

Jake felt a little silly in this position.

"This is our way of humbling ourselves before our Father," Tori explained. "Honey, what would you like to say to God?"

"Huh?"

"You just talk to Him like you talk to any other person."

Jake felt ridiculous.

"It's okay, honey. God understands. Just tell him what you're feeling."

"Dear God, it's me again. . . ." Feeling sheepish, Jake stole a peek at his wife. He'd half expected her to be laughing, but instead he found her with her eyes closed and her hands clasped together.

Closing his eyes, Jake continued, "I come before You to ask Your forgiveness, Lord. I would like to ask You to come into my life. I want to know You, dear God. Please come back into my heart." As he prayed, a warmth began to spread through him. Feeling more confident, he said, "Please give me the strength to be a good husband to Tori and a good father to our unborn baby."

Jake was starting to realize what his mother meant. He needed to let go of his inhibitions, his fears, his doubts. He needed to release control and allow God to move in his life. He prayed for patience and understanding. Jake also prayed for the power to forgive, because he knew only then would forgiveness come.

When he opened his eyes, he found that Tori was crying. Instinctively, he knew they were tears of joy.

"Doesn't it feel good?" she asked.

Jake smiled and nodded. It did feel good. The entire time he'd poured out his heart, he felt God's love for him. It was like coming home. His heavenly Father had embraced him, and that feeling was beyond words.

"Have you forgiven yourself, Jake?"

He knew Tori was referring to Tiffany's death. Jake nodded. "I need to go to Brunswick. It's time I visit Tiffany's grave. I've been away too long."

"Why did you come here, Sheila?" Tori asked as soon as she saw her standing on her porch. She was glad her husband wasn't home to deal with Sheila. This time she was going to put an end to this situation once and for all, Tori decided. "Jake's not home. And if he were, he wouldn't want to see you."

"I know. I saw him leaving."

"Are you watching my house now?"

"I think it's time you and I had it out. Jake wouldn't be acting this way if it wasn't for you, Tori. I want you to stay out of Madison Moore's business."

"Excuse me?"

"Tori, I know you don't like me, and I don't care about that. I'm not crazy about you, either. However, you're now interfering in my relationship with Jake. We are business partners."

"I realize that," Tori interjected. "It's unfortunate that my husband is stuck with someone like you as a partner. I expect that will soon change, however. Jake finally sees you for what you really are. He knows you for the manipulative witch that you are."

"I hope you haven't fed Jake all those lies," Sheila snapped. "I can't help it if you are insecure—"

"*Wrong,*" Tori cut in. "Sorry. That's not going to work this time. Sheila, you need to get a grasp on reality. Jake is my husband. He wants to be with me. Out of everything you've done to keep us apart—none of it has worked. *He wants me.*"

Sheila pointed to Tori's rounded belly. "Jake's only staying with you because of the baby. He doesn't love you."

Tori burst into laughter. "I hope you really don't believe that. Jake loves me, Sheila. I know it in my heart. All he feels for you is friendship. That's all. But now, he may not even feel that much for you."

"You are a liar. When Jake made love to me, you didn't even cross his mind. It was my name he called out. *Not yours.* He never ever talked about you when we were together."

Tori refused to allow feelings of doubt and insecurity to rise. "Call it whatever you want, Sheila, but to Jake, it was just sex. You were only a receptacle for his lust." Wanting to hurt Sheila as badly as the woman wanted to hurt her, Tori continued. "I explained to my husband how his actions possibly gave you false hope—"

"He discussed our sex life with you?"

"We had to talk about it in order for us to move on with our lives. Jake had to understand the consequences of his actions. He used you because you were simply available."

Tears filled Sheila's eyes. "I don't believe you."

"Jake could have divorced me a long time ago, but he didn't. When he decided to come home, he didn't tell you. Don't you think if he was in love with you, he would've told you? Why would he come home to me if he really wanted to be with you?"

Sheila remained quiet.

"Jake loves me, Sheila. He's always loved me. It's time for you to move on with your life."

"I love him with my whole soul. I loved Jake from the moment I saw him in college."

"He married me, Sheila. You have no right to interfere. If you were truly his friend, you would be happy for him."

"Like Nicholas is for you? He's a fool. Instead of going after you, all he does is stand on the sidelines, waiting to rescue you. You two are more suited to each other than you and Jake. Nicholas is a very handsome man, and I think—"

"I married the man I wanted to spend the rest of my life with, Sheila. That man is Jake. Nicholas is my best friend. That's all."

"It's not going to last, Tori. Your marriage is not going to work." She was crying harder now.

"If it doesn't, then it won't be because of you, Sheila. I will not stand by and just let you take my husband. If it's a fight you want—then you'll get it. Jake is my husband."

"She's right, Sheila."

Both women turned to face the doorway. Jake was standing there. He moved to stand beside his wife. Taking Tori by the hand, he said, "I am so sorry if I misled you. It was never my intent, Sheila. I'm sorry if I hurt you."

"You made love to me," she cried out.

"*I had sex with you.*" Jake took a deep breath and added, "It was wrong. I never should have—"

"Nooooo," she cried out in anguish. Grabbing him by the arm, she said, "We made love. You love me, Jake. I know you do."

"No, I don't," he replied as he gently disengaged his arm. "I'm so sorry, Sheila. I really am."

When Sheila dropped to the floor, crying hysterically, Tori's heart went out to her. It was clear that she'd placed all of her hopes and dreams in Jake, and now her heart was breaking. Why couldn't Sheila see that it had been doomed from the start?

Jake reached down to help her stand. "You've got to get control of yourself."

Tori was about to leave the room, but Jake stopped her with his words. "You don't have to leave. It's time we settle this mess."

"I'm going to get her a washcloth; then I'll be back," Tori explained. She returned a few minutes later.

Sheila was now sitting on the sofa, her face in her hands. Jake was sitting on the love seat opposite her. Tori sat down beside him.

"Sheila, I value you as a partner and I thought you were my friend. You don't know how many times I defended you to my friends and family. I thought they were wrong about you. I really did." Jake took Tori's hand and held it in his own. "You almost destroyed my marriage."

"You wanted me as much as I wanted you, Jake," she argued.

"That first time, I really believed you when you told me I seduced you. Now I don't. It was all a setup, as Tori suspected. You knew Tori was planning to come by the hotel, didn't you?"

"How could I have known that?" she countered.

"Because you must have intercepted the message I left for Jake. Be honest. You knew I was going to come to the hotel, so you planned on my catching the two of you in bed."

"Is that correct?" Jake questioned.

Sheila stared at him a moment before she finally nodded.

"And the lingerie? You planted them in my box?"

Again she nodded.

Jake's gaze never left her face. "You know it was only on this last trip that I realized just how manipulative you were."

Sheila frowned. "What are you talking about?"

"Tori and I found a condom. We also realized that it had been altered. It looked like it had been pricked by a pin."

Sheila's eyes widened in her surprise. "I-I don't kn-know anything about that. Maybe it was something left behind in the hotel by the previous guest."

Jake shook his head. "No, Sheila. They are the same type you carry in your purse."

"Well, I don't know anything about a pinprick." She glared at Tori. "Maybe she did it to set me up. To make me look bad in your eyes."

"Tori's not like that, Sheila."

"You make her sound like a saint. But I know her. She is not even close to being a saint. She pretends to be this weak needy woman so that you'll stay by her side, but I'm not fooled."

"You're right about that, Sheila. I'm not a saint. I am also not low enough to run after another woman's husband. I'm not manipulative enough to try to get pregnant by that man in hopes of ruining his marriage, either."

Sheila had no response to Tori's comments. She just sat there, staring down at her hands.

"I was a friend to you, Sheila," Jake said quietly.

"You used me."

"I'm sorry. I hope that in time you will forgive me."

Sheila glared at him. "You think that by apologizing, it makes it right?" She rushed to her feet then. "It's not okay, Jake. You took everything I offered. My friendship and my body. You can't tell me you didn't know how I felt about you. You did, but you didn't care. You used me until you got your precious Tori back. Now you want to discard me like trash. You treated me like a tramp!"

"I can't make you believe otherwise, Sheila, but that's not the way it was. I know my apologies aren't enough, but I think it's a start. I hurt my wife by my actions, too. None of us can go back, but I think going forward, everything needs to be on the table. Sheila, I love Tori. I have always loved her."

Sheila winced at his words.

"All I've ever felt for you is friendship. I need you to understand that. And now"—Jake paused—"I'm not sure I even feel that for you anymore."

"I suppose you want to buy me out." Her eyes filled with tears once more. "Jake, I love Madison Moore. Even more than I love you."

"I know that, Sheila. I love it, too."

She wiped away a lone tear. "So, what happens now?"

"I don't know right now. I really have a lot to think about. So do you."

Sheila nodded in resignation. "I-I think I'm going to take some time off. I'm going away for a while."

"I think that's a good idea. Our employees don't need to know what's going on between us."

"I agree." Sheila headed to the door. Just before she walked out, she glanced over her shoulder at Tori. Their eyes met and held.

"I hope you find your way, Sheila."

"Don't bother to pretend, Tori. You don't care anything about me," she shot back before walking out and slamming the door.

"She's very bitter," Tori acknowledged.

"I guess she has a reason to be. I handled this all wrong."

"Sheila has to shoulder some of the blame."

Jake gave a small laugh. "She once said that about you."

"I'm sure," Tori murmured. "She's probably said a whole lot of things about me."

Jake turned her around so that she was facing him. "I am so sorry for not believing you, Tori. I really believed that she was my friend. I thought she had my back."

"She did, Jake. It just wasn't for the right reasons. Sheila did everything she did because she was investing in you. She intended for you and me to get divorced; then she would have you all to her-self."

Shaking his head, Jake muttered, "I don't know how she ever thought I loved her."

Tori shrugged. "Maybe it was because you were having sex with her."

"It still bothers you, doesn't it?"

She nodded. "I can't help it. Just the very thought of you and her . . . Jake, it still hurts, and it makes me so angry. I'm trying to work through it, though."

"I guess we all have been betrayed in one way or another."

Tori agreed. "In time we will all heal."

Epilogue

Seven months later

Tori cuddled Jake, Jr., to her, kissing his cheek.

Jake entered the room, carrying a breakfast tray. She looked up and smiled. "What is that?"

"Your breakfast. Mom said you'd better eat all of it."

"Where is Mama?"

"She's downstairs in the kitchen. I'm going to put this little guy down for his morning nap, and then I'm joining your mother for breakfast. After that, I'm going to the church for Bible study."

Tori tried to hide her surprise.

"Go on and say it. I know it's killing you inside," Jake teased. He placed the tray on the bed, then gently took the sleeping baby from her.

She broke into laughter. "Honey, I'm not going to say anything. I'm just happy." Since the day Sheila had walked out of their house, Jake had been attending Bible study with her, and had even joined the church. "Very happy."

Jake met her gaze. "I am, too," he confessed. "For the first time in a long time, I feel like a heavy burden's been lifted off me. I finally feel at peace." He gave a light laugh. "You know, the night of the charity ball, Aunt Kate called me the prodigal husband. I

275

thought she was just referring to my leaving you, but then I realized why my coming home didn't take away some of what I was feeling."

"What do you think was going on?" Tori took a sip of her hot tea.

"I came home to you, but I hadn't come back to God. I hadn't allowed him into my life because I didn't think I needed him." Jake paused slightly. "I was so wrong."

Tori's eyes were bright with tears. "I'm so happy for you. I know when I stray from Him, I always start to feel such an unrest in my spirit. It remains until I find myself back on the right path."

"I'm not a perfect man, but I'm going to try to do right by you and our son. I intend to do right by God."

"Honey, just keep Him first in all that you do. If you keep your eye on God, you can't go wrong."

"Is it that easy?"

"No," Tori confessed. "I think it's real easy to live wrong. The challenge in life is trying to live right."

"Oh, there's something else. Sheila has come up with another idea. She thinks it's time we open another office. In New York. We have a lot of accounts there. She intends to move there and run the office. The corporate offices will remain here in South Carolina, however."

"How do you feel about it?"

"I think it's best for all concerned. After everything she's done to us, I'm not sure I can work with her as closely as before, but Sheila is a phenomenal businesswoman. I used to think that I couldn't work without her, but I realize I can. I don't need her to motivate me."

"I never thought you did, Jake. I felt like you were using her as a security blanket. You made some mistakes in the past, but you just have to keep trying. Madison Moore is a big success in part because of you. Not just Sheila."

"I wish things could be different, though. It's not going to be easy working with her on any level. I don't trust her, and I'm not sure I even like her anymore. I really thought she was my friend. I have forgiven her, though."

"She was in love with you, Jake," Tori said in Sheila's defense.

"Please forgive me for all the wrong I've done to you, Tori."

Smiling, she responded, "Jake, I have. And I want you to forgive me, too."

"What have you done?"

"I told you a while back that all was forgiven, but back then it wasn't. I was lying not only to you, but to myself as well. I hadn't realized it until recently."

"If you still want to have Pastor Allen counsel us, I'll go with you. I want our marriage on solid ground. Once and for all. There are some things about the both of us that we need to work on. Maybe a third party can help us. I love you with my whole heart, Tori."

Kissing him, Tori whispered, "Thank You, Lord. The prodigal husband has returned to Your fold."